Making SENSE

USA TODAY BESTSELLING AUTHOR

LILA ROSE

Making Sense Copyright © 2017 by Lila Rose

Photographer: Wander Aguiar
Editing: Hot Tree Editing
Interior Design: Rogena Mitchell-Jones

Making Sense is a work of fiction. All names, characters, events and places found in this book are either from the author's imagination or used fictitiously. Any similarity to persons live or dead, actual events, locations, or organizations is entirely coincidental and not intended by the author.

Second Edition 2019
ISBN: *XXX-XXXXXXXXX*

Chapter ONE

DATING WAS PAINFUL. My husband left us two years ago, and only recently, I'd gotten the courage to try dating again. Since the decision, I'd been on a few in the last couple of months, none of which had bloomed into something amazing. That was if something amazing still existed. I was convinced it wasn't out there for me.

My latest failed example was a man named Ronald, an accountant who happened to be sitting across from me. When I arrived at the restaurant, he seemed nice. I thought for the barest of moments he could be the one willing to do the honors of removing my hymen. Because I was sure that sucker had grown over again.

Ronald certainly looked like he'd enjoy the task of re-breaking my hymen. I could tell by how his hand was in his pants shifting his erection around. At least, I thought it was an erection; it could also be a cucumber, and he wanted me to think he was huge.

I just wished he'd leave it alone.

Huh, and my friend Molly was worried about my table manners.

Although, did I really care that Ronald was a wanker—*hee-hee*—or he loved himself more than anything in life? No, at least, not then I didn't. I also didn't give two hoots Ronald had a huge wart on the side of his nose.... If only I could stop staring at it, then I *really* wouldn't care.

"I'm sorry, Adalyn, I've been talking all about myself. Tell me, what is it you do for a living?" Ronald asked, shifting sideways in the booth to face me. What the heck? Did he just thrust his crotch up at me? At least his hand was out of his pants when he did it.

"Well, you see, I run my own jewelry store on eBay."

He smiled. "That's cute. Does it do well?"

Cute?

Seriously?

My items did extremely well, and they weren't cute; they were wicked.

"Yes, they do. I'm gaining more customers each day."

"Hmm. Is that all you do? Make crafty things?"

I had the urge to kick him in the teeth or knee him in the cucumber.

"No," I gritted out. "Though, it will be once my business gets noticed more."

"Right." He smirked. The assmuncher.

Gone were the thoughts of him getting anywhere near my hoo-ha. The idiot could just shove his hand back down his pants and keep touching himself, because that was the only action he would be getting that night.

Still, the least I could do was get a meal out of him and maybe a nice conversation.

Okay, I was doomed.

"I also work part-time in an adult store."

Of course, his eyes would light up at that.

He leaned in. "That's very interesting. Do you get to try some products out, to, you know, let customers know what they're like?" He smiled, and when he did, I saw a chunk of bread, from the breadsticks on the table, sitting in his teeth.

Internally groaning, I asked myself, *What am I really doing here with him?*

The thought of harming Molly was high on my list at that moment. She'd met Ronald in the coffee shop down the street from her apartment and, since she was already dating her high school sweetheart, she suggested Ronald contact me.

Thankfully a waiter appeared at the table with our meals and distracted Ronald from his question. Looking down at the ravioli, my stomach growled. It smelled amazing, and I'd been starving before I even arrived since I hadn't eaten much that day from the nerves. Even after Molly promised me he wasn't overly attractive. Something she'd supplied before I asked because she'd been witness to me when I was around a very attractive man. I became a bumbling fool.

As I forked a bite, I lifted it to my mouth and found Ronald looking at me with a slight frown on his face. He sighed. "You know, I could help you obtain a healthier diet. Pasta isn't really your friend with the figure you have already."

What in the ever-loving duck did he just say?

My hand was suspended in the air, my mouth already open for the goodness, but all I could do was look at him and hope he was joking. I wasn't one to curse, but I suddenly felt like it.

I knew I wasn't a supermodel. I had thighs, a belly, and a booty, even before my nine-year-old son Drew I had those, just not as much. Which was a major issue my ex had with me.

Well, bugger my ex and bugger the man in front of me. God, he didn't need to point out my weight to me. I knew I was bigger, and I was happy with the way I was. Shaking my head, I shoved the forkful in my mouth and chewed. I couldn't believe how he'd said it, as though he was being nice about it by wanting to advise me to eat right.

Screw that and screw him.

Ronald, not sensing my desire to stab him in the forehead with my fork, smiled and then said, "Excuse me a moment, I need to visit the lavatory."

I fought the urge to tell him to shove his head in the loo while he was in there and just nodded. He scooted around the booth and stood, making his way through the busy restaurant.

The need to leave came over me when my phone tinged in my purse. If it was Molly texting, I was going to warn her to protect her vagina when I saw her next because I would soon be punching it.

A year ago, Molly and I met at the adult store I'd just started working in. She'd been in there to buy some equipment, and we'd bonded over bondage. Since then, we'd been inseparable, and with Molly came Clinton, her high school sweetheart. He was just as amazing as she was.

Just as I pulled my phone free from my purse, a waiter passed by. "Excuse me," I called. He turned and came to stand in front of the table. "Can I please get this to go?" I asked and moved my plate closer to him. He looked to my dinner and then at the other one next to me.

He smirked. "Sure. I'll have it waiting at the front counter for you."

"Thank you." I smiled. However, I wasn't going to just disappear on pecker-face. I'd tell Ronald my thoughts before I left. After all, I knew I'd regret it if I didn't. Too many times had I kept my mouth shut and let things slip by, faking they didn't hurt me in some way. I wasn't that shy, fumbling woman any longer. Well, most of the time.

My attention went back to my phone. It was a text from my mom. I quickly opened it thinking something was wrong with Drew.

Mom: Yes or no to sexy time? Mom was all for me dating. In fact, I swore if she could, she'd shove me at the next available man. Though, I was sure it was just so she had something to talk about with her knitting club friends.

I snorted and sent back: **No!**

Mom: Damn. I need more grandkids. Then there was also that. She loved Drew and wanted more to cherish as much as she did my boy.

LILA ROSE

Shaking my head, I smiled down at the phone. My mom was a little crazy in her own way, but I loved her no matter.

Honestly, I never thought I'd find myself in a position of living at home again, especially with a child, but there I was, and at the ripe age of thirty-seven. It wasn't forever though. With the saving I was doing and the settlement I got from the divorce, I would be looking for a nice place in an amazing area, close to Mom. It would be for just Drew and me. And my ex-husband could go suck an egg.

When John had walked out on us two years ago for his personal trainer, I didn't know what to do with myself. I went through all the stages, and I was sure I was still stuck on anger. It was a douche move to leave the woman he married because she'd put on weight. Apparently, I wasn't taking care of myself, and his trainer, Dorothy, was. Didn't matter how I was doing all cooking, cleaning, keeping his books for his graphic design company and even working part-time myself as an assistant in a dental clinic. Didn't matter I was tired all the time and had no help at home.

What was worse, he deserted his son, only managing a phone call here and there while he was away on an extended work/vacation in Hawaii with his new woman. The thankful part about that was how Drew hadn't had the chance for John to shove Dorothy in his face.

Me: You won't get anymore either after the pain I went through. Childbirth wasn't a play in the park. It was a "rip you to shreds" kind of moment, and I wasn't ready to relive that anytime soon, as in never.

Looking up, I saw no sign of Ronald. What was he doing, taking a dump in the middle of a dinner date?

Mom: *Snort* It's easy the second time around. Now get rid of your date and come home.

"Sorry about that. I got a call while I was on the toilet."

My eyes widened. Did that mean he took the call while he was pooping?

My belly churned in disgust.

Placing my phone back in my bag, I turned to Ronald.

"Have you finished eating already?" His nose scrunched up at me.

Pecker-head.

"No. I got it to take home. I have to be honest here, Ronald. I'm happy with the way my body is, and my business isn't *cute*, it's amazing. I'm sorry, but I won't be calling for a second date." It was my turn to scoot along the seat.

"You don't want to have sex then?"

Laughter bubbled up and out. "Are you serious?" I stood beside the table with my bag over my shoulder and hands on my hips.

"Yes. You won't get anyone better than me with the extra weight you carry around."

Clenching my jaw, I placed my hands on the table, leaned in and bit out, "And you won't get anyone with the way you keep touching yourself and the huge hairy wart on the side of your nose."

His eyes widened. "I have no wart." He touched right where the wart was and when he drew his finger away, the wart came with it.

LILA ROSE

Oh, my mighty God. It was a monster of a booger, not a wart.

Didn't he look in the mirror in the bathroom?

When he stuck that snotty finger in his mouth, I gagged and made a run for the exit. Even forgoing my dinner. Snot-faced Ronald could deal with it all because I was suddenly not hungry.

The fresh air outside helped my churning stomach. Still, I lay a hand on it and rubbed. That was a sight I could have done without. Dragging my phone from my purse, I pressed the number saved to my favorites list.

"How did it go?" Molly asked as I made my way to my Cadillac in the car park.

"I hate you," I told her, and sniffed to double the effect.

Silence and then, "Really? I thought he wasn't bad."

"Not bad?" I scoffed. "Not bad?" I hissed, shaking my head. I continued in a whispered, annoyed tone, "Molly, I lost count of the times he touched himself, said something about my weight and then... Oh, God." I heaved, and the tart laughed.

"What?" she asked. She was probably enjoying my pain. I knew I would if the shoe was on her foot.

"H-he had a big clump of snot on the side of his nose. I'd thought it was a wart. When I pointed it out, he wiped it off, and then, *then, Molly*, he ate it." I gagged again and nearly smiled when I heard Molly do the same.

"Stop. Damn it, I nearly lost my dinner."

"And I hadn't had any. I also can't even stomach the thought of food right now, and that's saying something."

She giggled. "I'm so sorry, Addy. He seemed so normal at the coffee shop."

Sighing, I unlocked my car and slipped into the driver seat. "No more dates from you, Molly. I'll find my own, thank you very much."

"But earlier, I was—"

"No!" I demanded in a shout, throwing my bag to the passenger seat. "I swear if you try to set me up again, I'll wax your eyebrows off."

"Okay, okay. I promise no more dates organized from me." I could hear Clint in the background asking what happened. "Tell you later," Molly said, and then sighed when he pestered her again. "I swear he's the biggest gossip out."

"And you're only just noticing this?"

"Well, no." She laughed. "Okay, since your date was a disaster, why don't you come here for a pint of Ben and Jerry's? Those two men never disappoint a female, and it's still early enough before you have to get back to Drew." Clint yelled something, and Molly quickly replied in a bored tone, "Clinton is also a man who never disappoints."

"Gross, I don't want to hear any of that. He's like my brother. Anyway, I can't. I took Joe's hours for him later. I need to get home and sleep for a few before I start."

"But I thought you said you'd never do Joe's time again, due to Drew, and the fact those hours were the worst?"

"I did." I moaned. "But Joe's always had my back, and it's his birthday. How could I say no?"

"You're too nice, Addy."

"I know. This is a curse I must carry."

"Don't forget the jelly beans."

I groaned. "I have an extra huge bag at home." After all, I needed something to shove up my nose while I cleaned the booths. The adult store I worked in held booths at the back of the shop where horny men could visit and watch porn while they rubbed one out. I hated, *absolutely hated* cleaning them. Especially since I detested the smell of semen. But since it was a good paying job and I got to work school hours, especially as in those hours I hardly had men visit those rooms, it was worth it.

"Plus, I also have to spend some time with our new kitty cat."

Molly groaned. "I still can't believe you named the cat Puss-it."

Smiling, I started my car to warm it up, and said, "Well, when a cat shows up out of nowhere, and I couldn't find an owner, I really didn't want to look under it to see if it was a boy or a girl. It felt rude. So, of course, I couldn't call it Clementine, and then find out it's actually a boy so I should have named it Melvin. Puss-it seemed logical to Drew and me."

"Clementine? Melvin?" She sighed. "I'm sorry, but thank God jerk-off John named your son."

Laughing, I admitted, "That is true."

Walking through the front door, I found Mom sitting in the living room. "He wanted to wait up for you."

"Mom, it's nearly nine, and he's got school tomorrow."

"I know that, but he used the eyes on me."

Smiling, I rolled my eyes and made my way down the hall. One bad thing about living with Mom again was that Drew had her wrapped around his little finger. Which was another reason I had to find our own place or Drew would end up spoiled rotten. Though, when she'd stayed with Drew and me in our old house, the extra attention she delivered on Drew helped ease his loss of not having John around. She stayed until we sold the house, and then we moved in with her about six months ago. It was easier since I'd already been working in the adult store over her side of town the six months before moving in. I'd always wanted to eventually live in Mom's area, only it took me a while to convince John to let me change schools for Drew, to save the commuting back and forth.

He only recently started at his new school, and so far, so good. Although at first Drew hated the idea of being away from his friends, once we visited the new school, he fell in love with it all. What helped was the school having a basketball team. My son had been bursting at the seams to play basketball since he was six. His previous school only provided football, hockey, and soccer teams.

Stopping in the doorway to my son's room, I found him lying on his side with Puss-it curled into his stomach enjoying the attention Drew was lathering him with as he patted the cat's back.

My nine-year-old looked up, and a smile bloomed. His tired eyes crinkled in the corners at the sight of me. I loved seeing it—his face softening for his mom.

"My sweet boy should be asleep."

He yawned. "Wanted to see you, 'cause I won't in the morning." He knew I was working later. Only he thought I worked in a supermarket.

Grinning, I walked over to his bed and knelt on the floor. "Love that you wanted to see me, Drew, but I also would love it if you got some sleep so Nana doesn't have to deal with zombie Drew in the morning." I flicked his nose, causing him to laugh.

"I'll try not to be."

Pursing my lips, I then raised my brows. We both knew if he didn't get his ten hours he was a monster in the morning. His movements were sluggish and slouched, his replies were only ever grunts, which was why I called that side of Drew a zombie.

"Love you, my boy."

"Love you the most."

I scoffed. "Doubtful." I smiled and leaned in to kiss his cheek. "Get to sleep, and I'll see you after school tomorrow."

"'Kay."

As I stood, I picked up Puss-it, which Drew whined about. "Nope, I know you'll pat him all night if you had the chance. Maybe on the weekend he can sleep with you."

Drew sighed, but nodded. I threw him one last kiss, and he responded with his own, then exited his room, closing the door behind me.

I didn't know how I got so lucky, being blessed with such an amazing child, but I was, and I couldn't be more grateful.

Chapter TWO

SURPRISINGLY, THE NIGHT was quiet. I'd already tidied the DVDs, restocked the cock rings and had time to dust the vibrator boxes. Some women would hate the job, but I enjoyed it, except those back rooms. *Shudder.* Sex was something every person should enjoy, and sometimes with the added pleasure of toys, it made things more fun. I wasn't embarrassed about selling sex toys. I was confident in the job I did. Even if I hadn't tried out all the products, I still learned how they worked in case anyone had questions. Sex wasn't something to be ashamed of. It was a part of life... which was why I missed it so much. John had always been good in the bedroom. It was why I hadn't seen his cheating coming since he'd slept with me just two days before he said he was leaving. Yes, we fought, mainly over my weight, but if he couldn't take me for who I was, then he wasn't worth having in my life and bed. Something I told him after I slashed his tires and he called me a crazy bitch.

LILA ROSE

The bell over the door rang as someone opened it. I placed a wide smile on my face, only to freeze when my wet dream walked into the store.

Oh, God. He was... stunningly hot.

I was going to choke and burn.

He glanced over his shoulder and smiled when a woman entered just after him. I let out a whoosh of air that had caught in my lungs. When I knew the hot guy, like Clint, for instance, was taken, I was totally fine around them.

Although, I couldn't help but feel the sad dip in my belly knowing the man candy in front of me was taken. Then again, he was totally out of my league. At least he was entertainment for a few moments in the boring night.

"Hi," I chirped, and waved when they both looked my way.

Wow, his lady friend was also stunning. A little on the larger size like myself, and gorgeous, and seeing them together made me like the man even more because he went for a bigger-sized woman.

"Hey, hi, um, just looking," she spat, and then giggled nervously.

Aw, she was shy. I wanted to take her in my arms and hug her, tell her there was nothing wrong with being in an adult store.

However, I didn't. Instead, with my eyes holding hers, I said, "Let me know if you need any help. The other day our delivery came in with a shock therapy simulation kit for the nipples, clit and pussy mound. I've heard they do wonders to get you aroused." The woman blanched. But when the man beside her choked out a laugh, I turned to find him looking at me. I quickly averted my gaze back to the woman. Yes, I was okay with good-looking men once I knew they were taken, *but* his eyes, his warm, dark, luscious eyes wanted to hold me captive until I shouted my deepest darkest secrets, and I didn't think it would go down well when his girlfriend was standing right next to him.

"Um, thank you. I think. But really we're just looking. Filling in some time." She thumbed to the man next to her. "He dared me to come in while we waited—"

"What are these?" the man asked suddenly.

Dang it, I didn't want to look at him. My face was already starting to feel hot. I shouldn't have had that reaction since it was obvious he was taken, yet I was still acting like an idiot around him. Quickly, I flicked my gaze to see what he held. My eyes widened a fraction. Did he even read the packet? It was really self-explanatory.

Or maybe he couldn't read or he needed glasses to read.

Sucking in a breath, I called forth my sales persona and pasted on a smile. Talking to him didn't actually mean I had to look at him. I could fake it.

God, I hoped I could.

Clearing my throat, I made my way around the counter and started, "Its popping candy. I haven't tried it myself, but I've heard great things about it. Women love it when their partners use it in the bedroom." I stopped just beside the woman, and honestly, I knew approaching them to try and make them feel comfortable was a mistake. Her man smelled divine.

"How?" he asked. His voice being quieter and richer, deeper made my pulse race.

"Well, it's called BJ Blast. It's apparently designed for women, but I'm sure men would like it just the same."

"And this?" he asked, after releasing the candy and grabbing another box that I was sure he hadn't even looked at.

Smiling, I kept my professionalism at the front, even though I found the questioning a little strange. Not that people didn't ask me, they did. However, I was finding he was doing it in a way that was automatic. As if he didn't really care. Still, I replied, "Edible crotchless panties, unisex actually. Both men and women can wear them," I added, in case he was going to question what it meant next. Waving my arm around the store, I said, "All products in here add a little spice and fun in the bedroom. Feel free to look around, and call out if you need any information. I'll help as much as I can."

"You're—"

"Thank you," the woman interrupted, and took hold of her man's wrist, dragging him off to the wall of adult DVDs. Once there, they had a few private snapped words before the man sighed, ran a hand through his dark locks, and nodded.

I kind of felt weird standing there staring at the couple, wishing I was in the woman's shoes, so I went back around the counter and started to restock the sex dice on the stand near the register.

The bell above the door rang, and in stepped two men, one who looked eighteen and the other in his late twenties. Both looked similar with their blond hair and blue eyes, only the younger one wore glasses. Thankfully, they were both cute in their own way, but not overly hot to a point where I would get tongue-tied and stupid. In other words, they were nothing like the man standing in the porn area.

"Hi, welcome to Carnal Vice—" I broke off when the woman, still at the DVDs, started laughing loudly. Her man glared down at her. Turning my attention back, I offered a smile and said, "Sorry, my name's Adalyn. If you need advice on anything, please don't be shy to ask. I'm here to help."

The older one stepped up to the counter and said, "Hi, Adalyn, I'm Mike, and that's Sam. It's my younger brother's first time in this type of shop."

Sam blushed, and when I caught his eyes, I offered him a sympathetic smile. It was obvious he didn't want to be in the store with his older brother, who would probably tease like all siblings did. My younger sister, who I didn't really get along with, constantly had with me.

"Hi, Sam. Don't stress about your first time. Heck, when I first visited an adult store, I knocked into the dildo stand, and they fell to the floor. Everyone in that *busy* shop looked at me and laughed. I then had to pick them all up while they wobbled all over the place in my hand. It just happened to be the ten-inch stand." Leaning in a little, I added, "At least it's not busy here."

He chuckled and nodded.

"So congrats on it being your first time to the store, Sam."

"Thanks."

I threw out my hand and added, "Take a look around, enjoy, and there's no pressure or judging here."

They moved off, and Mike pointed something out to Sam; they both had a laugh about it. I thought it was sweet his brother had brought him for the first time.

"What DVD would you suggest?"

Just his growly voice had my heart jumping and lower half springing to life as if it were being born again and singing "Circle of Life." My hoo-ha wanted to offer itself up to the man in front of me.

Which was wrong.

So very, very wrong.

He had a woman at his side.

Looking at his chin, his very sexy chin, I stuttered, "P-pardon?"

He mumbled something under his breath, and said, "Which would you suggest?" There was a tapping sound, so I looked down to see his masculine hands on the counter, and one of his fingers tapped at a DVD of spanking. Next to it was one about gangbanging.

"Spanking!" I cried, and I felt my blush run down to my neck. I glanced at the others in the store; his woman was giggling behind her hand. Mike and Sam were smiling our way mischievously. Clearing my throat, I said, "Sorry, um, the one about spanking is good. Unless you like to share your woman, then I'd go for the other."

"I don't share."

That was good to know... at least, I thought it was. Only, I didn't know why I was thinking about it in the first place.

"Have you seen both?" he asked.

Why wouldn't he just leave me alone? His girlfriend had wandered away, and I wanted her to get her butt back over to us and drag him away.

"Porn is good." What in the world was I saying that for? "Ha, I mean, um, yes. I have seen them. We're sent an extra copy of each movie to watch so we know what we're talking about when people ask."

"Why are you patting your back?" His voice for once held humor.

Because I was proud of myself for delivering a coherent sentence around your stunning self, was what I wanted to say. Instead, I pretended to itch and say, "Ah, my bra strap was annoying me. I wasn't patting."

"So you would suggest spanking?"

Spanking.

He'd said it with his deep, gruff voice. I wanted him to say it again and again. If only I could watch his mouth form the words also. I honestly thought it would be possible to climax from it. However, I still wouldn't look him in the eyes, so I kept them down on the movies and nodded. "Yes. Spanking is good." My eyes widened. "I mean, the movie on it is."

Please, someone come in and murder me.

"Adalyn," thankfully Mike called. "What does this do?"

My whole body sagged in relief. "Excuse me, please. Unless you want to purchase...."

"Not right now."

Nodding, I left him to his choices and just about ran over to the brothers. They were holding up a dick pump, so I explained the use of it even while my mind was slapping myself mentally for acting like such an idiot around the customer when I clearly knew he was with his girlfriend.

I left the brothers laughing and turned back to the counter to find the man still standing there. On the quick glance around the shop, I saw his partner had gone.

Snap.

He stood with his arms crossed over his chest as I slowly approached. I got the feeling from the flick of my eyes to his face he wasn't pleased about something. Instead of going around the counter, I stopped just in front of him and asked, "Can I help you?"

"No," he clipped.

Okay then.

Maybe his woman ran off on him. He could come across as a big slong.

"My name is Vice Salvatore."

Oh. Shit.

"I can see by your expression you know who I am."

My mouth slammed shut. I nodded and then added in a whisper, "Yes." Taking a deep breath, I went on, "You're the owner of all Carnal Vice's stores." *Though why you would name them after yourself is kind of weird.* "And of all the adult films on the shelves."

My stomach dropped down into my toes. The stunning man was my boss.

"Exactly. Usually, I would have my assistant run the secret shopper program, but she's on maternity leave, and I told her I would fill in for the stores she had left."

Was he about to say there was a problem with my work?

"This was my last one, and I've found the service lacking."

Oh no he didn't.

Clenching my teeth, I breathed heavily out of my nose. The good-looking knob found me lacking.

Lacking.

"Not once did you meet my gaze when I asked questions. You seemed uneducated, not only on how to speak normally but on the items in the store— What are you doing?"

His question had come from me holding my hand up in his face. He'd just gone and peeved me off.

"I'm stopping you from continuing." Luckily, when I was fuming, I didn't care if the man was hot or not. If my blood boiled enough, I would stand up for myself. Taking a breath, I lifted my gaze to his and glared. Placing my hands on my hips, I said, "When you asked about the items I told you exactly what they were. I know about everything in this store. There is no way you can tell me I'm *lacking* in that area."

"You fumbled through talking about everything."

Damn it. I fumbled through it because of his stupid looks. Only there was no way I would tell him that.

God, I was an idiot.

LILA ROSE

With my anger riding high, I demanded, "Ask me anything, and I'll tell you." I knew it would be later my nerves would get the better of me over the fact I just spoke to the big boss that way, which could cause me to lose my job. There was also a chance it would send me to a mental hospital from having a breakdown.

His brows arched and then lowered into a scowl. "Fine." He rattled off some products, and I told him exactly what they were used for and how partners could enjoy them together or alone even. He then asked me to define the difference between each blow-up doll. Even though a blush lit my cheeks at the errant thought of Mr. Salvatore using one, I went on explaining with my head held high and my eyes meeting his very intimidating ones.

"So in conclusion, I would always suggest Veronica, her skin is smoother than most, so less chafing and more pleasure would be delivered."

"This will be your only warning. Act like you did with me with any other customer you'll be fired."

"I won't," I said with a snipped tone. It seemed Vice Salvatore may have cured me of becoming a stuttering fool with any good-looking man. All I had to do was picture him and how much he peeved me off to bring my anger forth.

Chapter THREE

Two weeks. It took me two weeks to calm my nerves and stop thinking Mr. Salvatore would pop back into the store and fire me. I needed and loved my job... well, until my own business was 100 percent profitable. Unfortunately, I couldn't keep the man out of my head. He even starred in some of the steamy dreams I had that involved spanking. No matter what I did, where I was, my mind conjured up the picture of him standing at the counter with his arms crossed over his broad chest, scowling.

Thankfully, it was Molly's thirty-fifth birthday, and we were headed to meet Clinton at the restaurant he'd picked, so I hoped with a few drinks and some inspirational words from my best friend, all thoughts of Mr. Salvatore would disappear. Not that I'd told her anything yet; I knew she would get annoyed on my behalf, so I was waiting for the drinking part of the night to begin, and for us to be around Clint; he seemed to calm her temper quickly.

Climbing out of the cab, Molly commented, "Wow, Clint's going all out tonight. Isn't that sweet." She smiled as we made our way to the door or the restaurant.

It *was* sweet, and it kind of hurt my heart because I wanted what my best friend had. Instead, I was always their third wheel, not that they thought anything of it. Like then, while we walked to the maître d's desk, I couldn't help but think I shouldn't be encroaching on their night. But then when I'd said I was staying in, they harped at me to join them, telling me it wouldn't be the same without me. I couldn't have asked for better best friends.

"Molly" was called before we could say anything at the front counter. Glancing to our right, we saw Clint standing beside a table. He was dressed in black pants and a white shirt, waving us over.

"He's all dressed up," I commented and heard Molly sigh in appreciation. I was glad I'd gone with a black cocktail dress for the occasion. Then again, the restaurant we were in held a five-star rating. Molly looked amazing in her dark red rock-a-billy dress, and by the way Clint's eyes were devouring her, he would also agree.

They greeted each other while I sat and placed a napkin on my lap. A hand landed on my shoulder. "Hey, Addy."

"Clint, good to see you going all out."

"Well, you only turn thirty-five once."

That was true. I turned it two years ago, yet I never did anything special for it. Neither did John.

God, since the visit from the big boss, I seemed to be in a depressing mood. The "lacking" comment must have got to me more than I thought.

Actually, I knew it had when I'd gotten home that night and cried into my ice cream. I had a real Bridget Jones moment while listening to music and thinking I had nothing going for my life. I had no one but my mom and son, who *had* to love me because we were related. Shaking my head, I cleared my mind, and instead of sinking lower into my pity party, I glanced to Molly who had just sat. I wouldn't bring the night down for her since she was sweet to also love me.

Her eyes widened. She smiled big and waved to someone. Before I got to see who, she took my wrist and Clint's, then pulled us up with her, dragging us over to someone she obviously knew.

"Grayson, long time no see. Hi, Kenzie, Dylan, Lori, and Mr. High." Molly greeted as I stepped up beside her. My eyes widened. It wasn't over the fact the table held two drool-worthy men and one good-looking older man. It was because Mr. Salvatore's girlfriend was sitting next to, and curled into, another man. That man who was soon standing and bringing Molly in for a hug.

"Molly, great to see you. When was the last time?"

"I think at Makala's baby shower." I could hear the smile in her voice. I didn't see it because I was glaring at Kenzie. Was she cheating on Mr. Salvatore? She glanced my way. Her smile dropped as she took in my scowl, and then her expression changed and she was grinning again. She glanced back to Molly, and said, "Wow, it has been too long since you couldn't make it to Makala first birthday a few months ago."

Makala? Who was that?

"Clinton, great to see you also, and who's this?" Grayson asked.

Molly gripped my wrist again and tugged my arm near out of its socket. I stumbled forward and moved my gaze from Kenzie to the man she was cheating with. "This is my friend Adalyn. Addy, this is Grayson, his wife, Kenzie, his brother Dylan, and Kenzie's sister, Lori, and Kenzie's and Lori's Dad, Mr. High."

Wait a second.

Hold the dang phone.

Kenzie was married to Grayson?

She wasn't with Mr. Salvatore?

Then...

"Oh, and I forgot to mention Grayson is also my brother's close friend."

No.

My wide eyes flicked to Kenzie. She was laughing, and then she nodded at me.

No, no, no.

"Molly, what are you doing here?"

That voice had me frozen.

"Vice," Molly yelled, turning and then throwing herself at my boss. I didn't turn. In fact, sneaking under the table so I didn't have to face him was the only option I could think of. Just as I'd started to crouch, Molly grabbed my arm, hurled me up and around.

"You," Vice clipped.

"You," I snapped back.

I could feel many eyes on us as we stood glaring at one another. My chances of hiding were shot, so I stood tall and crossed my arms over my chest. Mr. Salvatore's eyes flicked down and then back up, his eyes lowering into a scowl even more.

"What's going on? How do you two know each other?" Molly asked. "Addy, I've never had the chance to introduce you to my brother."

Shifting my gaze to hers, I said, "Brother?" But they had different last names.

"Stepbrother, but all the same." She smiled. "How do you two know each other?"

Looking back to Molly's brother, my boss, my gaze turned glacial when I said, "He found my services *lacking*."

Someone behind me choked on something, and then I heard, "Is she a prostitute?"

"Hang on—" Molly started.

"Well, they were," Mr. Salvatore replied, crossing his own arms over his chest and ignoring everyone else.

"They. Were. Not," I bit out each word slowly.

"Darling," a woman called before she slipped up beside Mr. Salvatore and placed her hand on his bicep. Of course, she just had to be beautiful, if you liked a woman with a slim waist, huge boobs, and brown hair that went on forever flowing down her back.

So, Mr. Salva-freaking-tore did have a girlfriend.

Go figure he went for someone like her.

"Vice—" Molly started.

"Who do we have here?" the woman asked as she glanced around at everyone.

Mr. Salvatore sighed, and then shook off the woman's hand, only so he could place his hand on her back. "Debra, this is my sister, Molly, her boyfriend, Clint, and that's Grayson, his wife, Kenzie, her sister, Lori, and Grayson's brother, Dylan. Also the ladies' father, Trent."

"Nice to meet you all, and who are you?" Debra asked as she looked me over while I still stood in front of her man glaring up at him.

"I'm not sure who she is. Molly?" Mr. Salvatore said. Totally wiping me off as no one important. I had an urge to pull back my leg and kick him in the shin.

I worked in one of his stores for goodness' sake.

Heat hit my back, and a hand landed on my shoulder. Then Clint's voice came from over my head. "She's a friend of ours, Adalyn Wallis. Now, I want to know how you seem to know her and why you're looking at her like you want to harm her."

Aw, Clint's gone into protective mode.

Mr. Salvatore's eyes snapped to Clint's hands on my shoulders before looking at Clint over my head. Dang it for being short.

"She works in one of my stores, and I'm unsure as yet if her employment will continue."

Molly stepped up to her brother and glared. "What did you do to her?"

He scoffed. "I did nothing. She stumbled over her words and wouldn't meet my gaze. My stores are meant to come across as professional, not some cheap, casual business."

Shit.

Yes, the moment was swear-word worthy because I knew what was about to come out of Molly's mouth when

28

she turned to me with humor in her eyes and lips twitching. "Really? Him?" she asked.

"Molly," I warned in a hissed tone.

She ignored me and faced her brother. "It's fine, Vice. I know why she was acting like that and believe me, she would never usually behave that way in a place she worked unless—"

I placed my hand over her mouth. "No. Nothing. She doesn't know what she's talking about."

"I'd like to know what she was gonna say." I glanced over my shoulder to see it was Mr. High who had spoken, and he was smiling.

"So would I," Mr. Salvatore clipped.

"Adalyn, relax and unhand Molly. Vice, her actions just meant— Oompf," Clinton wheezed as I elbowed him in the stomach.

"Nothing!" I cried. "I was having a bad night. That's all it meant."

There was no way I'd let either of them inform Mr. Salvatore that my actions were because I had been (note to self, I had said, *had been*, I wasn't any longer) attracted to him. Even if I had to take them to the ground so they didn't spill the beans, I would. Fancy restaurant be damned.

"What I would like to know is why you said you didn't know her when she works for you?" Debra asked, a slight frown on her Botox lips.

Good question, Debra. Let's see him get out of that one.

Molly shoved my hand off her mouth and added, "I also want to know when my brother branched out into opening stores without telling me."

Mr. Salvatore's brows dipped. "I thought I had told you."

"Nope." Molly shook her head.

"I was sure I did."

"About two years ago you mentioned you thought of branching out, not that you were serious about it."

He rolled his eyes. "Does it really matter? Can we get back to why Miss Wallis acted the way she had in the store?"

"No," I yelled, and then cringed when a lot more eyes came our way. "How about you all join us for dinner?" Grayson offered.

"Thanks, but... I, um. I think I forgot to turn the refrigerator back on. I'd been defrosting all afternoon."

"Liar," Molly helpfully—*not*—put in.

Sending her a glare, which she smiled at, I then said, "I have to feed my pussy." I paled and then felt, actually *felt* the heat bursting forward onto my cheeks. "I meant my kitty. He's new and hungry."

"For men or meat?" Lori called out. I looked to her to see she and Kenzie dissolved into a fit of giggles.

Mr. High started to grumble about how ungrateful his little shits of daughters were.

Shaking my head in amusement at their inside joke, I glanced to Grayson and said, "Thank you, but I should go." Looking to Molly, I added, "Have a brilliant birthday dinner, but I—"

"Fuck. It's your birthday?" Mr. Salvatore barked, causing me to jump.

Molly shrugged and smiled. "Don't worry about it. I know how busy you are."

"Please, sit and have dinner with us." He gestured to the table, which didn't supply enough room for everyone.

"I'll get someone to bring another table over," Dylan said as he stood and walked off.

Mr. Salvatore cleared his throat at my side. "And you'll stay for my sister since she obviously wanted to celebrate her birthday with you."

I ignored him, even when I knew he was talking to me. Instead, I kept my eyes on where Dylan had walked.

"Miss Wallis."

I didn't even bother to correct him on the Miss part. He didn't need to know I was still a Mrs. Well, I wouldn't be for too much longer. I was in the process of taking back my maiden name of Sage.

While Clinton and Molly talked—actually they were cooing at one another—I watched Dylan walk back with a smile on his face.

"Miss Wallis" was gritted out.

"Vice, can we sit already? Plus, I'm still waiting on an explanation to why you said you didn't know *her*." Debra had said *her* like I was some disease.

"Adalyn" was snapped low, and I finally graced him with my eyes. I was finding it fun riling Mr. Salvatore. *Call me lacking, will he?*

"Sorry, were you talking to me?" I asked innocently.

His nostrils flared. Grayson, who appeared from somewhere, slapped Vice on the shoulder and laughed, and then walked off to sit beside his wife.

Another table joined at the end, people shifted and made room for an extra three. Except I wasn't sticking around. Mr. Salvatore took Debra aside and started speaking quietly to her. I saw it as my chance to sneak out without him hindering me even more about sticking around when he forgot his sister's birthday in the first place.

I still couldn't believe Molly was my boss's sister.

She had spoken about her brother on occasions, only she never said his name. What she did tell me was that he was a local businessman and constantly busy. They kept in contact via e-mails and phone calls, but even those were sparse. Still, she loved him.

What she never mentioned, and I hadn't noticed until then was his name or who exactly he was. She'd even been into the store, so why hadn't she made the connection to her brother and the shop? Especially since the business was called Carnal Vice. Then again, maybe she thought her brother wouldn't be that conceited to name adult stores after himself.

I stepped up to Molly and Clint's side. "I'm going to head off. I'm sorry—"

"So...," she drew out, interrupting me. "You think my brother's hot?"

"Shh. I *did*, not since he called me lacking. In fact, now he just annoys me. He'll never be hot in my eyes again."

"Uh-huh." She winked.

"Seriously."

"Sure." She gave me the thumbs-up.

Rolling my eyes, I said, "None of that matters anyway. We're not talking about it any longer since I'm leaving." I leaned in and kissed her cheek. "Enjoy your night and have a drink for me—"

"Hold up," Clinton said, dragging our attention his way. I gasped and stepped back.

Oh. My. God.

Chapter FOUR

CLINTON DILMUN WAS down on one knee with a jewelry box in his hand. He held it up to his long-time girlfriend, Molly. Molly had her hand over her heart and tears glistening in her eyes. Warmth hit my back, and in my ear was whispered, with a gruff tone, "Now you'll have to stay to celebrate."

The man behind me seemed to like to think he could order me around. Well, I had news for him. "I'll be staying, *but* not because you said to. Instead, it's because I *want* to."

It was then I heard his low chuckle, and it sent a shiver throughout my body. I quickly stepped away. I couldn't afford to have any type of reaction to the man who was my boss, and my best friend's brother. Also a man who was already taken. The last part was the most important one.

Cheers went up around me, and it was then I realized I'd missed the whole proposal, all because of the stupid man on my mind. I turned to glare at him. His eyes were on me and he winked.

The gall.

Raising my upper lip at him caused him to throw his head back and laugh.

I was soon wrapped in arms by a screaming Molly. "I'm engaged."

A smile lit my face. Her excitement was contagious. We jumped around in a circle, gushing over the thrill and ring.

"Hey, waiter," I heard Mr. High call. "Drinks around the table, all on my son-in-law. It's time to celebrate."

Clinton stepped up and tucked Molly under his arm as others congratulated them. I took a seat next to Mr. High, and then to my horror, Mr. Salvatore sat next to me, while Clinton and Molly took up the next couple of seats at his side. My brows dipped. Where had Debra gone?

It was Grayson, from across the table, who voiced my question. "Your date seems to have disappeared."

Mr. Salvatore grunted, which Grayson smirked at. I turned my attention to the menu since it seemed my boss wasn't going to actually reply with a proper answer about why his date left. My stomach growled as I eyed the list of food. In the end, I narrowed it down between steak with salad or the mushroom chicken and salad.

"Adalyn, wasn't it?" Mr. High called beside me.

Glancing at him, I smiled.

"Yes."

"So tell me. How did Vice find your services lacking?"

"Dad!" Lori scolded.

"Come on, Jellybean, we all want to know."

"He's right, babe," Dylan said.

Grayson and Kenzie talked quietly, but their eyes were on me. My so-called friends were in their own world on the other side of Mr. Salvatore. Though, I couldn't blame them.

Since I was on my own, I told Mr. High, "I work in one of his stores, and he came in pretending to be a customer. I answered every question he asked, but apparently, I didn't do a good job of it."

Mr. Salvatore scoffed at my side. "If you had met my gaze and didn't mutter through everything, I wouldn't have had a problem."

Spinning to face him, I glared at his smirk and said, "I didn't mutter."

"You did."

"Well, maybe if you hadn't have been a big, scary ass, I—"

"Boss," Mr. High coughed into his fist. "Damn, that seemed familiar." He looked to Kenzie, who rolled her eyes.

Bugger, he was right. I couldn't call my boss an ass even if he deserved it.

"Anyway. It won't happen again." I grabbed a roll out of the basket in front of me and broke it apart like I was breaking the arm which was heating my back on the top of my chair.

What was Mr. Salvatore's game? To unnerve me? Well, he couldn't.

Grinding my teeth, I slapped some butter on my roll, squished it together and bit into it with a grumble under my breath about how stupid jerks smelt divine. Then again, I was sure most men from hell would smell tempting.

There were a couple of chuckles around me. One from the man I was trying to ignore beside me. I glanced at him and with a mouthful, asked, "What? Do you find my eating *lacking* also?" He probably had a problem with how I ate or the fact I ate at all. Especially if Debra was the type he usually went for.

"Not at all," he answered.

"I'm not lacking in any area," I stated with a huff. I placed the rest of my roll down so I could turn toward him and cross my arms. Why I was arguing about it there in front of everyone I didn't know. But the word lacking had hit hard.

"Really?" he queried. His lips trembled like he wanted to smile because he found me amusing.

I wasn't being funny.

The man before me got on my nerves.

"Yes, really."

"Then why wouldn't you look at me in the store, until of course at the end, when you became angry with me."

Rolling my eyes, I snorted and waved my hand aimlessly in the air. "No reason, nothing really."

"Then I guess you *lack* at telling the truth." He smirked like he'd won a round of boxing. I opened my mouth to tell him where he could shove the word lacking when Grayson cleared his throat.

"As entertaining as this argument is, I think it's time to order," Grayson announced.

I clapped, pointed to the man across from me, and said, "That's a grand idea."

Kenzie and Lori giggled. Dylan was smiling while Mr. High chuckled, and my *old* friends down the end were looking at me and grinning like they were enjoying a show.

When the waiter finally arrived, and after we ordered, Molly stole Mr. Salvatore's attention, which I was grateful for since he turned their way and dropped his arm from behind my chair. I used the time to get to know the rest at the table. They were amazing people, full of happy and laughable moments. Especially when I heard about Kenzie on cough medicine. Eventually we got on the subject of their children, Noah was two and Makala was one. I mentioned my divorce and then Drew. I didn't realize, as I was telling them my life story, the people to my right had grown silent and were also listening.

"Why would your dick of an ex leave a lovely lady like yourself?" Mr. High asked.

"Dad, you can't ask things like that." Kenzie jumped in.

His head jerked back. "Why not?"

"It's private. Don't mind him. He didn't take his not-to-be-nosy meds tonight."

Mr. High groaned. Honestly, there was no shame in the answer to his question. It was plain and simple. My ex left me for a younger, skinnier woman.

John had been the first to find me lacking.

Lacking enough to leave me.

He'd been gone for two years, yet it still hurt to think I wasn't enough for such a douchebag. He wasn't perfect either, but did I tell him about his flaws? No, I hadn't because I wasn't such a mean person.

Then again, John hadn't been mean throughout our relationship. We'd had happy times. Many of them. Except toward the end.

Honestly, instead of reliving the pain associated with the word lacking, I should think myself lucky. I had been married to a man who was so self-centered. A man who couldn't love me for who I was, no matter the shape I was in.

Yes, I was better off without a man like that in my life.

Pasting a smile on my face, I shrugged and glanced down to my watch. "Maybe another time I'll tell you, Mr. High, but for now, I really must be going."

No doubt Drew would be waiting up for me since it was Friday, even though I'd warned him not to be tired for his first basketball game. As I stood, Mr. High's hand landed on mine and gave it a squeeze. I sent him a warm smile and moved around my chair to push it into the table. Digging through my bag, I grabbed my purse and pulled it free.

"I've got it," his rough voice said. I looked to see Mr. Salvatore staring at me.

"No, thank you, but I can pay—"

"Do you have to argue about everything?"

LILA ROSE

My lips snapped shut. I didn't usually argue so much; it seemed Mr. Salvatore brought it out in me. Ignoring him, I pulled out some bills and—

"Adalyn," Clinton called. "I've got it, honey. I was going to buy anyway as a thanks for sharing this moment with us and being a part of our lives."

That was sweet.

Smiling, I blinked the tears away and nodded. I took the couple of steps to them and slipped my arms around each of their shoulders, bringing them in close. "Love you, guys, and congratulations again." Honestly, I wished I'd have known Molly and Clinton longer than a year. They were amazing people.

Standing, I placed a hand on each of their shoulders and said to the table, "Enjoy the rest of the night, and it was great meeting you all."

In their own verbal version, I got a goodbye from everyone. Only, when I glanced quickly to my boss, he didn't say anything. Instead, he tipped his chin up.

Molly tapped my hand. I leaned back in. "Thanks for coming. Love you, girlfriend, and don't fall over on the way out. He'll be watching." She grinned big, and I scowled back.

Why, oh, why, would she do that to me?

Great, I was going to fall on my face no doubt. She knew how flustered I got if I even had an inkling a stunning man was paying me attention.

Wait. No, I could do it. I could walk out normally, and nothing would happen because Mr. Salvatore didn't affect me. He annoyed me. I was over his good-looking self.

40

Yeah, and that was why my heart beat a million miles an hour. My stupid organ had been going crazy ever since I'd heard his voice, had him near me, and when his alluring scent clung to my nostrils all night long.

Damn the good-looking man.

I forced out a fake laugh, and then through gritted teeth, I said, "I'll be fine. Like I said… doesn't affect me any longer."

With a final goodbye, I turned, placed my bag strap over my shoulder, and with my head held high, I slowly walked toward the exit.

Easy. Simple. I can totally do this.

I would have been fine… if an idiot didn't push his chair back as I made my way through two tables.

I would have made it if that chair didn't slam into my hip and cause me to fall to the left, pushing a woman's upper body into her food, and then she turned abruptly with her arm out ready to defend herself. Yes, I would have stayed on my feet if I wasn't in her hitting distance and falling to the floor when she knocked the wind out of me with her elbow.

For once, it wasn't my clumsy fault, and yet I still made a fool out of myself.

I knew some of the laughter would be coming from Molly and Clinton. The rest I didn't have a clue. I lay on the floor dying from embarrassment and blinked up at the ceiling while people flittered around me.

Finally, my friend came to rescue me. With her hand out, I took hold, and Molly helped me stand on two feet. The man who pushed the chair into me came forward and apologized profusely, as did the woman who thought she was being attacked by her boyfriend's wife. After I assured them I was fine, I turned to Molly and asked an important question.

"Did he see?"

She was friendly enough she at least tried to fight her smile. "Yes."

Nodding, I bit my bottom lip and cursed under my breath. He must think I was a real head case.

"Not that I care if he saw," I quickly added.

"Sure," Molly drew out.

"I don't. I mean, let's be real here. He's my boss, your brother, and he's dating someone. Also, there is the fact his name is connected to adult films. Imagine if Drew ever found out." I faked a shudder.

"How about we talk about this later when you don't have a split in the back of your dress."

My heart stopped, my eyes widened, and I snarled, "You could have told me sooner." Reaching around, I covered my butt with my hands.

She shrugged. "It's hard to understand Clint's mime movements."

"Oh, God. They're all looking, aren't they?"

Her lips thinned. "Maybe."

"Kill me now."

"Addy, here you go." Clinton came up behind to cover me with his jacket.

Gripping the arms of the jacket tightly around my waist, I said, "We will never speak of this again. Any of it, except about the engagement part. The rest will be locked behind a solid vault."

"But Vice—"

"No."

"Adalyn, he's not so bad. I'm—"

"No." I shook my head, kissed her cheek and then Clinton's with a promise to clean his jacket and get it back to him. I then fled the restaurant quickly. Only it got the best of me. Just before I was out the door I looked back and saw my boss gazing at me with a frown on his annoyed-looking face.

If I had anything to do with it, I would never see Mr. Salvatore again.

With luck—*please shine down on me in this area at least*—Mr. Salvatore would never step foot in the store again, and if he did, it would be at the same hours as last time. Which was when I wouldn't be there.

At least I knew I would never see him at Molly's. I'd been visiting her place for a year, and he never went there. Ever.

Chapter FIVE

My dress was ruined, and it'd been the only black dress I owned. Mom said she could fix it, only she wasn't the best seamstress, and honestly, all I wanted to do was forget the night ever happened.

"Are you sure you don't want me to fix it?" Mom asked again as we sat in the seating area in the school gym. Drew was just warming up with his team. Seeing his infectious smile had me smiling also, even when my stomach was rolled up with regret from the previous night.

I didn't like feeling regret, but I was.

Not only over my drama spat with Mr. Salvatore, but the way I had handled him calling my work lacking in the first place. People had their own opinion. If he didn't like anything, that was his choice. I knew I hadn't been the best salesperson around him. I think I overreacted to the word and rolled my emotions over John up into that word when it had come out of Mr. Salvatore's mouth.

Usually, I wasn't that crazy.

Okay, so maybe I was, but I could have held it back a little where I wouldn't be worried about my future employment.

Shaking my head, I said to Mom, "No, it's fine. I've already thrown it out anyway." Even though John had had money, I'd never been one to spend it just for the hell of it. My parents had struggled, going from a week to week wage, but they did it happily. Dad passed away over five years ago, and it was a loss that hit us all hard. One I wasn't sure Mom could get over. The only blessing after his passing was the insurance my dad had placed. He wanted to take care of Mom even when he wasn't around.

"I worry about you, sweetheart. I want you to have what I had with your father. I thought you'd found it with John, but he turned out to be a dick. I know your sister won't ever find it. She's too wild to settle down, and I'm not sure a man could take her on full-time. But—"

"Mom, you do know happiness doesn't revolve around having a man in my life? I'm happy. I really am. I have a great job, people are loving my jewelry. I have Drew. I have you and my friends. I'm happy. I promise you. And yes, a good time in the sack wouldn't go astray, but I'll never count on my happiness to come from one person since I've already got it from everyone and thing around me."

"You're a smart woman, my Adalyn."

"I got that from Dad," I teased.

She mock scowled, and with a slap to the arm, she said, "Why I never, you rotten child. I'm taking it back now."

LILA ROSE

It was ridiculous how much I loved my mom, but I did. We were close, always had been since I was young and had been her shadow on everything she did. She loved Dad like it was their first date each day of their lives together. I wish she still had that. I also would have loved to experience that type of love for myself, but I hadn't, not even with John. Even though she kept herself busy, I still saw sadness lingering in her mom's eyes, and honestly, the love that they had for one another that sadness would always live in her, like it did me. I could only hope she was happy and content with her life, like I felt with my own.

"Do you... are you happy, Mom?" *Or do you feel you need a man to be happy*? Was what I left off.

She reached over and gave my hand a squeeze, knowing where I was coming from. "I'm happy, sweetheart. I'll always love and miss your father. The time I had with such an amazing man will be cherished until I take my last breath. My daughter is right, though. Happiness isn't something to be found in a man because I'm happy as I am. Though, an orgasm from a man instead of—"

I covered her mouth with my hand, my eyes wide as I glanced around to the people in the stands. "Say no more, I beg you."

A very manly chuckle sounded behind us. I glanced there to find a man who seemed to be around the same age as me, looking at me with a sweet smile. He was also a looker, and I would have thought my nerves would take over, but apparently, Mr. Salvatore *had* cleared them from my system.

"Sorry," I said. "Not really a conversation to have at a child's basketball game."

He winked. "Hasn't started yet, so all good."

"Oh, if you'll both excuse me, I think I need some refreshments before the game starts, and I need to call your sister," Mom spat out quickly, and she was up and gone even faster.

My mother.

I wasn't sure she'd actually call Camila, my sister, since Cammy never answered her phone when Mom or I called. She never liked being told what to do. In the end, her rebellion caused her to up and leave, only returning when Dad died and, even then, it was as though I didn't know my own sister. It saddened me to admit that. But I wasn't sure it would change until she did. Until she got over the "everyone hates me" complex. We didn't hate her. We just didn't like her choices, since one time it led her to a boyfriend who was a drug dealer. Thankfully, he wasn't in the picture any longer, or so we heard. I had no clue where we all went wrong, why she was angry with us all. If I knew, I would fix it so Mom wouldn't look at Cammy's photo with tears in her eyes all the time. Mom thought I didn't know, but I did, and her pain caused me pain.

Shaking my head to clear my thoughts, I said to the man, "Sorry."

He laughed and scooted down to sit next to me. "Not sure you need to be sorry about your ma giving me a chance to have a chat with you."

The man was smooth, and I grinned at his play.

He held out his hand to me. "Name's Den."

Taking hold of his warm, rough hand, I shook and replied, "Adalyn. Nice to meet you."

"You also. First time to the game?"

Placing my hand on each side of me on the bench seat, I nodded. "Yes. My son's just started. It's his first game today." I pointed out Drew.

"I'm sure he'll love it. My son, Rick, does." He pointed to a boy just a little shorter than Drew. He was a total opposite to my son, who had blond hair and blue eyes. Den's boy had black hair and dark eyes, much like his father, and was currently waving to his dad. Drew looked up at the same time, something passed over his face, but then he quickly smiled. He walked up to Rick and started to talk to him.

"Are you new to the area also?" Den asked.

Turning my attention away from Drew, I said, "Yes. We moved to my mom's for a while since I couldn't find a place I really wanted for Drew and me to live in."

"I'm sure eventually you'll find the perfect house."

Smiling, I nodded. "That's what I'm hoping for."

"So it's just you and Drew living with your mom?"

A snort shot out of me.

He chuckled. "Smooth, I know. But I don't see any wedding band on your hand."

My brows went up. "You've already looked?"

He shrugged and actually blushed. "When I see something I like, I don't care to hold back."

It was my turn to blush. "Um, okay. Wow. No, I'm not married. Divorced two years ago."

"Three for me." He bumped my shoulder with his. "Hey, sorry if I've made things uncomfortable already. I heard your speech with your mom, and I just wanted to get to know you."

"My speech?"

He grinned. "How happiness isn't about having a man in your life...."

Oh, no. What a jerk.

"Are you offering a roll in the sheets?" I whispered with a hissed tone.

He coughed, shook his head and held up his hands. "No. Shit. That's not why I caught your attention. I just liked how confident you sounded about your life."

All right, maybe not a jerk then.

"Oh."

He chuckled again. A whistle sounded and the game started. My heart jumped into my throat. I hoped Drew did well in the game.

"Sorry, ma'am," Den said, and I watched him stand as Mom stopped just at the end of our seats.

"No, no. It's fine. I'll sit just in front." She grinned.

My bloomin' mother.

She was probably already planning my wedding to Den, and the amused look Den gave me told me he was maybe thinking the same thing. Den sat back down next to me, his knee bumped into mine, and my heart went crazy for a new reason. He was closer than he was before, but I kept my attention on the game and cheered when Drew made a shot for the hoop, only to miss.

"You'll get it next time," I yelled. Drew sent me a thumbs-up and a big grin before his attention went back to the game.

"He's good," Den commented.

"He is, never played really, but always knew he wanted to."

"Must be in his blood."

"Must be." I grinned.

The game went on, and Drew's team lost by one. Even though they lost, my boy, my sweet son came barreling over to me as soon as I was standing on the main floor and shouted, "That was awesome."

Gripping the back of his neck, I applied pressure, and said, "You were amazing."

"I know." He smiled.

Laughing, I told him, "I think we need takeaway to celebrate."

"Yes!" he cried. "Nana, did you hear that? Takeaway. Mom, can we have tacos? I love tacos." Drew loved just about every kind of food. He ate enough to feed ten men, but he was a growing boy.

"Tacos sound good," Mom replied.

"Hey, Mom. Can Rick come?"

I flicked my gaze to see Den talking quietly with Rick.

"I'm not sure, honey."

"Please. He's not in my class, but he said we could hang at recess and lunch. He's really cool, Mom, and I think he'll be a good friend."

Gosh darn, since Drew hadn't really talked about friends from his new school, I was more inclined to want

Rick to come to dinner, but I wasn't sure I could get out of not having Den join us as well. His attention made me nervous, in a small way. It was nothing compared to Mr. Salvatore, but it was still there.

"Hey, buddy. I'm Den. Rick's dad. You did a great job tonight," Den said, stopping just beside me with Rick on the other side of him.

"Thanks, Mr. Den. I was just asking Mom if Rick could come have dinner with us. Tacos," he shouted.

"Yeah!" Rick cheered.

A smiling Den looked to me. "You okay with that, Adalyn?"

Glancing to Mom, who was nodding, I sighed quietly and said, "Sounds fine. Would you like to join us?"

His eyes twinkled with humor. He knew I was just being polite, yet he still said, "I'd love to."

The boys ran off talking a mile a minute while I followed slowly behind with Den falling into step with me, and my mom was somewhere behind us.

"Could be good our boys bonding."

Could it?

I wasn't sure.

"Yeah."

"Relax, Adalyn. It's all about the boys getting to know one another."

He was right. I was being rude thinking he was expecting something from me when I wasn't sure I could offer him anything but friendship.

"You're right. Sorry." I gave him a shy smile.

LILA ROSE

We drove separately to Taco Bell. It wasn't far from school. Mom was fanning herself over Den, about how sweet and cute he was. Thankfully Drew was in Den's car with Rick.

"Mom, I can't get involved with him. If anything bad happened, it could cause Drew problems with Rick. I won't risk anything, for Drew's sake."

"Darn. That's too bad. I was sure the way his eyes were glued to your ass on the way to the car was a good indication you would get some."

"Mom," I groaned.

"What about... what's that saying... friends with benefits?"

Laughing, I told her, "You're shocking, you know that, right?"

"Yes, dear."

Dinner was actually nice. The boys had a load of fun getting to know one another, and when they both found out they enjoyed Minecraft, a computer game I loathed, I was glad Rick would then be there to listen to Drew go on and on about it. I was sure my son knew I zoned in and out of consciousness listening to him talk about the game.

Den's company wasn't so bad either. I found out he worked for an insurance company that took him places all over the world when he had to check if claims were justified or not. He then told me traveling was the only perk in the job; the rest was boring as hell. I didn't mention my job at the adult store, I wouldn't in front of the kids, but I did tell him about my business. For once, a man acted like he wanted to know everything about it. At least that was

what I assumed when he asked me many questions about it.

Once we were back outside, Den pulled me aside and asked, "I'd like to have dinner with just you and me. What do you think?"

Biting my bottom lip, I told him honestly, "I'm not sure. Since Drew and Rick are…." I shrugged.

He sighed and then nodded. "I get it. You don't want anything to mess things up for the boys. Still, we could make it a dinner between two adults who enjoy each other's company."

I had enjoyed his time during the game and dinner.

"Sure, why not. As long as the boys know it's only as friends."

He grinned. "They will. Only it'll have to be next week. Rick is with me this week, and I like to spend as much time with him as I can."

"You've got my number," Den said. I had because Drew asked for it to plan a playdate with Rick. "So call me, and we'll make a plan from then."

"Deal."

Chapter SIX

DREW AND I stood outside Molly and Clint's apartment ringing the bell. We rang it a few more times when no one answered, which was strange because she was expecting us since it was her idea to take Drew to the arcade game place for some fun. She also liked to kick butt at the games she played against the teen boys who, if weren't totally in awe of her, would probably cry because they lost to an older woman.

"Mom, why are you dancing like that?" Drew asked.

Sighing, I found myself wishing I'd listened to my mom more when I was younger. She'd always said before leaving the house, even when I was young, to go to the bathroom. Usually I did, but I hadn't, and I was on the verge of peeing myself.

"I need to visit the restroom, my boy."

He started laughing. "Are you going to pee yourself again?"

The little twerp.

"That was only one time—"

"Three," he chirped.

I groaned. "Fine, cheeky, three times, and they were all because I got a fright when I was already busting to go."

He cackled like a madman, probably remembering the first time I peed myself. We'd been out at the park, and I hated, with a passion, using public facilities. Since Drew was having fun playing on the playground, I left it until I was desperate to use the bathroom and called him over. It was lucky we hadn't lived far from that park. We made it home, and I was just about nearing the bathroom when John showed up in the doorway scaring the heck out of me. I screamed. Drew came running to see if I was okay and he also got to witness the puddle I made on the ground.

The second time, Drew hadn't been around. However, John enjoyed telling our son the story just to see him lose himself in laughter. John and I had been out to lunch while Drew was at school. Again, I left things too late to tell John how I needed to pee because he would have insisted on me using the restaurant bathroom. He'd thought my issue with public restrooms was stupid. So when we'd gotten home, I ran to the front door first, jumping from one foot to another and yelling at John to hurry. Of course he was laughing and pretending to throw the keys at me to catch. Each time he did, I thought he'd end up losing the keys. I didn't actually believe it would happen; however, as his arm came out ready to throw, I screamed and peed when I saw a bird swoop low toward John's head. He dropped the keys, and they landed lost in the bush.

LILA ROSE

The third time, and last—I hoped—I had stupidly gone out trick-or-treating with Drew, and we were at the last house for the night. I would have been fine if Mr. Dangelo hadn't jumped out of nowhere yelling in my face. At that moment I hadn't known who it was, so I screamed my lungs out, picked Drew up, placed him under my arm like a football, and ran for the life of me. All the way home a trickle of pee ran down my legs.

Finally, the door opened and Molly appeared. "What are you doing down here?" I yelled, causing her to freeze halfway out the doorway. "You should have buzzed us up. I need to pee." I grabbed her keys, slipped through the door, and started for the stairs.

"Adalyn," Molly called.

"One second and we'll go."

"Adalyn," she yelled with a bit more urgency in her voice. I had no choice but to ignore it; my bladder was just about ready to explode. I ran down her hallway, and while cupping my sex, I managed to get her key in and unlocked it. Swinging the door open, I kicked it shut behind me and ran to the bathroom in the hall.

The door was closed, and it nearly caused me to lose my wee all over the floor. I fumbled it open, undid my jeans, and with a few hops and wiggles over to the toilet, I pulled my jeans down and flopped onto the seat.

Sweet, I'd made it to the toilet without an accident.

I was proud of myself and sighed in relief when my pee gushed forward. I moaned, and lifted my head, opening my eyes, which I hadn't even noticed I closed.

Then I screamed.

I grabbed the first thing, which was a towel in front of me, to cover my lower half. Only the towel I grabbed someone else had been holding it.

Someone else had been *using* it.

To dry themselves.

Oh dear God.

I had grabbed it, throwing it over me, which in turn gave me a view of everything.

As in *everything*.

"You have a penis," I yelled as I stared at the item in front of me. I hadn't seen one in the flesh in over two years.

Mr. Salvatore placed his hands on his hips and said, "It happens when you're a man."

"What... how... why?" I asked his penis.

"Miss Wallis."

"You...." I blinked.

Holy gosh darn. He was big.

And getting bigger. How was that possible? A whimper fell from my dry lips.

"Miss Wallis."

"I think...." What did I think? I liked it, that was for sure. I liked his penis. Could a woman not like the man but his penis instead? Well, obviously she could because I was doing it.

Two years without seeing one and all I wanted to do was touch it, stroke it, and maybe even lick it.

It was wrong on so many levels.

LILA ROSE

Mr. Salvatore bent. I scrunched lower to keep my eyes on his penis, but he stopped me with his finger under my chin. "Adalyn," he growled out low.

"Hmm?"

Bring back the penis, I wanted to demand on a yell, but I was suddenly lost in his eyes.

Then the realization came back to me. I was sitting on the bloody toilet while my boss stood naked in front of me, and my eyes wanted to make out with his penis.

Oh. My. God darn it.

I peed in front of my boss.

"I peed," I squeaked, my face heating. No, it wasn't heating it *was* burning.

He smirked. "Everyone does it."

Leaning forward, I whispered, "I did it in front of you."

He thinned his lips, only I was sure it was to hide the smile that was wanting out, if his twitching lips were anything to go by. He nodded. "You did."

Groaning, I slapped my hands over my face and demanded, "You need to get out."

"I think, due to the fact you've finished, it's you who needs to leave so I can finish drying myself."

My head snapped up. He was now standing with a hand over his junk. A disappointed sigh took hold of me before I shook my head and said, "Yes. I should go." But I couldn't move because it was then I took in all of his naked glory. He was buff, very buff, his six-pack was talking to me, and his muscular arms were crying for attention from my eyes as well.

"Can I have the towel?" he asked.

Nodding, I whispered, "Could you turn around first?" My eyes widened. "Not that I want to take a look at your bottom. I don't, but, I um, I have to do up my pants."

His brows rose. "You don't think it fair I get an eyeful since you did?"

"No," I yipped. "I'll close my eyes," I added.

He sighed, ran a hand over his face, then he gestured with his free hand. Closing my eyes, I heard him shuffle around. Of course I peeked, I wasn't a saint after all, and got a nice view of a grabbable butt. However, I didn't have time to take a good look. Instead, I quickly wiped, stood, and flushed before tucking the towel under my chin to hold it in place in front of me and pulled up my jeans. After washing my hands, I made my way to the door, folding the towel between my hands, worried I would soon be losing my job because I saw the boss naked.

"Adalyn," Mr. Salvatore called, just as I was closing the door.

"Yes?"

"The towel."

I thrust the towel back into the space. He took it, and I quickly slammed the door shut before making a mad dash for the front door. Molly needed more than one towel in the spare bathroom, not that I would tell her because there wasn't a chance I'd be saying I saw her brother naked. Or the fact I peed in front of him.

Heck, I never peed or did other things in front of John, and we'd been together a long time. The first time I farted, and he happened to be around, I was mortified. So was he. I made sure he was in another room if I had the need to let one go. Some people could do it in front of others. I couldn't.

My face was glowing. I knew it was when I stepped outside and Molly saw me. She took one look and threw her head back, laughing.

"Not one word."

"Did you pee yourself, Mom?" Drew yelled, just as an elderly woman was walking by.

"Drew," I scolded. "No, I didn't."

Drew shrugged. "Can we go now?"

"Lead the way, my man," Molly said, as she stepped to my side and threw her arm around my shoulders. Drew started off down the road, and Molly whispered, "What happened?"

"Nothing," I bit out coldly.

"Come on, you were like a lobster coming out. You have to tell me."

"No."

"Adalyn," she whined.

"What was he doing in your apartment, Molly?" I hissed.

She cackled. "He'd just been looking after Grayson's kids. As he was leaving, Makala threw up all over him. He thought he could put up with smelling like vomit on the drive home, but he couldn't. I'm close to Grayson's, so he stopped in, asked for a change of Clint's clothes and a shower."

It was nice of him to be looking after children. Still, I could have done without that whole episode. Again, I groaned and palmed my face. I peed in front of Mr. Salvatore.

Mr. Sophisticated himself.

"Was he still in the shower when you got in there?"

"No." I shook my head.

"Then where?"

"All my attention was on not peeing my pants. I didn't see him in there. I didn't see the steam or feel the warm room. I was busting."

She snorted, then giggled. "You didn't?"

"I did. I ran into the bathroom without seeing him, pulled down my pants and peed."

Another giggle. "Oh God. You had a piss in front of Vice."

Moaning, I shushed her, and stated, "You are not to mention this to Clinton. Do you hear me?"

"He won't say—"

"He's like my brother, I'll never hear the end of it."

"Okay, Addy. Relax, my girl. I won't say a thing."

Rolling my eyes, I knew she was lying. She told Clint everything, and I meant everything. Like the time we talked about our periods and how I craved cheese balls every time I was PMSing. One time I was at their place when Clinton got home and guess what I was eating? He'd walked in, took one look at me and paused. Molly had been in their room changing the sheets. He'd looked from me to the hall and then back to me. "Do I need to hide the knives since you're on your rag? Molly gets stabby when she's bleeding."

Glaring, I'd replied, "How do you know I have my period?"

He'd glanced down to the cheese balls and then looked back up with a smirk.

Mumbling under my breath about killing my friend, I'd yelled, "Is nothing sacred between you two?"

"Nope," he'd muttered.

WHEN WE ARRIVED at the arcade place, Molly disappeared with Drew, no doubt to teach him how to make others cry, and I took a spot in the cafeteria area, wallowing in embarrassment while drinking my Dr. Pepper.

Of course, my mind wouldn't jump past the fact I saw Mr. Salvatore's penis, or body for the matter. He obviously took very good care of himself. It kind of made me want to visit a gym... and then I laughed myself silly. Walking was my friend, anything else wasn't since I was clumsy half of the time. Sometimes I even fell over my own two feet. Leaning back in my seat, I wondered when I would stop making a fool of myself in front of Mr. Salvatore. I also wondered why in my head I kept calling him Mr. Salvatore?

Vice.

His name was Vice.

It felt naughty saying his name in my head.

God. I was losing my mind.

A shadow fell over the table. I glanced up and closed my eyes. "God," I groaned.

"No. Just Vice."

Opening my eyes, I noticed he wore casual clothes instead of the suits I'd seen him in, and dang it all, he looked amazing in casual as well. The jeans hugged him in all the right places, and the black tee showed off his upper body well. Bloody heck, I had to stop running my gaze over him.

Sighing, I asked, "What are you doing here? You shouldn't be here after what happened... not that we're talking about what happened, because we're not, ever. It shouldn't have happened." I needed to shut my mouth. "Do you by any chance have a time machine?"

His lips twitched. "Not on me, no."

"Darn," I muttered. He suddenly pulled out the chair opposite me and sat down, all serious once again. My eyes widened. "What are you doing?"

"Sitting."

"Why?"

Please, just go.

"I don't want you working in my store," he stated, his eyes dipping into a glare.

My jaw dropped. "You have got to be kidding me? You hunted me down to fire me?" Leaning forward, I asked, "Is this because you saw me pee or because I saw you naked?"

"You didn't tell me you saw *him* naked," Molly screeched behind me, causing me to jump. Twisting around, I saw, thankfully, Drew wasn't with her. Before I even asked, she pointed to the left, and I saw my son at the basketball game. "He's fine. So, you saw my brother naked?"

LILA ROSE

Sighing, long and loud, I thumped my head onto the table. "Yes," I mumbled into the wood. "And now he's here to fire me."

Chapter SEVEN

"You're here to fire her?" Molly screeched.

"Inside voice, Molly," Vice clipped.

"If I had known that was why you wanted to come here, I wouldn't have told you where we were. This isn't fair, Vice. You can't fire her because she saw your tiny, wittle peeny and you're ashamed."

Turning my head, I saw Molly standing over me with her hands on her hips scowling down at her brother.

"Jesus." Vice—who would be forever Vice in my head since he didn't deserve my respect of Mr. Salvatore because he was firing me—cursed again, then ran a hand over his face. His eyes met mine as I managed to place my elbows on the table and my hands up to hold my head since I was suddenly drained. Mentally.

He cleared his throat and stared at me. Was he waiting for me to defend his manhood because I'd seen it wasn't tiny? Well, he'd be waiting forever.

"Nothing to say?" he asked.

"Nope," I replied, making the p pop. "Well, not about that department anyway. What I would like to know is why you've come here, on a Sunday, God's day, to fire me."

"I'd like to know also," Molly huffed.

"It's not a place for a mother to work."

My eyes bulged. I glanced at Molly and asked, "Did you hear that?"

"I sure did," she replied and shook her head.

"First, it's a job to help bring in money. I know it's not a forever job, but it's one for now, and it's also a job I don't tell my son about. One I hope he never finds out about. Still, if that happened, I would deal with it. You can't fire me over the fact I'm a mother." I wasn't sure what I said was understandable. I had so many things rushing through my mind. Like how I wanted to kick Vice once again.

"I can, and I am. Besides, I've another job for you."

"I don't want it. I like where I'm at, and like I said, it won't be my forever job. I have my own business. Once that's 100 percent profitable, I'll be working on that as my forever job." *It also wouldn't lead me to jerkwads like yourself.*

"What is it?" he asked.

"Does it matter?"

"Yes."

"Why?" I snapped.

"Just tell me," he ordered.

I growled under my breath, and his lips twitched. "Fine. I make jewelry and sell it online."

"Right then, until you reach where you need to, you'll have another job in my company."

I coughed, and then blurted, "I'm not getting into porn. That's worse than selling sex toys."

Molly choked as the arcade attendant, a guy in his twenties who looked like he still lived in his mother's basement, arrived at the table with another Dr. Pepper just in time to hear what I said.

My cheeks heated. I lifted my gaze and stumbled through, "Oh, um, I, you didn't hear that, and..." I pointed to the drink. "I didn't order another one."

He winked. "I know. It's on the house."

"Leave now," Vice barked.

The guy gulped, nodded, and quickly disappeared. All of which Molly thought was hilarious. Vice then shifted the drink from in front of me to his sister.

"I'm not talking about the adult industry. I do have other businesses. However, the job I'm offering is the assistant position while mine is on maternity leave."

"Do you want to live?"

His head jerked back at my sudden question. "Yes."

"Having us in the same building all day long will not work out. One of us would end up dead." Clearly, he hadn't really thought it through.

"I'm sure we could handle it for the short amount of time."

"Thank you, but no thanks. I'll stay where I am."

"No."

Through clenched teeth, I asked, "What do you mean no?"

"You're no longer employed for that store. I've already informed them."

He'd already... he... I couldn't believe my ears.

"Molly?"

"His mom always told me he was dropped on the head a few times."

She was as surprised and confused as I was about the whole situation.

"She did not." He glared.

"She must have if you're pulling this shit with my friend."

"Even if she wasn't your friend, I'd still be pulling this shit. She's a mother. Doesn't matter how long she works in that place, someone in the school could find out and then there'd be trouble for her son and her."

Oh.

Oh, wow.

Okay, that had penetrated.

And it did, hard.

Vice Salvatore was taking care of me.

Why in God's name would he want to do that?

He was confusing.

My heart went wild in my chest. His words warmed me, yet terrified me. Why was the stunning man doing this to me, causing me to... God, like him, actually like him, when he'd been nothing but a tool around me.

Sugarplum on toast.

I was going gushy. I needed to get away from him. "Yes!" I shouted, their eyes coming to me. It was then I knew I should have kept my mouth shut and slunk off while they argued because as soon as I had his eyes, I was back in fantasyland seeing him naked.

Look away, Adalyn, before it's too late and you start drooling. Shifting my gaze to the drink in front of me, I noticed my hands shook, but I managed to grab it and twist it between my two hands without an accident.

"Adalyn?" Molly asked.

"I, uh, I mean. I'll find another job," I got out, eyes to my drink still. I heard Molly's laughter behind me. Never should have opened my mouth. She knew from the muttering and gaze, I was, once again, a goner. And I shouldn't be for goodness' sake. He was still a douche, in some ways at least. Definitely domineering by ordering me around so much.

"You don't need another job. I already have one for you," Vice bit out, his voice gruff and low, as if he was annoyed with me. Which he probably was. At least he didn't know I was attracted to him. I had to admit to myself his pull never left. I just hid it behind my crazy when he peeved me off. So, if I took up the job he was offering, it wouldn't work. I would become more infatuated with him, and since he already had a girlfriend, that would be awkward. He wasn't interested, and it seemed he could be just looking out for me because I was his sister's friend and a mother.

Internally groaning, I realized I was rambling to myself and honestly had no clue if I was making any sense.

Clearing my throat, I said, "Thank you, but no."

"Yes," he demanded.

"I can't. The hours I work already are perfect for me." There, that was a good enough excuse. I was sure his usual assistant would do nine to five, or later even. He seemed like he'd be a busy man.

"Nine thirty to three, those were your hours, right?"

"Yes." I nodded.

"Adalyn?"

"Yes?"

"Look at me when I speak to you," he clipped.

Stupid man.

I could do it. I could look at him without swooning over his full lips, his tanned skin, his charcoal hair, buff body, and how he acted like I was important enough to take care of, and that Drew's welfare, by giving me a job my son wouldn't be ashamed of, was just as important.

There it was. A lightbulb moment.

He wasn't doing it for me, but for Drew.

Rolling my eyes at my stupidity, I looked up and glared. "What?" *You stunning man, you. Darn you for letting me see you naked and for having a body of a Greek god.*

"You can do those hours as my assistant. Maggie will be back in a year. I'm sure we could keep it civil until then."

Why couldn't he just give up?

Even though I fought with my own body, my cheeks heated, and I wanted to glance away, but I couldn't. His good looks weren't going to win over me.

Bloody heck, I sounded like one mixed-up woman, and it was all because of the man in front of me. Honestly, why was I fighting so hard? Because I was attracted to him? I had to think of Drew. And Vice was right about one thing: if any parent or teacher saw me working in the adult store, things could get out, and boys were little monsters when they wanted to be. Then again, if they knew I was working for a man who made porn, it would still be a problem. God, I was so flipping confused.

"Wouldn't working for you be just as bad as working in an adult store?"

"No." He shook his head.

Was he going to elaborate? When he sat back and just stared me down, I knew he wouldn't continue.

Thankfully, Molly did. "What my brother is saying without words, is that he doesn't run his productions company. His minions do that. His other business of buying and selling companies is the one Vice mans."

"Oh" was all I said. So the job would be as a legit assistant for an aboveboard business. "Fine," I stated, and my tone sounded like I wasn't fine with it at all because I wasn't since I knew working so close to Vice would drive me crazier.

"Good," he barked, as if now I'd said yes, he wasn't sure about the whole deal himself. "You start tomorrow. Molly will give you the address." He stood.

"Mom, can I have more money for the machines?" Drew asked, stopping beside Vice. He then looked up, and up, until he met Vice's gaze. "Hey, I'm Drew."

"Hi, Drew, I'm Vice. Your Mom's—"

"Boyfriend?" Drew blurted.

"No!" I cried, then laughed awkwardly.

LILA ROSE

Both Vice and Drew were looking at me. Drew with a smile and Vice with his brows raised. Molly was still behind me, and once again laughing. Yes, I was a real clown. Ha de har ha.

"Drew, honey. Mr. Salvatore is my boss."

"Oh, cool." He glanced back to Vice, and when he saw he didn't have his attention because Vice was still looking down at me glaring, he tugged at his sleeve. "You play basketball? You're really tall. I like basketball. I had my first game yesterday. We lost, but Mom said I still did a good job. Hey, you should come to my next game. That's if you like basketball."

Where was a gag when I needed one?

My son, my sweet boy, who didn't know I had a crush and also disliked my boss—well, except for his penis— had just invited him along to watch basketball. I wanted to cry in frustration.

When Vice smiled down at Drew, I clenched my legs together. His smile was amazing.

"I used to play ball in college. Haven't for a while. I like to box."

"Yeah?"

"Yes. Still, I'd enjoy coming to watch you sometime, just not sure when."

Say what now?

Did Vice understand when saying something to a child they take it for truth? He couldn't tell Drew he'd be there and then not show.

"Cool." Drew's grin grew wider. "Mom, hear that? Mr. Vice said he'd come watch me."

My expression warmed at his excitement. "I did, honey. And I think you should call him Mr. Salvatore."

"Vice won't mind Drew calling him Vice," Molly put in, not helping me at all.

"Fine with me," the man himself added.

Great.

"Hey," I called, Drew's stare came from Vice to me. "How about another half hour and then we go get some lunch?" I grabbed some money out of my purse and handed it to him.

"Okay. Hey, Mr. Vice, do you want to come have lunch with us?"

Mr. Vice. I wanted to laugh at how cute my boy was adding in the Mr. Though, I was too busy praying to Satan to come up and take his minion back to hell. Meaning Vice, not my son. Though, there were days I did wonder about Drew.

"Drew," I started with an urgent tone. I calmed it, smiled, then added, "I'm sure Mr. Salvatore is busy."

"Actually, I am. So I'll take a raincheck on basketball and lunch."

"Cool," Drew cheered, which caused Vice to chuckle. My body shuddered.

Vice looked to me, and said, "Tomorrow."

Nodding, I offered up a lame wave. He said a quick goodbye to Drew and Molly, then left. Once Drew took off on a run to play all the games he could in half an hour, Molly took Vice's vacant seat, and asked, "You all right?"

"What just happened?"

"My brother happened. Just some advice, my brother always gets his way."

"Why would he want the likes of me working for him?"

She shrugged; however, I saw the glint of something in her eyes. She had an idea, but she wasn't going to share it, and I wasn't sure I would like what she thought anyway.

"What do I wear?"

"Dresses, skirts, slacks, blouses."

"Darn, no jeans?"

"No jeans."

"My life couldn't get any worse."

"Chin up, honey. I'm sure it'll get better."

"When murder comes into it."

"Pfft, please. And all those flushed faces, mutterings and not meeting his gaze meant nothing. You like my brother."

Scoffing, I slumped in the seat and shook my head. "No. I don't."

She made a rude gesture with her hand, like she was jerking off. I grabbed her hand and slammed it on the table. "Kids are around."

She pulled her hand free and patted the top of mine. "I wish you luck for tomorrow. Man, I can't wait to tell Clint about this."

Why would she wish me luck?

Actually, she was right. I would need all the luck in the world to get through my first day of being around Vice Salvatore for five and a half hours.

I may also need to take a change of panties, some ear-muffs, and boxing gloves, or just a sharp knife. Then a body bag for when he peeves me off and I kill him.

God, what was he thinking?

And what was I thinking by agreeing?

Chapter EIGHT

WITH LACK OF sleep, I made my way to the elevator from the underground parking garage ready to start my new job. A sure sign a panic attack was looming was how my hands shook as I pressed the button and waited for the door to open to then take me to the twentieth floor. Where Vice Salvatore would be.

The man hadn't even asked if I could do assistant work. For all he knew about me, I was only good at selling sex toys. What would I have to do as his assistant? I could make a mean cup of coffee, and answering phones was simple enough. Did I have to file? Would I be any good at it? Then again, it couldn't be any harder than when I took care of John's bookkeeping.

Right?

My breaths came faster and faster as the bell chimed for the arrival of the elevator and the doors slid open. *This is it. Doom day. Disaster day. Death day*. Any of those I was sure would be appropriate.

Stepping into the elevator, I pressed the number. My legs shook, and since my hands were still dancing their own jig, I tucked them under my armpits. My bag slipped from my shoulder, but I left it and closed my eyes breathing deeply through my nose and then out my mouth.

I needed to calm down or I would have sweat stains on my white blouse. Molly had said I looked great when I sent her a photo of myself dressed that morning. I again glanced down at my dark knee-length pencil skirt and second-guessed my choice. Not only were the clothes a little restricting, but I wore heels. Heels and I weren't friends because they always seemed to trip me up.

Mom had been giddy with the news of me getting out of the adult store. In fact, I was sure she was half in love with Vice already, and she hadn't even met him. She also assured me I looked amazing for my first day. Then she suggested I undo more buttons on my blouse to give the girls breathing room. Which was when I told her for the millionth time Vice Salvatore was annoying, bossy, my boss, plus Molly's brother. In other words, he was off limits.

The doors opened, and I had the sudden urge to vomit as I stepped out and into a room full of hustle and bustle.

"Hi, welcome to Tore Corporation. My name's Kylie, how can I help you?" a woman in her twenties asked at the front desk, just outside the elevator doors.

Walking up, I smiled. I knew it was a shaky one. "Yes, hi. I'm Adalyn Wallis and—"

"Ah, you're Mr. Salvatore's assistant." Her eyes ran over my body, and I saw the nasty smirk before she stood.

"Follow me, please." She walked around her long desk and then ducked behind the divider to the rest of the room. I quickly moved to catch up with her.

She swayed her hips as she moved throughout the room, saying hello to people as she went, and I saw those people give me a once-over. I was the new meat. I hated being new in any place because it felt like I had to prove myself. Oh well, if they liked me or didn't I wouldn't care. I was over caring about anyone unless they were close to me already, and then I would move mountains to make them happy.

"This will be your desk. That's Mr. Salvatore's office. He's in a phone meeting with a client right now so he won't want to be disturbed. Make yourself comfortable and go over the list Maggie created of things that will need to be done during each day. She left it in the top drawer." She turned, with a flick of her hair over her shoulder, only to spin back with a frown on her face. She asked, "You do know how to use a computer, right?"

"How old do you think I am?" I blurted.

She laughed. "About my mom's age."

The rude little.... "I'm only thirty-seven."

"Yes, well." She smiled and walked off.

What I would've liked to do was teach her some manners, but since it was my first day, I ignored her jeer and went around my desk, sitting down on the swivel chair.

I took hold of the handle of the drawer Kylie had pointed to; however, when I pulled, it only opened an inch. It seemed like it was stuck on something. I pushed it back in and then out again quickly. Again, it stopped. With my fingers, I felt in the small opening to see if I could find what was stopping the drawer to open but couldn't find anything.

Strange. Was there a trick to it?

I tried wiggling it, shifting it from side to side and still it wouldn't come all the way open. "You piece of poop. Open all the way," I grumbled and glared down at it.

Great, my first day and I couldn't even open a drawer. No, I wouldn't let some wood beat me. I grabbed the handle in a tight grip, banged my fist on the top of the desk and then with a big yank, I pulled it open. It came flying my way. I leaned back only way too far and, with the drawer still in my hand, it and I went shooting to the floor. Everything in the drawer tipped out all over me and my bruised butt.

"Shit," I snapped.

Of course, with the commotion, the office door behind me came open. I glanced there and saw Vice standing in the doorway looking down at me. His eyes widened, his lips twitched.

"Having fun?" he asked.

Nodding, I pushed things off me and said, "Grand time."

A few other people, who had desks close by, come over. A woman in her fifties asked, "You all right, dear?"

"Yes, thank you. Sorry to disturb everyone. The drawer was stuck."

A man, maybe in his forties, stepped up and held a hand out to me. "Let me help you. Maggie always had a hissy fit over the drawer, so don't worry about it. Boss was supposed to replace it." I took his hand in mine, and with ease and strength, he helped me to my feet again.

"Thank you..."

"Henley."

"Thanks, Henley. I'm Adalyn."

"Do you think we can all get back to work?" Vice snapped with his low growly tone.

Henley smiled down at me, since he was another tall man, and said, "Enjoy a great first day."

"Thanks, I'll try and not disturb anyone again." I laughed.

"All good. We won't mind at all," he replied before dropping my hand and walking off. I noticed his desk was only a few away from mine. At least two people, including the older woman, were nice. The others gave me dark looks and went back to what they were doing before I'd made a ruckus.

Turning to Vice, I saw he had his usual evil stare going as he looked down at me. I offered him a hesitant smile. "Sorry about that."

"Clean up the mess and get to work. I'm sure Kylie told you about Maggie's list."

"She did."

"Good. I'll have to call my client back now."

I winced. God, he'd probably been on an important call, and I'd interrupted it. It was no wonder he was in a foul mood. Then again, at first when he came out, he didn't seem too upset. He was confusing. And people said it was women who had mood swings.

THE REST OF the day went smoother than the morning. Actually, I hardly saw Vice, so that helped. He kept to his office, or if he did come out, it was either to head to a meeting or bark at me about something I needed to do for him. I ate my lunch at my desk, which thankfully I brought in since I wasn't sure there would be anywhere close to buy lunch from.

Deidre, the older woman who was nice to me, later told me there was a cafeteria on the first floor. It was good to know, except I didn't want to leave the phones, and besides, I was only there for five and a half hours. I didn't mind eating as I worked if it meant I got more work done. I found the work to be easy and similar to what I had done for John, so at least Vice wouldn't find what I did lacking.

I seriously had to stop with that word.

By the time I finished, he wasn't anywhere in sight. I said my goodbye to those who were friendly with me that day on the way out. I even waved to Kylie, the front desk girl, who in turn ignored me. With a shrug, I got onto the elevator and headed to pick up Drew, happy with myself and the job I'd done for the day. Truly, I was looking forward to continuing working there. It was challenging in its own way, and it seemed as though I wouldn't have to see too much of Vice.

The other great part about my new job, it was closer to Drew's school and Mom's house. When I worked in the adult store, I was usually five minutes late in picking up my son. That day I was early, so I parked in front and waited.

When the bell rang, my son took extra-long to come out the front. He probably thought I would be late. When he walked out with Rick at his side, he spotted me, said goodbye and ran to the car.

The back door opened. "Mom, you're here already."

"Sure am. From now on I'll be on time to pick you up."

"Sweet," he cried as he dumped his school bag on the floor and then did up his seat belt.

I started the car and backed out. Usually, he would be talking a mile a minute, so when he was silent, I knew something was wrong. "How was your day?"

"Good." I caught his smile in the rearview mirror.

"Okay, what's up, kiddo?"

He sighed. "Are you going out to dinner with Rick's dad?"

Bugger. I wasn't sure if Drew was ready for me to date, even though he knew his dad had a girlfriend already. However, from the look of it, Drew knowing I was going out with Den didn't sit well with my boy. "Yes. I hope that's okay, and we're going as friends, Drew."

He rolled his eyes. "It's okay, Mom. You can go to dinner with *men*." He whispered the word men as if it sounded like a naughty word. My kid. "But I liked Mr. Vice. You should go to dinner with him as well."

My head jerked back, and I swerved the car from the shock. "But... um, you only met both men once. Why do you say that?"

"He seemed cooler. Hey, do you know what Daniel sang today?"

Wait a second. I was still stuck on Mr. Vice being cooler than Den after just a short conversation with the man.

Still, I went with the flow; it was better for my sake anyway. "What did he sing?"

"Your momma, your momma, your momma sucks cock." Another swerve of the car. "Mom, what does cock mean?"

What in the hell were Daniel's parents teaching their child?

"Drew, I don't want you to ever sing that song again, please. It's disgusting."

"How? What does cock mean?"

Dear Lord, give me strength. "It means doodle."

He gasped. "Holy ship, that's terrible."

Of course, the one time I nearly said holy shit and instead changed it to ship was when Drew had been standing right next to me as I sliced my finger open.

"It is. In fact, maybe it might be best not to hang out with Daniel."

"I think you're right. He called you a loser for still living with Nana."

What a little monster.

Just another reason I needed to pull my finger out and up my searching for a perfect place we'd both enjoy living in. "You know, Drew, it's not going to be forever we'll stay with Nana. As soon as we both find a house we love, we'll move."

"But she makes awesome cookies."

Laughing, I shook my head and reassured him, "I'm sure she'll still make them for you even if we don't live with her."

"Oh, cool then. Can we go shoot some hoops this afternoon?"

"Do you have any homework?"

He looked out the side window and bit his bottom lip. "Maybe."

"Tell you what, Nana said she'd cook tonight. So when we get home, you can have a snack, get your homework done, and then, before dinner, I'll take you to the public court for a little bit."

Even though he sighed, like I'd just asked him to clean the whole house, he said, "Deal."

Chapter
NINE

MY FIRST MONTH working at Tore Corporation was surprisingly great. Just like the first week, the rest were pretty much the same. Except, in the start of the second week and onwards, each time I heard the office door open behind me, my heart would start pulsating in my chest, as if it was perking up for attention from a certain boss. Only it never got it. He was still his gruff, domineering self, but other than him ordering me to do or get him something, we didn't talk.

What was weird was how disappointed I felt. I think I even missed us going head to head about things. Although, it did help the crush I had on him to stay at a mild simmer when I saw him.

If only my dreams weren't filled with dancing penises that resembled Vice's nearly every night, then that mild simmer could be extinguished altogether. Thankfully, I hadn't thought about him naked during the day since I started.

Then again, I really shouldn't be pondering about my dreams while I sat at my desk because, when the door opened abruptly behind me, I spun my chair around and all I could visualize was Vice naked.

Darn it, my mind and eyes betrayed me because I was looking at his crotch.

"Adalyn," Vice called.

"Yes?" I asked. *Slacks really suited the man. They fit well to his form. He must get them all tailored.*

"Eyes up, Adalyn."

I snapped my eyes up to see his lips twitching. It wasn't funny. I was ogling the man, my boss, and he knew it. My face was like a furnace.

"I would ask where your mind was, but I think I know."

"Ha, no. No way. Um, I thought I saw a stain on your, ah, pants. I mean, I wouldn't want you to see clients with a stain."

He snorted. "Am I in the all clear of stains then?"

Do not look down.

My eyes flicked down without my brain telling them to and then quickly up again. "Yes," I squeaked.

"Thank you for making sure." He smirked and crossed his arms over his chest.

"Mr. Salvatore," Kylie called as she made her way over quickly on her tall heels. Her hand landed on his arm, and for a reason I wouldn't admit to myself fully, I wanted to rip her arm off and shove it down her throat. Then at least I wouldn't have to listen to her whiny voice.

"Adalyn?"

86

"Huh?" I asked, dragging my eyes up to Vice's gaze from glaring at Kylie's hand.

Vice shook his head. "Kylie, tell Mr. Delibe to come through."

"Right away," she chirped, sneered at me, and then danced off. Why she even ran over to tell Vice he had a client show up unexpectedly was beyond me. All she had to do was phone his assistant. But no, she had to place her hand on him and just annoy me instead.

"Adalyn, I asked if you could have the Monroe file on my desk before you leave."

"Yes, of course." I nodded, and then spun back to my desk. I heard Vice walk into his office, so when Mr. Delibe approached, I smiled and told him to go on through.

I wasn't sure why Kylie had a problem with me, but as each day passed, her glares and frowns directed my way were beginning to get to me. I wanted to ask what the issue was, but I didn't want to start trouble. I couldn't afford to lose the job. Well, unless Vice handed me another one on a golden platter in one of his other offices. If it came down to it, I would leave so I didn't drag any conflict through the building.

IT WASN'T UNTIL I was sitting in the car watching Drew run toward me that I remembered I hadn't left the file Vice asked for on his desk. I thumped my palm against my forehead. I'd have to make a trip back to the office. There was no way I would call someone to fix my mistake. Especially, if Kylie found out, I would never hear the end of it.

LILA ROSE

When the door came open, and Drew was in with his seat belt buckled, I started the car and told him, "One quick pit stop before heading home."

"Where we going?"

"I have to pop back to the office for a second."

"Cool, I haven't seen where you work yet."

Of course, there had been a reason before. Luckily, I was proud of my new job and the fact I could show it off to my son.

"Will Mr. Vice be there?" he asked eagerly. "Since he couldn't make it to my last few games, he might come to the one this weekend." I could hear the hope in his voice. *Please let Vice be out so my son won't feel the disappointment.* Drew's last three games of basketball had been at a loss also. He'd been a little down after it, not that it lasted long, but still, I hated to see him upset in any way, and I had a feeling Vice had only been acting politely when he'd agreed to come watch Drew one time.

"We can certainly see. Though, he is a very busy man."

I caught his nod and how his mouth dipped. "I know, Mom. Like Dad's always busy."

Goddang John for not calling last week or remembering to call him back when Drew had tried to reach out. Drew missed his father and loved getting calls from him. John had been a great dad when he was around, but since his absence, it was like he'd forgotten he ever had a son. It hurt me to watch Drew go through his own pain.

"This is where I work, Drew, and I have to park under here." I drove into the underground parking garage. "Hey, did I tell you there's a cafeteria in this building, and they have the best ice cream? Maybe we could get one after I drop a file off."

Finally, a small smile appeared. "'Kay."

"Awesome, let's go." I grabbed my bag from the passenger seat and climbed out of the car. Drew was already out and bouncing from one foot to the other.

"Are there scary clowns hiding down here?" he asked. That dang clown video a boy from his previous school showed him had Drew scared for months of any dark places.

"No. They're not real, remember?"

He nodded but clutched my hand tightly as we walked to the elevator. Someone must have just gotten off since it arrived quickly. I told Drew what floor to press. He did and came back to my side then placed his arm around my waist to lean into me. It was moments like those, and many others for that matter, where I wished he wouldn't grow up. I knew the day would come when he'd be too embarrassed to be seen with his mom or hold my hand, kiss my cheek and hug me when he wanted to.

The doors opened, as did Drew's mouth. "Wow, Mom, this place is huge." He stepped off before me and spun in a circle to take it all in.

"It sure is, but come this way, and I'll show you my desk." Hand in hand we made our way past Kylie, who seemed surprised I had a little boy with me. She mustn't have known I had a child. I was sure after I'd told Deidre, it would have been around the office. After all, from what Henley had said, she was a gossiper around the floor.

LILA ROSE

"This place is cool, Mom," Drew said as he sat in my swivel chair and spun around and around. Ah, the things that amuse young minds. Maybe if I didn't have that chair, he wouldn't be thinking it was as cool.

"I like it too, Drew." I smiled and grabbed the file near the computer. "I'll just be a second, then ice cream."

"'Kay." He beamed with a spin of the seat.

The steps I took found my heart getting excited, yet my brain wished he wasn't about. His door was always closed so I couldn't tell if he was in or not. I knocked anyway, just in case, and when I heard no answer, I sighed in relief, only my belly bottomed out in disappointment.

With a need to get out of there quickly in case he arrived back, I opened the door and stopped dead.

My boss was standing up against the wall with his back to me. If it wasn't for the feminine hands at his waist, I would have been wondering what he was up to or thought he was going crazy by staring at the wall.

His head turned as I entered, but he didn't move. His eyes widened in surprise from seeing me. He opened his mouth as if about to speak, but I got in before he could. "Sorry, I just forgot the file." I waved it in my hand and quickly stepped in further to place it on his desk. Spinning, I made my way back to the door as my heart made nice friends with my feet.

"Adalyn," he called.

I didn't pause. "Got to go. Have fun." Seriously? Have fun? I didn't give two hoots if he was going to have fun with some floozy in his office.

"Adalyn," he clipped, just as I closed the door. Then I thought I heard him curse, but I wasn't sure because I was moving fast to Drew's side.

"Was that Mr. Vice?"

"Yes, honey, but he's busy at the moment. Come on, let's go get some ice cream." I held out my hand and Drew jumped up taking hold. We started for the elevator as I asked, "What flavor do you think you'll get?"

A door banged opened behind us. Drew turned, and it was another time I wanted to haul him under my arm and make a run for it.

Instead, his face brightened, and he yelled, "Mr. Vice, hey." My hand got dropped, and Drew disappeared back toward my desk.

Welcome to a very awkward moment.

Sighing, I slid my eyes to the floor and wished it would just open up and eat me. Instead of that happening, I lifted my head and turned to see Drew talking rapidly to Vice, who stood outside his closed office door. At least he had the thought to shut his girl in so Drew didn't have to see her.

"Drew, let Mr. Salvatore get back to work." To his woman actually…. God, why was my stomach churning over that thought? I didn't know what was going on in his office. She could be a really nice person. Then again, since I didn't see who it was, it could have been Debra, and she hadn't seemed that nice at the restaurant.

Dang it, body, it's just a little crush.

Vice could be with whomever he wanted; it had nothing to do with me. I was just his assistant. I had to stop obsessing over his penis and start finding another way to fill my dreams with something or someone else.

"Drew," I called again.

My son looked my way, grabbed my boss's hand, and dragged him toward me. Vice's stunned expression would have been laughable if I wasn't thinking it was right about the time to make a run from the annoying goddang scene. To make matters worse, I sensed people around the office were watching.

"Mom, Mr. Vice said he could come get ice cream with us, but he'd meet us down there."

Shit. Fuck. Shit. Bugger.

Through clenched teeth, I bit out, "Don't you have a meeting soon?"

"I'm sure I can reschedule."

Was he talking about the woman in his office or an actual meeting?

Either way, I didn't care. I just didn't want him to come.

"You're busy," I stated, with a do-not-screw-with-me tone.

"I'll be free shortly."

"No, I'm sure you won't."

It was then his office door opened, and I saw a woman around the same age as Vice stroll out. She looked polished, swaying her hips our way and, if it wasn't for the sadness in her eyes or the fact they were red, I would have hated her on sight because she was more than beautiful. She was gorgeous.

Before I knew it, my brain not registering my movements beforehand, I slugged Vice in the arm and hissed, "You made her cry?"

His eyes widened for a second, his jaw clenched, and maybe if it wasn't for Drew being around, he would have been strangling me like his sudden glare told me he wanted to.

The woman stopped beside Vice and giggled. "He didn't, but thank you for sticking up for me. I'm Monica, but my friends call me Nica."

Hmm, that didn't explain who she was to Vice and why she'd been crying. However, the answers to those questions were none of my business.

"Nice to meet you. I'm Adalyn, Mr. Salvatore's assistant, and this young man is my son, Drew."

"Hey, lady," Drew said, with a tone that told me he wasn't impressed. Why, I didn't know since we'd never met her before.

"Ms. Monica, Drew."

"Hmm." He rolled his eyes and ignored me. My son was never rude, unless he felt there was a reason for it.

"Anyway, we must be going." I smiled apologetically at her.

"Yeah, Mom has a date again."

I blanched. What was my son playing at? He was nine for goodness' sake. "Um, no I don't." I laughed humorlessly.

"Yes, you do, with Rick's dad again."

What the...? Den and I had gone out a few weeks ago. I enjoyed the time I'd spent with him, but for me, there wasn't an attraction. Then again, feelings could grow, so when Den had asked me for a second date, I'd agreed.

"Um, no—"

"But, Mom you said—"

Holding up my hand, I ground my teeth together, took a breath, and finally corrected, "That isn't until Wednesday, Drew." Why he brought it up in the first place was a puzzle... unless, no. He couldn't possibly be matchmaking and trying to get my boss jealous?

Laughing to myself at the ridiculous thought, I glanced at Vice to see him with his arms crossed, glaring at me.

My eyes widened. He couldn't actually think less of me with Drew bringing up the date, could he? I blurted, "I didn't tell him. Rick mentioned it." Did he honestly think I would mention to my son about my dating life if it weren't a serious relationship? There wasn't a chance in hell.

And anyway, it was none of Vice's business, much like the woman standing at his side, who was smirking and looking from Vice to me and back again, was none of my business.

"Yeah, Rick's my friend from school. We met him and *his dad* at basketball."

Monica giggled. I turned my shocked expression from my son, who was grinning evilly, even if I did say so myself, up at Vice, while Vice was glancing down at my son with a tick in his jaw.

It was time to fly the Popsicle stand before my son had the chance to mention where and what time my date would be, and then wondering if I'd be home that night to

tuck him in.... Honestly, it could happen. I wouldn't put it past my conniving son.

Reaching out, as my face heated, I grabbed Drew's wrist and gently tugged him my way. "Ah, the file, on your desk. Sorry again for the interruption. We have to go." Turning, I dragged Drew along with me to the elevator. Of course, my son just had to yell behind him, "So I might see you this Saturday at the game?"

I didn't hear a reply, but Vice must have done something to make Drew turn back around with a proud smile on his face.

Stepping into the elevator, I pressed the button, and once the doors were closed, I turned to Drew and stated, "No ice cream, mister."

He had the gall to look up at me sheepishly, like he didn't know what he'd done, and yet, he grinned and said, "Okay."

What in the world had just happened?

It was then I regretted saying no ice cream because I could have done with some. My son was too smart and tricky for his own good to get what he wanted. He wanted Vice at his basketball game for some reason, and he threw me under the bus to get it. Still, I wasn't sure it would happen in the end.

Chapter TEN

SINCE I DIDN'T get a lot of sleep the previous night, I chose to use the hours to work on some jewelry, as well as organizing deliveries ready for Mom to send off. As I walked to my desk, I was my very own version of a zombie. People said hello, and I pretty much grunted back. Heck, I wasn't even sure if I dressed normally. Had I put on panties? Guess I'd find out when I went to the restroom.

Great, the thought of a toilet had my mind conjuring up the thought of my visit to Molly's bathroom while Vice was in it... *naked*.

Running a hand over my face, and probably trailing makeup everywhere, I groaned and warned my brain to not go there. I wasn't in the mood.

At least the lack of sleep gave me the opportunity to create some beautiful pieces. Well, I thought they were, and when I uploaded them to Facebook, as well as Instagram saying they were coming soon to my e-store, they gained a lot of great feedback.

Sitting on my seat, I rolled the chair up to the desk and blinked at the screen. Then blinked once more. And blinked again. Right, turning on the computer could help start the day. And coffee, lots and lots of coffee were in order probably for the rest of the day.

Vice's door opened with a swooshing sound, and my stomach turned. I thought if I stayed still long enough, he wouldn't see me, but of course, luck hated me. I heard his intake of breath, and then he barked, "Adalyn, office now."

He'd never called me in there before. He always came out to order me about. Not that I minded since it was my job. So why was he calling me in? Had Drew and I embarrassed him in front of Monica?

Slowly, I turned in my seat to see he'd already made his way back into his office. Taking a gulp of courage, I stood and walked toward the door, then inside.

"Close the door," he demanded to his computer screen.

My pulse kicked into hyperdrive, but I did as he asked, and then went over to sit opposite him. Would it be worth apologizing? Then again, what would I apologize for? His ignoring me, while he tapped away on his keyboard, was starting to peeve me off. He'd called me in for a reason, and it wasn't just to ogle him in his swanky suit. Another formfitting one. Goodness, even his hands looked good that morning while they typed away.

Breathe, Adalyn, and stop looking at him. Look around the office. You're not in there much. Oh look, a plant. I wonder if a woman gave him that. I can't see Vice picking it out himself. Aw, I do like the painting on his wall. Actually...

turning my head sideways... *is that an abstract art of his penis? It's long and thick like that, or could it be a sailboat? Heck, I don't know Mozart from Da Vinci.... Wait, did they both make art? I really should have paid attention in art class or history at least.*

A scream burst from my mouth when a loud clap caused me to jump. Spinning my gaze to Vice, I saw his hands part, and he placed them on his desk. He was smirking, until he took me in.

"You look terrible." He winced when he realized what he said.

"I didn't get much sleep. What did you need? Am I fired?"

His head jerked back. "Why would you think I'd fire you?"

The way his eyes seared into my soul wasn't good. I quickly looked away before I blurted something I shouldn't. Instead, I shrugged and told the tall plant over his shoulder, "For coming into your office while you were busy. I didn't know you were in here. I did knock. Then again, I should have just placed the file under your door or did it as you asked in the first place before I left."

"Adalyn?"

I glanced at his chin and raised my brows. There was that tick again as he clenched his jaw.

He sighed. "Sometimes I really don't understand you. One second you're hitting me, telling me off, and then the next you won't look at me, and you're muttering."

"Um, I guess I'm just hard to understand."

"That is true. Right then, straight to the point. You're busy Wednesday night for—"

"What?" I interrupted.

"As I was saying—"

"Why Wednesday?"

"If you let me—"

"Can't it be any other night? Then again, I don't work at nights, you know this."

"I need—"

"I'm sure Kylie could help with whatever you—"

"Enough!" he yelled, my eyes snapped up to his, and we glared at one another.

I stood. My hands landed on his desk, and I leaned in to snap, "Do not yell at me, Mr. Salvatore."

He cursed and ran a hand over his face, then stood also. "Finally, it seems I just have to piss you off to get you to look at me and show me some fire back."

The man was a confusing, stunning jerk.

"Yeah, well...." I had nothing because I didn't understand why he would want to light a fire inside of me in the first place.

He rolled his eyes. "Sit down, Adalyn, and let me finish."

Grumbling under my breath, I sat back down and crossed my arms over my chest.

He nodded and sat, then placed his hands on the desk. "Wednesday night you will accompany me to a business meeting. I haven't asked much of you since you've started, but I need you to do this."

"But you know I was busy."

He snorted. "I'm sure you can reschedule."

I could. I knew Den would be fine with it, but still, a business meeting with Vice wasn't a good idea for me. It would be at least an hour or two where I would have to sit in his presence, and then there was the possibility the extra time with him could cause my mild crush to grow into something more. That was a scary thought.

Who was I kidding? I was screwed no matter. He was on my mind all the time, and for some stupid reason, I let the thought of him liking me back a little run away with me. I tried to deny it, to tell it to shut the hell up. However, I couldn't help but notice the way his eyes traveled my body each day or even how he gave me the job so I could protect my child. And then there was the fact when in the bathroom that day, he didn't yell at me to look away or get out. He'd been playful in a way.... So, so screwed, that was what I was, because thinking he had some type of feels for me was ridiculous or as Donkey from *Shrek* would say ridonkulous. *Ah, Disney movies, I love them.*

Realizing Vice was waiting for an answer, I muttered, "Fine."

"Fine." He smirked. His eyes twinkled in the light, and I was once again lost in them.

"Right." I nodded, not really knowing what I was saying.

"Glad we have that sorted."

"We do." Did we? What were we talking about again?

"Adalyn."

"Yes?"

"You may get back to work now."

Before he could see the blush rising from sitting there like an idiot staring into his eyes, I nodded and quickly exited the room, closing the door behind me.

Great, the man once again got me to do what I didn't want to do. How did he do that? Was he a Voodoo master?

VICE

Damn infuriating woman. Since the first time I saw her, I wanted to know everything there was to know about her. She was a puzzle. How could one woman go from sweet, clumsy, and muttering one second to a bull-headed, stubborn, pain in my ass? And yet, I didn't want it any other way. What she needed was a good spanking.

A smile crept onto my face. Spanking reminded me of how she'd acted when I'd asked about the adult films at the sex shop. She'd acted crazy, but I was charmed by it.

I even wanted to get to know Drew, and if my opinion was correct, he also wanted to get to know me. In fact, I had an idea Drew wanted me for his mother. Luckily enough, I also wanted that, but how to go about it was something, for once, I had no idea about. She seemed attracted to me. Hell, when she saw me naked she couldn't keep her eyes off me, well, one part of me. But then there were those times when she wouldn't look at me at all.

Confusing.

Still, no matter, I liked a challenge, and I usually got what I wanted, and what I wanted was Adalyn Wallis.

LILA ROSE

Picking up the desk phone, I called Grayson at work. "Jackson Media, this is Makenzie, how can I direct you?"

"Hello, sweetheart." I smiled. I adored Kenzie. She was sweet and perfect for Grayson.

"Vice. What are you up to?"

"Just need to speak to the man, please."

"Well, since you said please and didn't bark down the line, I'll put you through."

I had to chuckle. I was abrupt always. Most times I couldn't help it. I had many businesses to watch over, and yet the first time I met Kenzie, she put me in my place about my attitude over the phone. She was the only one I'd let speak to me that way, besides my former assistant and sister.

"Vice. How's the new assistant?"

"A pain in my ass," I grumbled.

Grayson laughed long and loud. "I remember those days with Kenzie. What can I do to help?" Dylan, Grayson's brother, had given Makenzie the job as Grayson's assistant without his knowledge. It was fortunate how it all worked out. They were since married and had two children together. I never thought I would've seen the day Grayson was taken by a dark-headed beauty, but he was, and the time he gave her to get over her ex had been long and trying on his part. At least I didn't have anything to stand in my way.

Well, with the exception of the Den douche, which was why I fabricated a dinner meeting. I couldn't have competition. So before they even had a chance to go on another date, which would lead to more, it was time I moved on with the catch and claim.

"Glad you asked. Wednesday night if you're busy, you're now not. I need a fake meeting to bring Adalyn to."

He snorted. "Why?"

"She was going on a date."

"Ah, I understand. Well, since I have new music for you to listen to, it won't be so fake. Dinner, our place at seven. The children will be in bed by then, and we can relax a little more." Grayson was a music producer and made all the background music for my adult films, only we'd been friends a lot longer than that.

"Thanks for this. See you then," I said, and then hung up. Next, I grabbed my cell and shot off a text to my sister. There was something that had been on my mind for a while, and I wanted to know.

Me: Why did Adalyn act the way she did when I first met her?

Molly: Because you were a jerk no doubt.

Damn younger siblings.

Me: Molly, tell me.

Molly: I can't. It breaks the girl code.

Interesting.

Me: What would you say if I wanted to date your friend? Would you tell me then or order me to back off?

Molly: OMG! You do?

Me: Yes.

Molly: I thought so. You wouldn't just fire her and then find her another job that's close to you for no reason. You're not that kind.

Sighing, I clenched my jaw. **Me: MOLLY.**

Molly: Well, you're not, but I think you would be amazing with Adalyn and good for her.

"Just fucking tell me," I muttered to myself.

Me: Waiting???

Molly: I really can't. She'd kill me if she ever found out.

Damn it, I really had to know, and I knew one way to get to my sister. **Me: I'll pay for your honeymoon.**

Molly: Holy shit, you don't play fair.

Me: You know I never have. For years I hadn't known about Molly and her mother. My father had had a side family, and they were it. I knew he wasn't faithful. I just didn't realize it could lead to having a half-sister. Once I found out, after Grayson had someone follow him, I met with my dad after and demanded him to pick. He chose neither. Instead, he left with his veterinarian, his *male* veterinarian, and none of us had heard from him since.

My mother had been fine with his choice. They'd drifted apart a lot in the years before, and she hadn't been happy for a long time. Of course, I couldn't leave his disappearance alone, so I approached Molly and her mother, and told them who I was. I never thought I would gain an annoying, but kind sister and a second mother. It was difficult over the years to keep in touch when I was building up my businesses, but we had somewhat, and I made sure all women in the family knew I would be there for them if they ever needed me.

Molly: She acted the way she did because she gets nervous around attractive guys. Not that I think you're good-looking, YUCK, but she does.

Very interesting.

Molly: If she finds out I told you, I'll kill you.

Me: Her nervousness changes, why?

Molly: If you piss her off, she'll ignore everything and tell you how it is.

Me: So she likes me.

Molly: Why do I feel like I'm back in elementary school? Yes, Vice, she likes you... well, no actually. I'm not sure if she likes you, but she thinks you're hot. Then again, she could need glasses.

Me: Smartass.

Molly: And yet you still love me.

Me: Unfortunately. Thanks for the information.

Molly: Be careful with her. If you break her heart, I'll cut off your head.

Me: (Thumbs-up)

Molly: Dork, you know there are things called emojis you can just send a thumbs-up.

Me: And one day I will learn such a juvenile thing. For now, I have to work.

Molly: Later, loser.

Placing my phone on the desk, I leaned back in my chair and smiled. It was great to actually know, instead of thinking, Adalyn was attracted to me as I was her. Then again, it was hard not to notice in the bathroom. So all I had to do was get her to like me for me and not my body or looks.

It could be tricky. So far, I was sure she thought me a jerk, but if I could add her attraction into the mix of things, I may figure out a way to get her to fall for me.

Grayson had said once, that when he first saw Makenzie, he fell for her in seconds. He told me it would happen one day to me. Of course, I'd mocked him and rolled my eyes at the stupid suggestion.

Only, he'd been right.

Adalyn had stopped my heart at first sight, and everything she'd done since that day had drawn me to her even more. Warmed me to a point I could only see a future with her.

It was time to win her over.

Chapter ELEVEN

WEDNESDAY NIGHT I found myself pacing my bedroom and freaking out. I'd forgotten I'd thrown out my black dress, so I had all my clothes scattered all around my bedroom trying to find something suitable to wear. Only I didn't have anything. What type of dinner meeting was it? Fancy? Casual? Semicasual? I didn't even have Vice's number to message him and ask. Although, having Vice's number could be a bad thing. Especially if I ever got drunk. One night I drunk dialed my ex and told him everything I thought about his limp dick. It was just lucky he'd somehow managed to damage his phone the next morning, even before he'd heard my message.

Me: SOS.

Molly: What???

Me: What do I wear to a business dinner?

Molly: Jesus, I thought something had actually happened. Bitch. What business dinner?

Me: I don't know. Your brother just said I had to attend one tonight, and I didn't think about clothes until now.

Molly: Were you too freaked about being alone with my brother? Aw, so cute.

Me: TELL ME WHAT TO WEAR.

Molly: Relax. What time is he picking you up?

I nibbled my bottom lip, looked at my bedside clock, and gasped. **Me: In half an hour.**

Molly: Fucking hell. At least tell me you've shaved, showered, done your hair and makeup????

Me: Yes.

Molly: Thank God. Okay, you remember that dress you wore six months ago and you refused to wear again?

Me: I AM NOT WEARING THAT!!!

Molly: Stop shouting at me. It'll be perfect!

Pushing a button, I placed the phone to my ear and when she answered, I asked, "Are you out of your mind?"

She laughed. "No. I loved that dress. If was perfect for your figure."

"My boobs nearly popped out half the night."

"So? It'll keep the clients happy."

"I'm not even sure who this meeting is with. What happens if it's some old-timer and I bend over, my boobs drop out for all to see, and I give him a heart attack?"

"At least he'd die happy," Clinton yelled in the background.

He was obviously sitting next to her and listening in. "You two are terrible."

"Wear it," Molly ordered.

"No!"

"Wear it, Addy," Clinton called.

"You're both crazy," I told them before ending the call.

Thank God, Mom and Drew were out of the house. I hadn't wanted Drew to be around when Vice picked me up in case he got the wrong idea, so Mom had taken him to get ice cream. I also didn't want them to see what a tizzy I was in over a business dinner. When I told Drew I had to cancel on Den, which Den was understanding about, Drew had been excited, especially when I added I had a business thing to go to instead of on a date with Den. Another reason why I wanted Drew out of the house because I hadn't said the dinner would also be with my boss. All I'd said was it was with a colleague.

I glanced at the dress Molly mentioned. I had once thought it to be too hookerish, so why was I actually thinking of wearing it? Okay, I was overexaggerating; the dress wasn't too bad. The worst part about the dress was the dipping neckline; the rest was perfect. Still, I was on the verge of hyperventilating, and Vice would be arriving soon.

Throwing caution to the wind, I grabbed the red dress and slipped it on. Grabbing one girl at a time, I lifted my boobs into place and gave them a jiggle. Nodding to myself, I admitted they did look amazing in the dress. I could only hope I wasn't overdressed or Vice hated the way it flaunted my girls. I raced to add my own jewelry I poured my heart and soul into—a black beaded necklace, rings on nearly every finger, and a charm bracelet.

LILA ROSE

When there was a knock at the front door, I yelped and glanced at the clock again. He was early. Quickly, I slipped on some black ballet flats, which were still dressy enough to wear, and grabbed my bag before bolting to the front door.

My head was down and going through my bag to check I had everything when I opened the door. I heard a choke and looked up to see Vice's eyes were fixed on my cleavage and he was scowling.

He glanced up and asked, "Are you trying to kill me?"

I tilted my head to the side in confusion. "Sorry?" And in that time, I took in his clothes. He was wearing another suit, a dark gray one, only he didn't have a tie. Instead, the top button was undone, tantalizing me with his tanned skin, and neck.

"Nothing," he clipped. "Do you have a coat? It's getting cool outside."

Shaking my head to clear the Vice fog, I said, "Oh, right," then spun back around. My feet tangled and I tripped, stumbling forward where I landed on the arm of the couch. Vice must have tried to stop my fall because I felt his heat on my bottom and hips.

"Ah... Adalyn dear, not a good position for Drew to see you in."

Glancing over my shoulder, I saw Mom in the doorway and noticed Vice was right, as in *right* behind me, with his hands on my waist. And apparently, in the stumble, my dress had kicked up, so my panties were on show. Vice moved fast to place my dress back down, step back and helped me stand.

"She was going to fall," Vice explained. What would have helped was if his lips weren't fighting a smile.

Bloody heck, my face must have matched the color of my dress.

"She's always been clumsy. Hi, I'm Jenny, Adalyn's mother, and you must be Vice." Mom's hand came out. Vice stepped forward and shook it.

"I am. It's nice to meet you, Jenny."

"Nana, I got all the mail." Drew came bounding into the room and stopped still at the sight of Vice.

Great. Just great.

"Mom," I bit out. "I thought you were going to be longer."

"And miss meeting your boss? Not a chance."

"Hey, Mr. Vice. What are you doing here?" Drew asked, passing the mail to his nana.

Vice glanced at me with a frown.

"Mr. Salvatore is picking me up for the *business* meeting I mentioned," I explained.

"Adalyn, I love that dress. Don't you like it, Vice?" Mom just had to ask.

"Yes. It's very nice." He leaned into me and added on a whisper, "So was your underwear."

I gasped, only to choke on it. Then once I recovered, I clapped my hands and said loudly, "Right! Time for bed for you, after you have a wash of course, and it's time for us to go." Walking to Drew, I pushed his cheeks together with both hands and shook his head. "Be good, or I'll rip your legs off."

He chuckled, and there was a manly one added to it from behind me. "'Kay, Mom." I kissed him, and he rolled his eyes. "Have a good night," he said, and then moved around me to ask, "Hey, Mr. Vice, are you coming this Saturday?"

"I'm sure—" I started.

"Wouldn't miss it, Drew."

"Cool!" Drew cried. Then he hugged me, hugged his nana, and to my surprise and my boss's, he hugged Vice, who returned the gesture. Then with a pat on his head, Vice said, "You better get ready for bed, kid."

"Night." He smiled up at Vice, and the whole scene had me holding my breath, while my heart swayed from side to side with how sweet it was. I glanced to see Mom with her hand over her heart and her eyes glistening.

"Good night, Drew."

"Night," Drew called to us with a wave before he ran off down the hall.

Speechless.

I was at a loss for words. So when Vice looked from the hall to me, to my mom and then back to me, I cleared my throat. Then did it again. "Um. We'd better go."

"Yes." Mom nodded. "Can't be late for the business meeting." She moved away from the door and swept her hand toward it. Stiffly, I started for it with Vice at my back. His hand to the small of my back made my breath catch. John had never done that. Once out the door, Mom called, "Have a good night."

Glancing back, I smiled and said, "Thanks, Mom."

"Good night, Jenny."

"Night, handsome."

Holy ship, my mom did not just call my boss handsome. From Vice's chuckle, I was certain it was real, and I hadn't heard things. At least he got a laugh from it.

When we were both seated in his large car—I didn't have a clue what sort, I wasn't a car person, but it was big—I turned to him about to apologize for my mom, but he was already looking at me and frowning. So I asked, "What?"

"You forgot a jacket."

"Oh." I glanced down. "I did."

"One moment." He got out of the car, raced up the pathway and knocked on the front door. Mom opened it and nodded at something Vice said. She disappeared from sight only to return with my long, oversized fluffy jacket. One I wouldn't have worn with the dress and one which was more for snowstorms instead of a chilly night. Vice made his way back, and Mom waved from the front porch, then gave me a thumbs-up.

Rolling my eyes, I turned to Vice when he got back in, and stated, "It's not that cold. She could have gotten me a shawl instead."

"No" was his only comment, and then he started the car, driving off.

We drove for ten minutes in silence, which I thought would have been awkward, but wasn't. I was happy to sit there around him, if I didn't look at him, and listen to the soft music playing.

"Tell me about your business."

"My store on eBay?"

"Yes."

"Um, sure." I could do that. "Since I was young, I liked to put together my own jewelry. Of course, back then I wasn't so good at it, but over time I got better, and it's something I love to do. It's relaxing in a way, creating new pieces, and then it's exciting when someone wants to buy something you've made with your bare hands."

Had I said too much? I didn't mean to say that much. But once I started talking about it, I couldn't stop.

"And your store does well?"

Nodding, I fiddled with my bag on my lap. "It does. I mean, it was slow to start out, but it's getting there."

"How long has your store been open?"

"Just over a year. John, my ex, thought it was just a hobby. He didn't trust people would like my work. He didn't want to look like a fool if it failed, so he asked I never told anyone about"—I used my hands for air quotes—"my hobby."

I was fascinated when I saw his hands tighten around the wheel.

"You must be happy to prove him wrong?"

"Oh, he doesn't know I've started it. He left about two years ago, and that was when I began. Sometimes it's hard to work, fulfill my jewelry making and be sure Drew has his mother there for him all the time. Which is also why we moved into Mom's. She helps with the business, so now all I have to do is make it, and she does the rest."

"Your ex sounds like an ass."

Laughing, I wiped under my eyes, and said, "He is. He's missing out on Drew."

"So really he's worse than an ass. Your son is a good kid."

"Thanks," I whispered. I couldn't actually believe we were having a normal conversation without glaring or arguing or having me act weird. It was nice. Actually, I liked it a lot. "Um." I flicked my gaze to him and then back out the front window.

"Yes?"

Looking to him, I asked, "How did you get into the adult film industry?"

When he turned to me and smiled a smile that had my nipples perking up, I glanced away. He still answered, "I was a young boy with a dream." I laughed at that. "Honestly, moving into the adult industry hadn't crossed my mind until five years ago. Grayson and I had been complaining about how terrible porn movies were—"

"Did you watch a lot?" Oh, my God. I couldn't believe I'd just asked that. He chuckled at my shocked expression.

"Actually, I've watched quite a few over the years. I came up with an idea of classy porn, with people who could actually act and storylines that were hotter than anything out there. It seemed to work out."

"How many businesses do you have?"

"A few." He smirked.

"No wonder you're always busy."

"I like to stay busy. I'm not one to sit around and watch movies. Unless I had a special someone to do it with."

What about Monica or Debra? I wanted to ask, but it wasn't my place to, so instead, I just nodded.

A nervous laugh escaped my mouth when the thought of Vice and me cuddled up on a couch watching some lame movie popped into my head.

"What are you thinking?" Of course he had to ask, and the growling tone he used had me wanting to spread my legs and ask him to sing my hoo-ha a song.

"Nothing!" I blurted, and with a quick look, I caught his smile before looking away. "So, um, where is this dinner meeting?"

"Here." He gestured with his chin to the building he pulled up in front of.

My eyes widened. I thought Vice's building was big; I was mistaken. The one in front of me was the biggest I had ever seen. Only I was confused, because the place looked like a business, not a restaurant. What was Vice leading me into?

Chapter
TWELVE

AFTER VICE PARKED in the underground parking garage, one that seemed scarier than the one I used every day at his building, he led me toward the elevators and pressed a button.

"Name?" was snarled from the panel beside the elevator, causing me to jump. Vice's hand came to my lower back, which didn't help my nerves at all.

"Vice Salvatore."

"Right, doors will open soon."

Why would the building have someone control the elevators? Vice must have seen my confusion and worked out what I was puzzled about because he explained, "It's top security here. Grayson wouldn't have it any other way once the children were born."

"This is Grayson and Kenzie's place?"

"Yes."

"But—"

"Their security is manned mainly at night, but they do have some in the front entrance as well since this is also Jackson Media."

"Jackson Media?"

Vice glanced at me, surprised to find me still confused. "Yes. Grayson Jackson, music producer. He has to be safe also for all his clients' sake. Especially when there's a guest floor where his artists sometimes stay."

"Grayson's a music producer?"

His lips twitched. "Yes."

The door opened, and Vice led me in, but I was still lost in my thoughts. I never knew Grayson was so famous. *Should I bow in front of him?* No, that was plain stupid. Oh, wow, I wondered who his artists were. They'd seemed so normal, all of them, and yet I had been sitting among the rich and famous that night in the restaurant.

Shit on a stick. I'd split my dress in front of the rich and famous.

They've seen my panties.

"I can't go in there."

"What, why?"

"I made a fool out of myself last time." Shifting to Vice, I leaned in and whispered, "They saw me fall... and my *panties*."

He chuckled. I slapped his stomach, and he took my hand. My body shivered, and my pulse kicked up. "Yes, we have to work on your coordination."

"That's all you have to say?" I asked, my pitch higher, and then I melted when his thumb started to circle my wrist.

"Relax. We're here to have dinner, and they're normal people like you and me. Shit, we forgot your jacket."

Wait.

Hang on.

Pulling my hand free, I turned fully to him with my hands on my hips. "Forget the jacket. You said this was a business dinner. I did get that right, right?" He didn't answer, so I went on, "Why are we here? I canceled with Den for this?"

"We'll get to that, but, Adalyn—"

"I was sure you said business dinner," I mumbled to myself, searching the floor for answers.

"Adalyn—"

Glancing up, I asked, "Why would I have to come to a business dinner in the first place? And while I'm asking the question, why in God's name did you name your sex stores after yourself?"

A throat cleared. "Vice, Adalyn, so good to see you both."

Shit.

Dropping my head, I sighed, and then raised my gaze and turned with a smile.

"Hi, Grayson, Kenzie, and Mr. High." I waved lamely.

Grayson's lips twitched. What was it with these men and their cute lips action? It drove me crazy when Vice did it to a point I wanted to kiss the twitch right off his face.

"Hi, Adalyn. Thanks for joining us. I, um, ah, I asked Vice to bring you so I wouldn't be bored when they talk business. Hope you don't, um, mind. By the way, you look lovely."

LILA ROSE

If I didn't already think Kenzie was really terrible at lying, then Mr. High's words would have confirmed it, "What the fuck you talking about, Puddin'? Vice wanted her—"

"Dad!"

"Trent," Vice clipped.

"Drinks," Grayson shouted.

What in the world was going on?

"Shit," Mr. High muttered. "Yeah, son. I'll take one of those drinks." He followed Grayson to the bar, and I took the chance to step off the elevator and look around the room. It was amazing, big, beautiful, and fancy.

As if she read my mind, Kenzie said, "This is the formal lounge, where Grayson puts on small gatherings." While Vice made his way past us, heading toward the other men, Kenzie stepped up to my side and pointed to the left, and added, "That's the children's side, with two bedrooms. We cut the third room out to make a larger playroom for them. Don't worry, the place is huge, but we have cameras everywhere linked to our iPads, so we know what the kids get up to. To the right is mine and Grayson's bedroom, a living room, and another spare room. And in through that door is the kitchen and dining area."

"The place is amazing."

"Thanks, we think so. Here, let me take your bag." She pulled it from my shoulder and placed it on the side table by the door.

"Where does Mr. High stay?" I asked.

"Sweetheart, call me Trent. Mr. High is so formal. We ain't that around here. And I stay on the guest floor. That place is bloody huge," Trent explained as he made his way to us carrying a glass of champagne.

Smiling, I took his offered glass, and replied, "Thanks, Trent. So where are the kids?"

"In bed." Makenzie picked up an iPad on the side table near the couch and tapped it. I snatched it out of her hands and cooed over the cute little bundles.

"They're adorable. How do you get anything done? I'd keep watching them sleep or play or eat." I glanced up to see everyone watching me. "Um, I'm a mother, and I do love children."

Kenzie laughed. "I totally understand."

Trent snorted. "Just thank God you didn't have two little girls. That's stress right there."

"We weren't that bad, Dad, and I'm telling Lori you said that."

Trent threw a hand out. "See, they always ganged up on me. Anyway, I wanna get back to Vice naming his shops after him. What's it called, sweetheart?"

My eyes met Vice's, and I was sure a slight blush coated his cheeks. Then I told Trent. "Carnal Vice."

Trent threw his head back and roared with laughter. "Oh, shit. Wait until I tell the boys."

Boys?

Kenzie leaned in and whispered, "He means the security guys. He goes down and plays cards with them all the time. Oh." She gasped. "I better check the food." She took off toward the kitchen, and I took one look at the remaining men, all who were good-looking in their own way, even Trent. So knowing I didn't want to be left alone with so much testosterone, I stuttered out, "I-I'm, um, going, to ah, help, Kenzie."

"Adalyn," Grayson called, I turned back. "Vice lost a bet."

My brows rose. "Sorry?"

"We made a bet. He lost, so I got to name the stores for him."

My mouth dropped open. I was surprised Vice actually stuck to the bet. "What were you going to name them?" I asked my boss.

He coughed on his sip of beer. Trent slapped his back. Vice laughed, rubbing the back of his neck. "Let's just say it was probably good Grayson made the bet. I'm never good at naming things."

"Come on, what would you have picked?" I smiled.

He cursed, looked at the roof and then back to me. "Pleasure Center." Both Grayson and Trent cracked up. I let a small giggle free and then covered my mouth.

"Hmm, I think you're right. It was lucky Grayson won that bet." I grinned and then walked into the kitchen.

A thought popped into my mind. If Vice and I had a child, we'd have to seek someone else to name them.

"What's that smile for?" Kenzie asked as I stepped up to the counter.

"No reason."

She rose her brows but left it alone. "Do you like your new job?"

"I do. It's pretty easy. I used to do the bookkeeping for my ex-husband, so that helped a lot."

"Really? What does he do?"

"He's a graphic designer."

"I was married before I met Grayson. Actually, I was still married when I came to work for him. I left my husband because I couldn't take his personal jabs any longer. They were sinking deep to a point I thought they could be true."

"At least you were strong enough to leave him."

She let out a huff. "It only took me six years. At least I found my happily ever after now."

Snorting, I asked as she potted around the kitchen, "Do they actually exist? And do you need a hand with anything?"

"No, thanks, just sit, relax, and drink your drink. Also, to answer your first question, I do believe they do. Lori and I have both found ours, and I'm sure you will one day."

Shrugging, I said, "One can hope."

"It's good to hope. Do you want a refill?" she asked.

"Um, no, at least not yet. I'm a cheap date. I hardly drink so alcohol goes straight to my head."

She laughed. "That could be a good thing."

"Not when I'm around Vice it wouldn't be," I muttered to myself.

"Pardon?" she asked.

"Oh, um, I'm not sure it would be appropriate at a business dinner."

"Pfft, we're here to have fun, too. Do you know, on my first business dinner I asked if I had a sign on my forehead that read I hadn't had sex in a while?"

A shout of laughter fell from my lips. I covered my mouth. "No?"

"Yes." She nodded. "And I hadn't even had a drink."

"I like you, Kenzie."

Her smile was warm. "I like you, too, Adalyn. And I've been meaning to ask where you get your amazing jewelry from?"

My hand reached up to my necklace, and I looked down to my rings and bracelet. She called them amazing. I grinned. "I made them."

"No way, really?"

"Yes. I could make you some if you like."

"I would so love that, but I'll pay for them."

"No." I shook my head. "Friends rates, meaning they're free. But you can take a look at my online store, to see if anything interests you on there. However, if I find a purchase from you, I'll cancel it."

She laughed and grabbed a pen and paper from the drawer. "Write down your store, and I'll take a look."

Once I wrote it, I passed it back. "One thing you can do, if you know anyone who'd be interested in my product you could share."

"Oh, I will."

"What are you two conniving about?" Vice asked as he entered with Grayson and Trent.

"How to take over the world." Kenzie winked.

"Sounds interesting." Grayson deadpanned.

"Glad you all came in. Dinner is ready. Let's eat," Kenzie announced. I helped her take the cooked chicken, roast vegetables, and warmed rolls to the table.

"This looks amazing, sweetheart," Vice said, and kissed Kenzie on the forehead before taking a seat next to me. Trent sat at the end of the table and on my other side, while Grayson and Kenzie sat opposite Vice and me.

The room fell silent while we dished up our own meals, and then Vice took the time to share, "Did you tell Kenzie about the time you saw me naked?"

"Shut up!" I screamed. The roll I had just picked up went flying through the air and knocked Trent in the face.

"Puddin', do not dish out rolls. I seemed to always get one in the face."

Grayson chuckled. Kenzie's eyes widened, and then she giggled. "This I have to hear."

Vice retold the time in the bathroom. All three had tears in their eyes from laughing so hard. I took my drink and skulled the rest, shocked he'd told them. Then again, they were his friends and not just business associates. Which reminded me, why had I been invited to come in the first place? It didn't make sense.

"Adalyn, would you like another drink?" Vice asked. He moved, ready to stand. When I didn't answer, he faced me. "Adalyn?"

"Kenzie, can you please tell Vice I'm no longer speaking to him?"

She looked from me to Vice and back to me. "Um, sure." She glanced to Vice. "Vice—"

"I heard." He sighed, but his lips twitched, and I caught his look to Grayson, one I didn't understand.

"Adalyn girl, don't stress over it too much. We share in this family. It's how it is. Why, I'm sure Grayson has some stories to tell you about Vice back in college days."

Family.

Trent was including me in their family. Why? Even though it spread good fuzzy feelings inside of me, it still confused me.

"This is true. I have many." Grayson nodded and smirked at Vice.

"Don't you dare," Vice warned low.

"Payback is a bitch as they say."

"Yes, please tell me." I grinned. It would be good to have some dirt on the man who drove me crazy, and it was a welcome distraction from overthinking about the invite there.

"Right, where to begin." Grayson rubbed his hands together. Vice groaned, but he didn't stop Grayson any further.

Chapter

THIRTEEN

DINNER WAS AMAZING and the company even better. The stories Grayson had on Vice were thrilling. He hadn't always been the serious, gruff man he was since I'd met him. He'd been shy, cute, and skinny. It wasn't until after dinner that Grayson pulled out some old photos, ones that caused my stomach to ache from laughing so much. Never would I have guessed Vice had a mullet back in the day, but I had the proof in front of me. Even when Vice tried to take Grayson to the ground, so I didn't see, I still did. Vice Salvatore had had a mullet. He also wore short shorts, though those looked good on him as he leaned against his old car at the ripe age of eighteen.

"I'll be sure to ask your mother for some old photos," Vice grumbled beside me. Even his arm at the back of my chair couldn't put me off the good time I was having and turn me into a bundle of nerves. I was enjoying myself and was glad I'd come out.

"Oh, no. She would never show you or I'd disown her."
I took another sip of my new glass of champagne. "Actually," I started turning to a smiling Trent, "I think you and my mom would get—"

His smile died. "Do not even go there, sweetheart."

"But—"

"No."

I glanced to Kenzie to catch her eye roll. "I've tried to get Dad dating for a long time. He just won't be in it."

Nodding, I said, "Same with my mom."

We stared at each other for a moment and then started giggling. Yes, I was sure we were on the same page, and somehow, we would get Trent and my mom in the same room to see what happened.

"I'm not liking the look you two are giving each other. Stop it. Now! Jesus, no laughing. Forget it, pains in the ass, the both of you." He stood from the table. "I'm heading out. You two get your women under control."

Your women?

All laughter subsided.

I wasn't anyone's woman.

Even though I found myself wishing I was. But it couldn't and wouldn't happen. Vice was... well, amazing, and all types of wrong for me. I wasn't in his league.

Then why am I here?

God, I didn't know and that kind of freaked me out.

"Night, Dad," Kenzie called. He replied with the middle finger.

"Adalyn, would you like a refill?" Grayson asked, standing.

"No, thank you. I, um, really should be going." It wasn't lost on me when Grayson slid his gaze to Vice with another look I couldn't decipher, and Vice answered with a chin lift. Meeting Kenzie's eyes, she shrugged and then smiled softly at me.

Vice stood. "I'll get you home then."

"No, I, ah. I'm going to help Kenzie with the dishes."

"Don't worry about it, Adalyn. We've got it," Kenzie offered.

"But—"

"Come on," Vice interrupted.

Great, I felt bad for abruptly wanting to leave, but Trent's comment confused me because why would I be classed as someone's woman when we weren't even dating? We hardly knew each other. He didn't know how I liked my coffee or that I loved eating Cheerio's without milk for breakfast while I got myself and Drew ready for the day. He didn't know I loved watching horror films, even though they scared the heck out of me. I loved the thrill. And also, I didn't know those such things about him. Well, except for his preference for his coffee, white with one. But what did he do in his downtime? Except work on that magnificent body, because no man could look like him without working out. So then where did he work out?

All those things ran through my mind as we walked to the elevator, after I grabbed my bag. When Vice pressed the button, I turned and leaned into Kenzie for a hug. I also kissed her cheek.

"Thank you for an amazing dinner," I whispered.

"Thanks for coming. We'll have to do it again."

Stepping back, I glanced at Vice and then back to Kenzie. "Um, sure. Maybe we could have a girls' day with Molly and Lori also?"

"That sounds wonderful."

My nerves started to play on me, but I still walked up to Grayson and got to my tippy toes to kiss his cheek. "Thank you."

"Pleasure." He smiled.

Vice said a quick goodbye, and we stepped into the elevator. It was then I remembered and gasped as I spun to Vice, "You didn't get any work done."

The doors closed, and I was sure I heard Grayson laughing.

"Vice?"

"Hmm?"

"Don't ignore me. We went there for a business meeting, but you didn't talk about work at all. Did I ruin the plans? Was I supposed to do something?"

"No." He shook his head and leaned back into the wall.

"Then...?"

"We'll talk on the way home."

"Oh, God. I *was* supposed to do something, and I failed, didn't I?"

"No."

Facing him fully, I placed my hands on my hips and glared. "You're starting to annoy me, Vice."

His lips twitched. "Do you know this is the first night you've called me Vice. It's always been Mr. Salvatore."

My arms dropped before my body stiffened. He was right. I had been using his name all night.

"I'm sorry, I—"

"It's fine."

"But—"

"Adalyn," he growled deeply. "If you go back to Mr. Salvatore, I swear I will make you pay."

My head jerked back.

Pay?

How would he do that?

Spanking? My mind whispered the naughty thought, and fire spread over my face.

"Adalyn, Adalyn, Adalyn... what would I give to know what just popped into your mind."

"Nothing!" I shouted just as the doors opened, and I made a bolt for the car. Great, just bloody great, I still had the drive home to put up with, and the fact Vice would be closer. Also, since the thought of spanking popped into my mind, I couldn't stop playing that one word over and over.

I was screwed. One hundred percent.

With my hands clasped in front of me, holding my bag, I stared down at the car and waited. The beeping of locks caused me to jolt. Just as I reached down to take hold of the handle, a body hit my back.

"Let me get that for you," Vice said *right* into my ear. My pulse spazzed out, and I stopped breathing as he leaned into me, grabbed the handle, and opened the door slowly. So very slowly. "Breathe, Adalyn," he ordered, and my lungs complied.

His warmth left me. I heard his footsteps as he walked casually around the car, as if he didn't just turn me into... heck, I didn't even know. I was still frozen on the spot.

Blink. Breathe. Blink. Breathe.

"Adalyn," Vice called from over the car. My big eyes flicked to his amused ones. "Climb in."

Looking to the seat, I wasn't sure if I should.

God, I could still smell him behind me, and he wasn't even there. I peeked to see he was still standing on the other side of the car watching me and smirking.

"Do I need to come around and help you in?"

"No," I cried, and quickly slipped into my seat. I closed the door and did up my seat belt while listening to him chuckle as he also got in the car.

With my eyes ahead, I heard the car start and felt Vice reach his hand to the back of my seat so he could back out, even though there was a perfectly good reverse camera he could have used.

When his hand gently brushed my arm, I was gone. My nerves overtook, and I couldn't sit still. I shifted one way and then another. I nibbled on my bottom lip and then took to biting my fingernail, only to switch it up and play with my blonde locks.

What was Vice doing by acting that way?

Was he just being a gentleman and opening a door for me? Did he have to get so close to me though? Had he done it when he'd picked me up? No, he hadn't, so why then? Heck, what was he thinking? I wanted to know. I needed to know. Out the corner of my eyes, I kept looking at him while he watched the road with a small smile upon his luscious lips.

It wasn't fair he had lips like those. Ones that were just kissable.

Stop! I had to stop thinking about him.

I hadn't realized I'd been lost in my thoughts until we pulled up out the front of Mom's house. I fumbled with the seat belt a little before flinging it off. I nearly had the door all the way open and ready to make a run for it when Vice called my name.

Pausing, I closed my eyes and then opened them slowly. I shifted enough to see him. "Y-yes?"

"We were going to talk."

"Um, that was supposed to be on the way home." I shrugged. "It didn't happen, so...." I got out of the car, peeved with how rude I was being when he hadn't really done anything to gain that type of treatment. All he did was brush up against me, and I was acting stupid.

"Adalyn," Vice called, but I kept on going. I heard his laugh and then his car door being slammed. My dang hands shook so much I couldn't get my keys out of my bag. A hand gripped just above my elbow. Before I could shake it off, I was spun around fast and found Vice looming over me with his hands on the door on each side of my head.

"I'd like to talk now," he demanded in his rough tone.

I faked a yawn. "Tired."

He smirked. "What is it you're afraid of?"

Snorting, I shook my head. "I'm not."

"You are."

"I'm—"

"Addy," he interrupted again.

Having Vice use my nickname had my belly dipping in pleasure for some strange reason, so I blamed that for why I breathed "Yes?"

"I'm going to kiss you now."

My eyes near popped out of my head. I went into panic mode. "Why on earth would you do something like that?"

"Because I wish to," he bit out and then started descending.

If he kissed me, I would lose it.

If he kissed me, that would be the end, and my mild crush would switch to a full-blown one.

"Debra!" I yelled.

His lips, inches from mine, stopped. His breath from his sigh ran over my lips, and I licked them just for a taste since I wouldn't be getting one because I'd thrown a cold bucket over the moment.

"What about her?" he asked, but what he didn't do was move back.

"Um, she was your date."

He blinked slowly and stared down at me. "And?"

"We can't, you know, because of her."

"She was never anyone to me. An actress wanting to look good on my arm for the night and that was all."

"What?"

"Adalyn," he clipped. "I haven't seen Debra since that night," he stated in a final tone and began again to lean further in.

"And Monica?"

He groaned. Touching his forehead to mine, which was sweet, he said, "An old friend who was in town and had lost her husband recently."

"Oh, that's terrible."

"Yes. And what's worse is how my lips aren't on yours."

"But—"

"Enough," he bit out low and grumbly. Then he slammed his lips down onto mine. My eyes widened for a fraction of a second and then closed when his head tilted, and he molded us together more. His hand slid from the door to my neck, then into my hair where he gripped. A moan trembled from my lips. I hadn't been touched this way in so very long.

Gently, still unsure, I placed my hands on his waist. He hummed under his breath when I tilted my own head.

"Open," he demanded against my lips. I smiled, only it was wiped away when his tongue ran over my bottom lip, and then he bit down. Whimpering, my hands tightened against his waist before I ran them up to his chest. He pulled back, looked down at me with hooded eyes, and growled, "Fuck."

"What?" I breathed.

He shook his head and kissed me again. It was a new one, a bold one, and a very heated one. He opened my mouth under his and coaxed my tongue out to play. They tangled, swirled, and danced with each other. Wrapping my arms around his waist, I held strong, unsure if my legs could keep me standing much longer.

His lips trailed from mine to my cheek, and, holy ship, to my neck. I arched to make it easier for him. His hand went from my hair and skimmed down over my shoulder to around my waist where he tugged me forward.

Was that?

Yes, yes it was.

My dream penis.

He was hard, and our kissing had done that to him. It had also soaked my panties, but I was more occupied thinking about his long, thick length against my lower belly.

Would it be too forward to snake my hand down the front of his pants for a feel?

His head rose, his forehead touching mine again. Both of us panted with need. "We should stop," he said.

"Huh?"

His chuckle was rough. "I haven't made out on the front porch of someone's mother's home in a fucking long time, Addy."

"Right. Mom."

Oh, shit.

She was probably looking out through the curtain.

"Yes, your mother."

"I'll be moving out soon," I blurted, and then cursed under my breath for saying it in the first place.

He laughed. "Good to know. Where will you be moving to?"

"I don't know yet."

"Go to dinner with me tomorrow night." He wasn't asking, he was telling me, and I wanted to. Though, I was still confused on what exactly was happening. Vice was interested in me... right? That kiss meant he liked me... right?

Flicking my eyes to the left and then back again, I said, "I can't. I was away from Drew tonight, so..."

"I understand. Shit, it means I'll definitely have to go out of town tomorrow until late Friday." He was going to put off going out of town to have dinner with me?

Wow.

"Oh."

"Saturday. I'll come to Drew's game—"

"You don't have to do that."

"Adalyn, I want to for Drew. I'll come to the game, and then after, we'll take Drew somewhere for lunch or dinner, depending on the time of the game."

My heart swelled. "It's an afternoon one."

"Dinner then."

"Um, okay?"

He touched his lips to my nose and then backed away. "Go inside, Addy, before I take your mouth again."

I didn't move and was rewarded with a huge smile. "There will be more of that soon. We also need to talk about what just happened."

"What *did* happen?" I asked, worrying my bottom lip with my top teeth.

"Talk soon. Get inside now, Adalyn."

"Okay," I whispered. With a trembling body, I turned and unlocked the door, stepping inside. I didn't close it because I looked back once. He was still standing there, waiting until I was all the way shut inside. It was another sweet moment of my life because no one had done that for me. Waving, his smile turned into a grin, and he tipped his chin up to me before I closed the door and leaned against it.

Chapter FOURTEEN

"I WOULD HAVE asked how it went, but I can tell it went well," Mom said, as I looked up to see her sitting in the living room with Puss-it on her lap. She was smiling so big it kind of looked scary, adding to it was how she stroked the cat like she was some evil genius.

"I don't know what just happened," I admitted, because that kiss confused me even more. Maybe I'd been right, and Vice did like me. Well, he wouldn't kiss me if he didn't, right?

"I think what happened was your handsome man made a play for my daughter."

"Hmm." I nodded.

"Oh, sweetheart. Don't think too hard about it and just let things happen."

"But I have Drew to consider."

"Adalyn, it's plain to see Drew adores Vice."

"He's only met him a couple of times." How could my son like a man already? Why would he want me to date?

Did I look lonely even to a nine-year-old? If that was the case, I was kind of pathetic.

"That was the first time I've met him, and I already like the man."

Throwing my hands up in the air. I made my way to the couch and asked, "How? Why?" As soon as I was close, I slumped down onto the cushion, leaning my head back, eyes to the ceiling.

"Because the way he looked at you."

I slanted my head to the side so I could see her. "What way?"

"Like you were his dinner and he wanted to gobble you up."

"Mom!"

She laughed. "It's true. John never looked at you like that."

I wasn't sure if I knew the look she was talking about. To me, Vice glared, scowled, and maybe looked at me with humor in his eyes, but other than that, I hadn't seen what Mom was talking about on his face. Yes, he checked me out a few times, but he quickly stopped it, and I honestly thought he didn't realize he was doing it himself.

"I just don't know, Mom."

"Well, I do, and I say stop stressing over it and go with whatever happens. What did he say when he left?"

"That we'd talk soon about, well, um, he kissed me and said he was out of town for a couple of days."

"Talking is good. Did he plan to see you again?"

"He's coming to Drew's basketball game, and he wants to take Drew and me out after it."

Mom's smile was huge.

"Don't." I held my hand up and sat straighter. "I-I can't think too much into it until we've spoken."

"Why?"

"Because... I don't know what he wants. He may only want a fling of passing passion." Mom snorted, but I went on, "Which means I honestly shouldn't have agreed to this dinner Saturday night because it could also get Drew's hopes up. Not that I understand why Drew has taken such a liking to Vice." I sighed. "It's all confusing."

"I don't think you have anything to worry about, but I understand, and I'll keep my glee for when he takes you as his."

I scoffed. "I'm not sure—"

"Adalyn. Go to bed. I know you won't get much sleep, but try and think of something else and not worry about your man."

"He's not—"

Her hand came up, and she rolled her eyes. "Not another word of fear out of you."

"But—"

"Bed, young lady."

"Geesh, Mom, I'm thirty-seven not ten."

She winked. "When you still live under my roof, I get to boss you around."

Snorting, I stood and kissed her on the cheek. "Night, Mom. Love you." I gave a quick pat to Puss-it, which he yowled at, and then started down the hall.

"You too, sweetheart. Oh, by the way. He has a nice tush."

Stopping still, I groaned, "Mom."

"Well, he does."

Shaking my head, I left her to her show. She loved watching the late-night programs. It was probably where I got my liking of late hours from. I bypassed my workroom and snuck a look in on Drew, who had somehow managed to shift his whole body sideways and was sleeping with his head and feet off the bed. Tiptoeing in, not that I really had to—he slept like the dead—I maneuvered him back around to lay on it properly.

Suddenly he sat up. "Mom, did you check the kitchen?"

"What for?" I asked, knowing he was sleep talking. He'd always done it from a young age.

"The cat ate my cereal."

"Well, I'll get you some more."

"'Kay." He nodded and flopped back down. Giggling, I walked out of his room and into mine, which was opposite my son's.

I threw my bag on the bed. It was then I realized I'd forgotten my jacket in the back of Vice's car, I knew I hadn't needed one, but Vice was still sweet enough to get it for me.

Vice.

His lips were... heavenly against mine.

Reaching up, I trailed my finger across my grinning mouth. Vice had been there.

My phone in my bag rang. I quickly grabbed it out, and without looking at the caller ID, I answered, "Hello?"

"Hi, Adalyn."

"John?"

"Of course." I could hear a smile in his voice.

"It's late, John. Why are you ringing now and not when your son is awake to talk to him?"

"I know, I'm sorry, but I actually wanted to catch you, and I promise to ring Drew in the morning."

My stomach bottomed out. He wanted something; it was the only time he wished to speak to me. What I wanted to do was hang up, but I didn't because that would lead to John turning into a jerk and name calling, so I asked, "What do you need?"

"School holidays are coming up. I know I'd said I'd be home for them, but I don't think I can get away."

I ground my teeth together. "John—"

"Wait. Before you start yelling, just hear me out. I was hoping Drew could come here for a week of the holidays. I stay right on the beach, and you know how much he loves the beach."

"I'm not sending our son on a plane alone, John."

"No, I wouldn't suggest that. I thought you could fly over with him. I'll pay for your flight also. You could stay and enjoy the time in the sun. I know it's starting to get cold there."

"I don't think—"

"Please, Adalyn. Just think about it. Drew would love it, and I really want to spend time with him, I miss him a lot."

God, it was his choice to move so flipping far away in the first place.

"John—"

"Please. Just think about it."

Sighing, I ran a hand through my hair. "Fine."

"Thank you."

"The holidays aren't for another couple of months, so I'll let you know in the next few weeks."

He cleared his throat. "I kind of need to know by the end of next week. The deals on the flights end by then."

Darn him.

"Okay."

"I appreciate it, Adalyn, and I'm sure you'll both love it here. It's so peaceful and beautiful. Everyone is always relaxed. I get so much more work done, so I'm really busy all the time, and if you fly him over, it will help a great deal."

"I do have a new job, John."

"That's fantastic, Adalyn. I never liked you working in that store. What are you doing now?"

"I'm an assistant, which means I'll also have to check with my boss about the time off, that's *if* I can do this. But since I'm new, I'm not sure it will be possible."

Really, I shouldn't have said that because I didn't even want to spend any time in the same place as him and his tart. Honestly, it should be John flying out to pick up Drew and then flying back with him instead of me.

"Talk to your boss at least and see. I'm sure she won't mind." I didn't correct him about my boss being a he and not a she.

"Maybe you should fly here to get Drew, and then—"

"I wish I could, Adds babe, but I seriously can't. I want to get all my work out of the way before Drew arrives so I can spend all my time with him."

Adds babe?

I cringed. He used to call me that when we were married, so why would he call me it then when his woman could be there? Not unless she was out. Thinking of her had me wondering if she knew John's plan in the first place.

Drew. He was the most important person in this decision. I would think everything over good and proper for Drew's sake.

"I'll see what I can do, John, and get back to you. Does Dorothy know you want Drew there and that you've asked me to bring him?"

"She does. It'll be fine."

Strange. I wouldn't have expected her to be. From the two times I'd seen her, she'd glared daggers at me.

"Right. So you'll call Drew in the morning?"

"Sure will."

"Okay. Well, I'm heading to bed."

"Great, thanks again for thinking about it. Night, Adalyn."

"Good night," I said, and then hung up the phone. God, was I being too nice? He was the one who screwed Drew and me over for another woman. I didn't know what I should have done. Said no and tell him to flock off? To deal with his own time with Drew without me being involved in any way?

It wasn't in me to do that because if I did, Drew would miss out or he'd sense something else had happened between his father and me. I didn't want any animosity with John when it was Drew we both had to put first and think of.

At least one thing about having a phone call from my ex, it stopped me thinking about Vice and worrying what would happen next.

I was his assistant, and he'd kissed me.

Great, I'm yet again thinking about Vice.

Groaning, I slipped out of my dress and put on flannel pajamas. After a quick bathroom visit, I went back into my room, turned off the light, and slipped into bed.

Then lay there.

Blinking up at the ceiling in the pitch black.

Vice Salvatore had kissed me.

Heck, what would Molly think? Should I tell her? She knew I kind of liked him, but would she be shocked and disgusted her brother kissed me and how it could lead to more… like both of us naked?

My clit spasmed at that thought. Maybe a quick flick of the bean would make me tired, and I'd find sleep. Only it felt wrong doing it in the same bedroom from when I was young.

Mom's just down the hall.
But I'm so wide awake.
Mom down the hall.
But Vice kissed me.
Childhood home.
But Vice's penis.

LILA ROSE

Screw it, go for it.

Slipping my hand into my pj pants and panties, I closed my eyes, and a picture of Vice naked was already in my mind. We were in the bathroom, only I was sitting on the vanity with my legs spread, Vice was getting to his knees in front of me, his eyes heated like they had been after our kiss. He leaned in and kissed my thigh, telling me how beautiful I was and then...

"Goddamn it," I whispered through the room as my orgasm burst out of me.

That went too darn fast.

God, imagine if Vice did get his hands on me. I'd be a screamer in seconds, and that would be embarrassing. So it would be wise to keep my skirts down, my pants up, and not let Vice near my privates or I'd be a blushing, fumbling fool running from the room after coming from one touch.

I hoped I could stay true to my word and stay away from Vice Salvatore.

But if he kissed me again like he had on the doorstep....

Bloody heck, I was totally screwed.

At least, after a quick wash, I did go back to bed and slept the whole night through.

Chapter
FIFTEEN

VICE

"I'm sorry, say that again?" I demanded, slamming my near empty coffee mug on the table in the living room of the hotel.

Molly giggled. "She went to dinner with this Den guy, but Vice, it wasn't her idea. He called Jenny up and invited them all around for a friendly dinner so the kids could play."

Friendly my fucking ass.

Douche Den wanted in Adalyn's pants.

I'd been gone a day, and he'd moved in. Maybe he found out Adalyn had been out with me instead. Kids talked, and Drew seemed keen to have me around so he could have shared that with his friend, then his friends would have told his dad.

However it went down, I didn't care.

Adalyn was mine.

LILA ROSE

It was sly going through Jenny the way he did. He wanted to play dirty, I could too.

"Doesn't matter what way it went down, Molly. He'll soon get the picture." Again she laughed. "Now, tell me, did Kenzie get in touch with Evelyn?" She was a popular country singer and married to Ethan, another country singer, and both were clients of Grayson's.

"She sure did. Kenzie's going to see her today and show her Adalyn's site."

"Again, be sure I only want Evelyn to buy something if she truly likes it and is willing to spread the word about how much she likes it."

"I just texted Kenzie before to make sure that message was passed on."

"Thanks. Has Adalyn talked to you about our date?"

She snorted. "No. She's still calling it a business dinner, and she never mentioned anything happened between the two of you. I'm only guessing something did if you're moving to get her business noticed more."

"Never should have put that clause in the contract at work." Then again, if I hadn't stated a strict no dating policy, I knew Kylie and a few other women would have been gunning for me. I wasn't blind to the looks they gave me. I just wasn't stupid to think they were my type. A lot of women I dated only did it for the money and a step toward the people I associated with. Which was why the only serious woman I had was ten years ago and, since then, the rest had all been hook-ups.

Until Adalyn.

Christ. That woman, that kiss, her blushes, mutter-ings, and anything about her really was made for me. There was something deep in me that knew she was it. She was my forever. Even if I sounded like a complete pussy for thinking it, I didn't care. Never felt it before, even after one sight of a woman, but I did for Adalyn, and I was probably an ass because... well, I was an ass most times, but she was annoying me by not looking at me when all I wanted to do was stare at her and her stunning blue eyes.

Each time I saw her, spent time with her, I found it wasn't enough. I wanted to be around her every chance I got, and even Drew. He was a cute, smart kid, and spend-ing time with him, I knew was going to be fun.

"At least, if things go well, and Evelyn shares about Adalyn's work, her business will boom, and she'll leave your employment."

"That's the plan."

It was either that or fire her, and somehow, I knew firing her wouldn't go down well. Besides, her work on jewelry was superb. After I'd gotten home from our din-ner, I'd looked up her items and checked everything out. She was underpricing herself, but I knew she was doing it so she'd get noticed. She'd have to leave it for a while longer, even after things progressed with the business. A price increase wouldn't look good right after everything took off.

All I had to do was hope Adalyn didn't see this as me taking control of her life. Instead, I wanted her to realize it was me seeing to taking matters into my own hand so we could be together.

At least if she didn't, I'd eventually wear her down to see sense, because we'd be good for each other. I also knew I had people backing us. Grayson and his family, Molly and her man, and I was sure I even had Jenny and Drew gunning for Adalyn and me to be an us.

"Things will work out in the end and, when they do, I'm going to stop sharing shit with you because she's my girl. But for now, and until she sees the light with you, I'll help. You'll be good for my girl, and she'll keep you grounded."

"Can only hope, Molly."

"So do I or else I'll have to hurt you."

"How many times you going to threaten your brother?"

"As many as I want so he knows not to screw my friend over."

"Won't happen," I said with a determined tone.

"You're serious."

"Yes."

"Good." I could hear the smile in her voice.

"I've got to go, Molly, but know I'll handle this Den guy when I get back."

"How?"

"He'll get she's taken when I attend the basketball game."

"Can I come and watch?"

"No."

"Party pooper. I'll let you go. Talk soon, brother."

"You will and, Molly, thanks for everything."

"I'm just happy to help you both and to have my brother sort his life out where work isn't everything for him. Bye."

"Later," I said and then ended the call. I would have liked to have called the office and talked to Adalyn, actually barked down the phone with how pissed it made me to find out she was in the company of another man who wanted to fuck her. But I couldn't since she wasn't the one who told me. She was too damn sexy for her own good, and the shit part about that was how she didn't see it. To my shock, she was oblivious to the men in the office blatantly checking her out, and if it wasn't for the clause in their contracts, they would be up in her grill wanting to take her out. I was sure she thought they were just being nice to the new person, but they weren't. Kylie could see it, which was the main reason Kylie was such a bitch to Adalyn.

Running a hand through my hair, frustrated, I sighed and sent off a similar e-mail to yesterday's to Adalyn stating what I needed done at work. There was no mention of the kiss or her friendly dinner date. I kept it professional. I had to because I had my tech guy going through all employee e-mails and such to know there wasn't anything untoward going on.

Since I was the boss, I couldn't exactly send an e-mail to Adalyn saying I wanted her. Even though I was exempt from Chad, the tech guy, going through my computer, I had to hold to my own standards. Didn't I? I did, I admitted reluctantly. It wouldn't be right to e-mail Adalyn wanting to know what color her panties were.

Jesus, just the thought of her panties had my cock stirring. I'd lost count of the times I'd jacked off over her, imagining taking her in every way possible. Even when I'd picked her up from our date, not that she knew it was a true date, and she'd tripped where we ended up crushed together with her bent over the couch, I'd pictured slipping her black panties down and thrusting into her. That was until her mother walked through the front door. I knew neither woman looked, but if they would have glanced down, they would have seen my raging hard-on.

I had to know everything there was to know about Adalyn and I wanted to share the same back.

Stupid fucking rules.

Hell, I was the boss. I could change them and then have other women think I was doing it for them. No, it was safer to wait. I had to keep it in my pants until she was no longer an employee.

I smiled to myself, however. It didn't mean I couldn't start finding out things about her. E-mailing wasn't the only way to communicate.

Me: I just sent you an e-mail. Did you get it? I fired off to Adalyn. Dammit, I forgot she didn't know I had her cell number, but I'd taken it down the day she started and filled out all the forms.

Adalyn: Who is this?

Me: Vice.

Adalyn: Sorry, Mr. Salvatore, I didn't realize you had my number. I did get the e-mail. Thank you for checking.

Back to Mr. Salvatore. Then again, she was being professional. I was the only one who messaged for a different reason.

All I had to work out was how to lead this into a different direction instead of anything about work. I couldn't exactly ask what color her panties were, or tell her I wanted to see her naked. Or even ask for a boob shot.

Ever since I was young, I was a boob and ass man, and Adalyn was perfect in both areas.

Grinning, I typed in another message: **What time is Drew's game?**

Adalyn: Four PM. Again, you don't have to go if you're busy.

Clenching my jaw, I released an annoyed breath. Why did she do that when I'd already said I was going? Didn't she understand I wanted to be there for Drew, but also for her? I'd thought I'd made it clear. At least, I'd thought it was clear when I'd kissed her and showed my intentions of wanting her. Maybe I hadn't, that or she just couldn't understand I would be interested in her in the first place.

What had the men in her past done to her to think she wouldn't be worthy of attention?

Me: I'll be there. Looking forward to it actually.

Adalyn: Really?

Shaking my head, I smiled. **Me: Yes, Addy, and for dinner that night.** I was also looking forward to showing up and having a friendly chat to douche Den, telling him to back the hell off from Adalyn.

Adalyn: Okay.

Snorting, I stood and made my way to the door. I had another meeting I had to get to. Even though I wanted to just sit back and text Adalyn for the rest of the day, I couldn't.

Me: I have to go to a meeting now, Adalyn. Enjoy your day, and I'll see you Saturday.

Adalyn: Okay.

Laughing, I walked out the door and down to the elevator. Just from her texts, I could tell she was nervous. I was uncertain which part she was nervous about: seeing me, having me at the game when Den would be there, or maybe she was worried I'd kiss her again, which was likely to happen. Only when Drew wasn't around. Surely a kiss wasn't breaking the clause. At least I wouldn't be at work when it happened. Even if it was, I didn't care. I couldn't wait to have her mouth again.

ADALYN

Okay?

Okay?

That was what I sent back, and I could have hit myself. I nearly pooped my pants when he texted back saying it was him.

I didn't know he even had my number, nor did I understand why he would text me in the first place when he hadn't done it the day before when he e-mailed me.

Unless... no, he wouldn't know I went to dinner at Den's. That was just stupid to even think he knew and was reaching out to remind me of him. I was already freaked out by going to another man's house for dinner—even though Mom and Drew were there also—especially as I'd just kissed Vice the night before that. I was sure Vice was a man who wouldn't understand it was a friendly dinner and was mainly a chance for the boys to play Minecraft.

My stomach had already been full of humming bees even before his text, and after, it had ramped up its speed to where I was in a state of losing my breakfast.

What would Saturday bring? I didn't know, and I wasn't in the right space of mind to even think about it. What I did know was that I would have to let Den know I wouldn't agree to another date, even if it would be a friendly one. At least, not until Vice and I had spoken.

I considered booking myself into a mental hospital before the weekend. I already had the stress of John calling, like he'd promised, and then telling Drew I was thinking about us flying over to see his dad on the holidays. I wanted to kill John for even mentioning it to our son in the first place when it wasn't set in stone. Drew's excitement was off-the-charts high. It made saying no all the more impossible. How could I break his heart or stop him from seeing his absent father? I knew my son would eventually understand, but I didn't want to disappoint Drew by not giving him a chance to spend some time with his dad at the beach.

So the upcoming weekend stress just added to the amount I already had, causing me to seriously consider a mental hospital, that or I'd suddenly come down with an illness and have Mom take Drew instead.

Though that'd just make me a chicken, and I wasn't one.

Usually.

Chapter
SIXTEEN

My heart was about to beat out of my chest to scurry off into hiding as I made my way into the basketball stadium beside a peppy Drew. He didn't know his mother was about to lose it, I hid it well, so he was bouncing beside me and asking a million questions per second.

"What time will Mr. Vice show? Will he be here from the start? Where are we going to dinner? I can't believe he wants to take us to dinner. When are the school holidays? Maybe Vice can come with us. I know it's only a week, but it'd be fun. Do you think I should ask him?"

"Drew," I called, and with a hand to his shoulder, I turned him to face me. "Please don't say anything to Mr. Salvatore about the holiday with your dad. I need to ask for time off first, and I'm not sure if I can get it. Though, no matter what, you'll be going. I've already spoken to both Molly and your nana. They said they could take you on the plane if I can't get the time off."

"'Kay." He smiled, then skipped off toward the double doors.

Slowly, I followed him. My gaze kept flittering around to see if I could spot Den before Vice showed. I wanted to let him know about Vice coming. I should have said something the night we'd been to his place for dinner, but I hadn't. Actually, I was surprised he didn't already know via Drew and Rick.

Stepping through the doors, I spotted Den sitting in the second row of the seats. I made my way over and caught his smile when he spotted me. Waving, I kept going until an arm came around my waist and halted my progress. Den lost his smile, and he got up, heading down the stairs.

Shit, shit, shit.

I already knew who was at my back; his scent was a tell-tale sign. More of his heat hit my back as he leaned in and whispered in my ear, "Addy. Good to see you." My body quivered.

"Adalyn, everything okay?" Den asked, stopping in front of Vice and me.

"Um, yes?" I tried to shift to the side, but the arm around me wouldn't move. So I thumbed behind me, and said, "Den, this is my boss, Vice Salvatore."

Vice's body stiffened. "Den, was it?" His free hand came out to shake Den's.

"That's right. Vice, was it?"

"Yes."

"And boss?" Den added, his gaze sliding down to Vice's arm.

"Yes," Vice clipped.

"Mr. Vice!" was yelled from Drew over the other side of the court before he took off on a run toward us. It was then Vice took a step to the side, dropping his arm from around me.

I had shifted enough to see Vice smile at Drew, who came to a stop in front of Vice and beamed up at him. "You made it."

"I sure did." He ruffled Drew's hair, and added, "I'm excited to see the game."

"Cool. You can sit with Mom."

"I will."

"'Kay." He grinned. I watched Drew flash a quick glance to Den and then back again to Vice before he asked, "Where we going for dinner tonight?"

Vice's smile matched my son's. Then he chuckled. "That's a surprise."

"I like surprises."

"I'm glad."

Drew's name was yelled. "Gotta go."

"Have fun," Vice called.

"I will," Drew yelled over his shoulder.

Vice moved back to face Den, and to my utter shock, Vice said, "We need to talk."

"What why?" I asked, my tone reaching fearful.

"I think we do," Den replied. Both men ignored me.

"And I think the game's starting soon, so we'd better sit down," I snapped.

"Outside," Vice ordered.

"Right," Den supplied before he walked past me.

LILA ROSE

When Vice went to follow, I grabbed his arm, and hissed, "What are you doing?"

He grinned. "Just having a word with your *friend*."

My eyes narrowed even though I was about to hyperventilate. "Why?"

"Don't worry about it," he said, and then, *then*, he leaned in and kissed the tip of my nose. My arm fell away as he walked off.

Would it be best if I followed, so I knew what Vice wanted to talk to Den about? However, I didn't. Living in a bubble of denial about them talking was better for my sanity. Instead, I stalked to the seats and sat down.

It didn't stop my eyes from hovering over the door waiting for them both to enter back in though. Or the fact I couldn't keep still; my brain, body, and heart were fighting a war. A part of me told me to go out there, another told me to stay put, and then another, anyone could guess which part, was swooning over Vice wanting to talk to Den and letting me believe Vice was warning Den away from me.

BOTH MEN ENTERED just as the game started, and both wore frowns. My knees bounced up and down as they made their way toward me. What did they talk about? Of course I didn't know, and when they sat, one on each side of me, I didn't want to ask. If anything, I thought about sliding to the floor to be away from them.

"Drew plays a good game," Vice commented.

"Uh-huh." I nodded, keeping my eyes on the game. The other team made for a shoot, missed, and my baby, *my* boy stole the ball. "Go, Drew," I cheered, clapping.

Drew made it down the end of the court and then passed it to Rick, who shot the ball to the hoop. I held my breath, watched it hit the back of the board, and then slide through the net. "Woohoo!" I yelled, standing and throwing my hands in the air. Drew looked our way, his smile the biggest I'd seen, and then he rolled his eyes at me. Next, his thumb came up, with his arm in the air. I glanced beside me to see Vice grinning and doing the same back to Drew.

Cute.

Shaking my head, I sat back down. Den leaned in to say, "They work well together."

"They were amazing."

Den chuckled, bumping his shoulder into mine, which knocked me into Vice because we were all sitting close. Out the corner of my eyes, I saw Vice clench his jaw, his nostrils flare, and then, it was as if in slow motion, he reached out to lay a hand on my thigh before turning to me and saying, "So I thought we could head back to my place for dinner."

"Um—"

Den leaned around me. "They came to dinner at my place the other night. It was a good time. Right, Adalyn?"

"Um—"

"Of course, I remember Adalyn couldn't make it to the *friendly* dinner on Wednesday you'd planned because she was with me. So glad you could reschedule it."

"Wait—"

"It was. I even got a chance to get to know Jenny, her mother."

"Jenny's such a nice lady. Baby, do you remember what she called me Wednesday night?" Vice laughed, and I wanted to crawl up into a ball to die.

Den made a sound in the back of his throat. "Drew and Rick had a great time that night too. It's great they're close."

"Speaking of close, do you know Molly? She's Addy's close friend and also my sister."

Please, please, please someone kill me.

"Will both of you stop whatever this is? We're here to watch the game, and that's it."

"You're right, sorry," Vice agreed with a glare toward Den.

"Yes, sorry, Adalyn."

Were they seriously going back and forth for me? Why?

My nerves had me biting my fingernail. I hated they were acting like possessive idiots because I also despised the fact I would have to let Den down. No one was in competition against Vice-freaking-Salvatore, and the jerk probably knew it.

Thankfully, they stayed quiet throughout the game, except to comment on how it played out with Drew and his team winning. I quickly made my way onto the court just as Drew was flying my way. He was crushed in my arms in seconds.

"I'm so proud of you and your team. What an amazing job. You all worked well together like that." As Rick came up, and after he hugged his dad, I added, "Great job, Rick." I held out my hand which he high-fived.

"Thanks, Miss Sage."

I caught Vice's brows dipping together. I hadn't yet told him I'd changed my last name back to my maiden name. It had finally been completed two weeks ago.

When Drew's body detached from mine, I glanced down to see him fly at Vice and hug him tightly, then pull back to look up. "Did you see, Mr. Vice?"

A smiling Vice was an amazing Vice. He looked down to Drew with affection written all over his face. "I did. Fantastic job, all of you."

"Thanks!"

It was then I happened to glance at Den. He was watching Drew with Vice, and something flashed across his face before he hid it, met my gaze, and nodded with a small smile on his lips. I wasn't sure I understood that look, nod, or smile. However, Den then turned to Vice and held out his hand.

"It was… good to meet you, Vice. I'm sure I'll see you here next time."

Vice studied Den for a moment, then grinned and nodded. "Wouldn't miss it." Another male looked past between them before they stepped away. It was then I realized Drew was still at Vice's side with his arm slung around Vice's waist, and Vice had his arm over Drew's shoulders, his hand resting on the opposite one.

"You two ready to go?" Vice asked.

"Sure am." Drew nodded. After a goodbye to Rick and Den, we made our way out into the car park.

"Mom, can I ride with Mr. Vice in his sweet car?" Drew asked.

"Why don't we all go in mine, I can drop you back after dinner?" Vice suggested.

"Ah, no, thank you. I'll take mine and follow you."

He smirked, probably knowing my nerves were once again present or how the kiss we shared kept rolling around in my mind. My body wanted a replay, and if I was in close proximity to Vice, even with Drew about, I wasn't sure I could trust myself. I wanted nothing more than to reach out and touch him, which was why throughout the game I kept my hands under my thighs.

"Drive safe," I called on my way to my car.

"Always, precious cargo on board."

Oh, wow.

That was sweet.

The man was winning more and more points with me. It unnerved the heck out of me because I still couldn't understand why he would show any type of interest in me. Heck, I drove the man insane most days.

Unless… was he a masochist?

Grumbling under my breath as I climbed into my car, I realized all the wondering wasn't doing me any good. I needed to talk to Vice. It would have to be when Drew wasn't around, though. So all I had to do was get through the night and maybe ask him to lunch one day so we could clear the air, and I could find out where we stood.

Chapter
SEVENTEEN

"THIS PLACE IS the bomb!" Drew yelled as he ran off. When Vice pulled up to a large ranch-style house, just on the outskirts of town, I was pleasantly surprised by his pick of home. Despite the fact it was my dream home, one I'd always wanted since I was a little girl, it was also close to town so it wouldn't take me long to get back to Mom's.

Maybe he'd want to sell it to me. Although, once I walked in, I knew it would be way out of my price range. My mouth dropped open, my eyes popping out of my head, and it was only when Vice said, "Breathe, Addy," that I took in a lungful of air.

"Ah." I blinked slowly. Shook my head and asked, "Where's Drew going?"

Vice chuckled. "I told him about the game room I have down the hall."

"I better see he doesn't—"

"Adalyn, can I show you around first?"

Alone with Vice in his house...? No, that wouldn't be good.

I licked my dry lips when the thought of seeing his bedroom conjured in my mind. A giggle just about fell from my mouth, but I clamped my lips together. I'd pictured myself touching his sheets, maybe even smelling them.

That's wrong on so many levels, Adalyn.

"Mom, Mom, Mom. You have to see this," Drew popped his head out from a doorway down the long hall to the left.

Smiling, I looked at Vice. "I guess I have to look at something. Then, um, you can show me around." Would asking to avoid his bedroom seem suspicious? How many women had been in his house, his room, his bed? God, the thought churned my stomach.

Shaking my head, I made my way down the hall. I didn't look around too much, well besides when we'd first entered. Which had been straight into a living room the size of Grayson and Kenzie's formal lounge, only Vice's was more homely. The living room held two couches, one to the left of the room and the other just inside the front door. The ginormous TV was to the right and hung on the wall, while to the back of the room was a panty-wetting bookcase, floor-to-ceiling high, and on each side of that were windows. Since it was dusk outside, I was able to see decking and a lot of land. There was a doorway to the right of the living room, and I was certain it would lead to the dining and kitchen area. I'd wait until the official tour to see it.

Drew had disappeared from sight by the time I made it down the hallway to the doorway I'd last seen him in. When I stepped around into the room, my mouth once again dropped open.

"Holy… wow!" I gasped.

There was a ten-pin bowling lane, pinball machines, a pool table, a poker table, a bar, some old video games, and in the far corner, there was also an Xbox, PlayStation, and a Wii. No wonder my son had been so dang excited about seeing it all. The room was about the same size as Vice's living room… just how big was Vice? No, I meant his house. How big was his house?

Looking up at Vice, I said, "You do realize I'll never get Drew to leave your house again?"

He shrugged with a smirk on his lips.

"Mom, I love this house," Drew cried loudly.

"It is amazing, Drew. Be careful with what you play with, okay?"

"I will. Mr. Vice, do you want to play pool? I've never played before."

"You're on, Drew. I'll just show your Mom around quickly and come back."

"Awesome!" He ran over to the game area and plopped down on a beanbag.

"Shall we?" Vice asked, his hand gestured out to the door. Nodding, I turned and walked out, only jolting once when Vice's hand touched my lower back. "We'll start down the end of the hall."

I wasn't sure why it never really registered in my head, it should have, but it didn't until Vice showed me his house. Then it slapped me in the face. Vice was rich. Very rich.

The hall, Vice talked about, went around to the right. It explained why his house looked smaller on the outside. Of course, the room he picked first just happened to be his bedroom. I blushed. He chuckled as he showed me his space. My gaze landed on his king-size bed, my cheeks heating even more before I focused on the two armchairs which sat in front of another big TV. His room-size walk-in closet, and his en suite, which was another bedroom-sized room with a Jacuzzi, were something to be envious about.

Flustered, I was glad when we walked out of his room. My hand had inched toward his bedside table to see if it would be his underwear drawer. We made our way back down the hall, my skin finally cooling. As we walked, he pointed out his study, and four spare bedrooms. Then there was the game room. I poked my head back in to see Drew's attention was still on some car game, and he was driving like a maniac. Beside that were the swimming pool room and a gym. Then finally, we returned to the living room.

"You've hardly said a word." Vice came to a stop at my side and faced me.

That was because I was still stuck back in his bedroom. His sheets had looked soft. Stroking them was high up on my thoughts still, which led me to think about stroking Vice in a very naughty way. Then of course when I saw his bathroom, it brought me back to the day I peed in front of him and saw him in all his naked glory.

I was sure I was sweating from keeping my mouth shut and not shouting, "Take me, take me now," before flinging myself on his bed, or vanity, or floor. I wasn't too fussy where it was.

"Sorry," I muttered. "I'm loving your place. It's very big." His brows rose. Another blush took over my cheeks. "The house, your place, it's…" I widened my hands out to my sides, "huge," I finished.

"It is, but I like it."

"Oh, I didn't mean to sound like I don't like it. I do." I nodded.

He laughed, and said, "Come on, I'll show you the rest and then get back to Drew before starting dinner."

I gawked at him. "You're cooking dinner?"

His lips twitched. "Yes. I do know how."

"Um, okay." I nodded, and once more blushed because I imagined Vice in the kitchen with nothing but an apron on. Jeepers, my lady bits needed some attention.

"I really wish I could read your mind sometimes," Vice commented, as he ushered me through the living room and toward the door.

"That wouldn't be good at all."

"Hmm, and why is that, Adalyn?" he asked, smirking down at me.

"Because it's kind of crazy up there." I tapped my temple and nodded, then walked into the dining and kitchen area, only to come to an abrupt halt.

If I could marry a house, I would pick Vice's.

My eyes flicked from the large bay windows to the door beside it that led to the deck, to the large wooden table and chairs, and then to the monster of a kitchen opposite the windows. So many cupboards, so much space, just so much to take in and drool over.

Vice's hands on my shoulders caused me to jump. He leaned in and said right in my ear, "I take it you like it?" His breath tickled, and I shuddered as need pulsed through me.

Clearing my throat, I said, "Like does not compute. Love would be a better word." I bit my bottom lip when his hands rubbed my shoulders, only to then thin them tightly when his thumbs dug into my muscles. Like a hussy, I wanted to scream and moan.

"I'm glad you love it, Addy." Over my shoulder, he pointed further into the room to another door. "Through there and to the right is the cinema room. To the left is the utility room that runs into the garage."

"A movie room?" I loved watching movies.

"Yes, with recliner seats and all," he teased wickedly into my ear.

"Oh, my," I breathed. *Lick my ear, suck it, bite it, and I'll scream I'm yours.*

Bloody hell, I needed a cool cloth.

His chuckle was low. "Do you want to see it?"

What? What did he want to show me? His penis?

"The movie room, Addy?"

Oh, movie room, that was just as exciting. I looked up at him with wide eyes, and asked, "Can I?"

Grinning, he started to lean in as he said, "You can look anywhere you like."

"Your dick?" I gasped. "I mean deck? I wanted to look at your deck also." His eyes lit with hilarity right before his lips touched mine.

"Mr. Vice, you coming?" Drew called loudly.

Vice pulled back. His warm eyes met mine before they dipped to my lips and then back up. "I'll have more of that later. But for now, I'm going to play pool with Drew while you look at my *deck*." He tapped my nose and spun, exiting the room, only to come back to poke his head around, and with a teasing smile, he added, "Though, if you still want to look at my dick, I'll see if we can fit it in later." He boomed with laughter when my jaw dropped. His laughter followed him as he walked off to play a game with my son.

That man was going to give me a heart attack.

The movie room was ginormous. The large wall-to-wall and ceiling-high screen caused me to gasp, and the reclining seats had me giggling in glee. I skipped over to the left side of the wall where all the DVDs were. At first, I thought he might have had some movies he'd produced displayed. He didn't. Instead, there was a wide range of films, from horror to sci-fi and suspense, and to my surprise, he even had some romance. Some were old, a lot new, and all I wanted to do was rest back in a recliner and eat popcorn. However, I didn't. Instead, I went from the dining room door right onto the deck, and what I saw stole my breath away.

There would have to be at least ten acres I stared at in awe beyond the deck, which was the length of the house, and in the middle was an outdoor setting. Just near the deck, there was an outdoor pool. Further on, a play area with swings, slides, and a climbing frame. Then there was a fence, but over that fence were horses.

Horses! I cried internally like a little child.

I loved horses—not that I knew how to ride—but I loved them all the same. The sun was just setting, and even though a chill started, I sat myself down onto one of the deck chairs and watched the sun disappear altogether.

The door being opened, and the bright light flashing over the yard pulled me out of my daze. I glanced there to see Drew run out, nearly tripping over the blanket he was carrying as he came my way.

"Mom, Vice won, but he showed me some cool moves. Here." He thrust the blanket at me. "Vice said you need to wrap up because it's getting cold. Can I go and play on the playground for a bit while you watch? Vice is inside cooking. He said I could, but I had to check with you first. Isn't this place awesome, Mom?"

I would have laughed at my very excited son if I wasn't touched by Vice telling Drew to bring a blanket out for me, one I wrapped around my arms. It didn't go unnoticed that Drew was calling Vice by his name instead of Mr. in front of it.

"Can I?" Drew asked again. I was about to tell him he needed his jacket, but it fell from my lips when I took in Drew. My face softened as my heart warmed, then melted.

"I guess you're all set with that sweater," I commented.

Drew picked up the too-big-for-him sweater and dropped it again. "Yeah, Vice gave me one of his because I think we left mine in the car."

Vice dressed my son to keep him warm.

Oh, wow!

"Go play, but only for a short time. I should see if Vice needs some help."

"'Kay." He grinned and bolted off, holding the warm sweater up as he ran.

I smiled, with tears in my eyes. Never would I have thought Vice to be such a sweet, caring man, especially when at first all I saw him being was gruff and mean. I liked how he could be all of that. Although, looking around, I couldn't help but think I was out of his league. If something happened between us, I would need him to know I wasn't in it for his money. I'd sign anything I had to for him to understand that.

Chapter
EIGHTEEN

DREW SPRINTED BACK over when I called him. He was great like that. I'd seen kids throw tantrums over not wanting to leave a place or not getting what they wanted. I was lucky Drew had never been like that. He might pout and glare, but never had he thrown his body down to kick or scream. It could be because he knew he'd be in more trouble if he even tried it.

Without saying a word to me, he went right to the dining room door and opened it. I quickly followed, seeing he'd left it open for me, and I didn't want the cold to get in. I found Drew at the kitchen counter, on a stool opposite Vice who was cutting something up, and again, Drew was talking a mile a minute. Vice was smiling down at him and answering in his gruff, hot voice.

Then he glanced up. My lungs seized.

Everything in front of me I wanted.

Vice standing in a kitchen.

Vice grinning at my son and me.

Vice talking with Drew.

Vice advising and taking care of Drew.

I wanted it all, but most of all, I wanted him as mine.

It all slammed into me, and I stumbled forward. If the table hadn't been there, I would have fallen.

"You okay?" Vice called.

Nodding, heat hit my cheeks as I straightened. Placing the blanket over a chair, I made my way over to sit next to Drew. "D-do you need a hand with anything?" I asked, while my heart thumped in my chest.

"I've got it all organized. Hope you like pork chops with salad?"

"I do." I smiled, only I couldn't look at him and stared at his chin instead. He chuckled. I wanted to know what was so funny but didn't ask.

"Drew, what's your favorite meal?" Vice asked as he diced some tomatoes.

"McDonald's."

"I should have guessed," Vice deadpanned. "What about you, Adalyn?"

"Chocolate."

Vice and Drew laughed, but Drew voiced, "That's not a meal, Mom."

"Okay then, um…" I tapped my chin, thinking. "I'm not sure. I like a lot of things. What's some things you like, Vice?"

"Let's see. I love a roast, any type of meat." I snorted. Typical man. "Pizza is a must."

"Yes!" Drew shouted.

"And what about hobbies? What do you do when you're not working?" Since my nerves about my epiphany had calmed somewhat, I glanced up.

His brows shot up. "You mean I could be doing things besides work?"

Drew cackled. I smiled.

"I like to work out and box. I enjoy watching movies and reading. I do dine out a lot since I'm not a fan of cooking for one, but I do enjoy cooking."

"You don't have to eat alone. Mom and I can come here every day if you want," Drew said, his tone serious.

Reaching over, I tickled him. He wiggled and giggled. "You only want to come to play with all the games."

"And swim in the pool." He nodded. "And play outside. But I also want to spend time with Vice."

Vice cleared his throat, and if I had a guess from his expression of shock, then warmth, he liked Drew had said that.

"I'd like to have you here anytime you want, Drew." His stare turned to me. "You also, Addy." I opened and closed my mouth like a dying fish. I couldn't form a sentence. He smirked. "Let's head to the table, and I'll dish up dinner."

Once we all had our meals and started eating, Drew asked, "Do you have any family, Vice?" It seemed my son wanted to know things about Vice as much as I did. It was sweet and brought a happy smile to my lips.

"I do. Did you know Molly is my sister?"

"What? No way. That's totally cool. She's like my mom's bestest friend." I was sure I'd mentioned it to Drew, but I mustn't have.

Vice nodded. "I know. I also have her mother and my mother in my life."

Drew looked confused. "Two moms? Is that like if my dad was to get married, I'd have another mom?"

"Ah." Vice glanced at me with an apologetic frown and then turned back to Drew. "Yes, in a way. But she'll be your stepmom. Though, no one could be as amazing as your mom."

"I know. She's really cool." Drew grinned at me.

I winked. "So are you, kiddo."

"What subjects did you like most at school?"

What was my son doing? Giving him twenty questions to see if we were suited?

"Math and history."

"We don't really do history yet, but I like math. Mom said she used to like art and English."

"Did she?" Vice glanced at me, smirking.

"She did, but that's okay. We can't all like things everyone else does."

"This is very true." Vice nodded.

"Drew honey. Eat up."

"Then maybe we could watch a movie?" he asked.

"I'm sure Vice has other—"

"No," Vice interrupted. "I really don't, and since it's the weekend, I'm sure you'll be okay if Drew stayed up to watch just one movie here?"

"Please, Mom. Please?" Drew used his hands to pray in front of him.

There was no way I could say no. "Okay." I grinned.

"Cool!" Drew cried and then started eating with more gusto.

"Slow down, kiddo, before you get heartburn," Vice said.

My eyes slammed into his. He raised a brow, and I knew he was asking if it was okay he called Drew kiddo like I had. Biting my bottom lip, I nodded. I thought it sweet and would have sobbed over it if I hadn't stopped myself. However, I saw Vice's brows dip and I wondered why he suddenly looked concerned.

We finished dinner with a few more questions Drew drilled Vice with. I told Drew to wait for us in the movie room while we cleared the table. I took mine and Drew's plate up and placed them on the counter, ready for rinsing. When Vice's hand grabbed my wrist, I looked at him.

"Did I cross a line before?" he whispered, his eyes flicking to the movie room and back again.

"No." I shook my head.

"You looked upset over it."

Dang, I must have, and I didn't want Vice to think it was because I wasn't happy he called Drew kiddo. So I said, with a small smile, "I thought it was sweet. Sometimes I become emotional when things touch my... heart."

He reared back, his eyes open in shock. "It touched your heart?" My gaze was drawn to his Adam's apple as he swallowed.

"Yes," I whispered.

"Good." He nodded, his eyes lowering to my lips. "I'd really like to take your mouth about now."

My heart did a summersault in my chest, and I licked my lips, but I said, "You can't."

"Why?"

"Drew. In the other room."

"I think he'd be fine if he caught us kissing." Then he shook his head, let go of my wrist he'd been caressing, and said, "However, you're right, we can't."

"Why?" I stupidly blurted.

He smirked. "We'll talk about it soon."

"When soon?"

His hand came into my view, and he ran his thumb over my bottom lip. I shivered. "Soon," he stated, and then went back to stacking the dishwasher.

The thought of kicking myself for saying we couldn't in the first place was high. Maybe if I hadn't said no, he'd be in my arms and his lips would be on mine. Still, I couldn't help but wonder why he'd put a stop to it as well. What did we have to talk about? Why would *he* want to hold back?

We seriously needed to sort things out. I was so mixed up. What I did know, at least I thought I did, was Vice Salvatore liked me. He wouldn't come to a basketball game for my son or invite us to dinner to his place otherwise.

Maybe the hesitation had something to do with work? Or the fact I was friends with his sister. It could also be he didn't want anything serious in case things went sour and caused a problem in their family. Although, that couldn't be it because he wouldn't have involved Drew if that were the issue.

So it had to be with work... right?

"Adalyn," Vice called for my attention. "I'm not trying to send you mixed signals or anything. I'd like to see where this goes between us."

Moving my wide gaze to the floor, my body trembled from all the thoughts running through my mind.

He wanted to see where it went between us.

He *did* want me.

Holy shit!

He stated it.

Right there, with the last plate to stack in the dishwasher in his hand.

"Um, I think that would be good," I said to the floor.

He teased my ears with another chuckle, and my legs wobbled. "Good. Although, for now, for your sake and Drew's, we need to take things slow."

"Okay," I whispered to the floor, again. I was worried if I looked at him, I'd jump him or cry. Both were a possibility, so I'd probably cry while jumping him and get snot all over him, and that wouldn't be good.

Vice's body hit the back of mine. His fingers threaded through my hair, causing my body to hum all over. With his other hand, he pushed my hair from my neck and touched his lips there. Then he said, low and husky, "I like you, sweet, shy, clumsy, and fiery Adalyn, and I can't wait to see you after I've made you come."

My body spasmed along with my hoo-ha. He chuckled. "I think you like the thought of that, baby."

Baby.

I melted into a puddle.

"Um…" I started. Then he nipped at my neck, and a moan dropped from my lips. "Yes. Now?"

He wrapped both arms around my waist. "Jesus, baby. I wish we could. I don't mind Drew seeing a kiss between us, since I want you both in my life, but anything else would traumatize him."

Blinking like crazy, I asked, "Why do you want both of us in your life?"

Another kiss on my neck before he replied, "Because, since the first time I met you, I can't get you from my mind. With you, comes Drew, and I wouldn't want it any other way. He's a great kid, Addy."

"He is."

"And you're an amazing woman," he added.

"I am?" I was?

"Christ, yes."

"Okay."

With his hands on my waist, he shifted me to face him. My eyes focused on his chest. But with his fingers under my chin, he raised my head to have my gaze. "Now you know I'm not fucking around, I want you to never look away from me. Need your gorgeous eyes, Addy."

Pulling my bottom lip between my teeth, I bit. Was it time to admit the truth?

"Adalyn?"

Scrunching up my nose, I went for it. "You're kind of hot, and I get freaked. I also sort of like you, and that again freaks me out. I don't understand why you'd like someone like me. I know that sounds like I'm putting myself down or have issues. I don't. At least I don't think I do because I'm happy with who I am. I love who I am, what size I am, and the people around me. The people already in my life I can understand liking me, but you and all that"—I gestured with my hand in a roundabout way over his body—"I don't understand."

He smiled softly. "Give me time, and I'll make you understand."

"You will?"

"Oh, yeah."

"Time?"

"Yes, and in that time, I still want to have your eyes."

"Okay." I nodded.

He had just started to lean in when we heard the movie room door open and Drew yelled from within, "You two coming?"

Chapter NINETEEN

JOHN: CAN YOU please let me know by tonight.

Sighing, I bumped my leg up and down under the desk and glanced at Vice's door. It had been nearly a week since Drew and I went to Vice's house. The week had been a busy one, which was good and bad in some ways. Good because I was busier with my business. There'd been an intake of purchases, some I had to make from scratch, which helped keep my mind busy from Vice at night. Bad, because I hadn't spent any quiet time with Vice. At work nothing changed, except Vice didn't bark as much or even order me around. He asked. I was surprised by his change, and I noticed some of the workers also were, but no one said anything.

Me: I'll let you know shortly. I had just pressed Send when Vice's door came open.

"Um. Mr. Salvatore?"

"Yes, Adalyn?" He stopped beside my desk, and I watched his fingers tap into the wood on top.

Wood.

It made me wonder about Vice's morning wood.

"Eyes," he ordered low. When I looked up, he smirked. "What are you thinking, Adalyn?"

With big eyes, I quickly glanced around the room. Some were looking our way. "Nothing. But, um, I do have something to ask, and if it's a no, I understand because I've only been here a little over a month. I also have a backup plan, so don't feel you have to say yes."

"What is it?"

Licking my lips, I whispered, "My ex wants Drew for a week over the next school holidays. He's asked for me to fly Drew over and stay the week so I can fly Drew back. He said he was too busy to leave. I told him I'd think about it, but I need to reply today. However, that doesn't mean I actually *need* to go. Molly and Mom have said they could take him for me since John is paying for the extra flight no matter."

"I'm not sure time off right now is an option, Adalyn."

Nodding, I sighed in relief. I was glad he'd said no. I hadn't wanted to go and have to bend all of my will for John's sake. "Okay," I chirped. His head jerked back.

"You're okay with it?"

"Yes. Totally fine with it, and I'll be even better when I tell John I can't go, and that my mom will be taking him. He hated her, and she hated him. Let's hope they don't kill each other in front of Drew." I didn't even try to hold back my glee.

He laughed. "Yes, let's hope. I was worried—"

My fingers ran over his quickly. To others, it would seem I was only reaching for my stapler. "I felt I had to ask anyway for Drew, and under normal circumstances, I wouldn't have been able to go since I am a new employee. So I'm glad you said no, Mr. Salvatore."

"Good." He nodded. Then he made way out of the office for a business meeting.

After sending off an e-mail, I picked up my phone.

Me: Sorry, John. I can't get the time off, but Mom's willing to bring Drew and stay for the week.

John: But I thought it would have been good for the three of us to spend time together for Drew's sake.

Me: I'm sure Drew will be fine without me and busy wanting to spend time with just you. Will you be introducing Dorothy to him while he's there? I ground my teeth together. I hated the thought of it but knew it had to be done.

John: No. Not this time around. I didn't want to confuse Drew.

Me: John, it's been two years. Drew knows adults date and that you have a girlfriend. It's bound to happen for me too.

My phone started ringing, I quickly answered it. "Are you dating?" John demanded down the line.

"Sort of, why?"

"I don't think it's appropriate."

My body stiffened. "What?" I snapped harshly into the phone.

"For Drew's sake, his mother shouldn't be out dating. Does he know? Is there more than one man? You shouldn't bring this around our son."

Honestly, I was flabbergasted he had the nerve to say that to me.

Still, he went on, "You're with Drew all the time. Do you parade men in and out of the house? Or do you leave him with your *mother* and then go out to get some before—"

"You need to stop right there," I seethed through clenched teeth.

"Adalyn, I have every right—"

"You don't," I bit out, standing, and started to pace my area. "You lost any right to question me about my private life when you left me for another woman."

"You're right. I did lose the right, but when anything in your life has to do with my son, I can question you then."

"Bullshit. My dating has nothing to do with Drew to start with. Until I meet someone who I'll spend the rest of my life with, then it'll be Drew's business. If that time comes, I will introduce Drew to him, and still, you won't say or do anything because my life doesn't involve you. The man I fall for... love will also love Drew, and no harm will come to him. I will make sure of it while you're off screwing your hussy." I ended up screaming at the end.

"Adalyn," his tone held a warning.

"No, John. From now on, anything to do with me has nothing to do with you. If it's something about Drew, I'll keep you informed. Please contact me via text only from now on. Goodbye."

"Av—"

I stabbed the End button and glared down at the phone. My temper got the better of me, and I regretted it being at work. Slowly I glanced up, to find people staring at me.

Damn John for getting to me once again. At the start of our separation, we'd be at each other's throats all the time. Only we kept it well hidden from Drew. Though children were smart, he would have sensed the tension between us.

It wasn't until John actually left that I calmed enough to realize he'd done me a favor. Even though I wasted fifteen years on the man, I was still better off having him out of my life.

"Adalyn, are you okay?" Henley asked, appearing in front of me.

Sighing, I shrugged. "I'm not sure." And I wasn't. Did I just make matters worse for Drew's sake? Or was John overreacting? I had to believe he was because seriously, what gave him the right to dictate when I could date?

Henley took my arm. "Come on." Still in a daze, I let him lead me into Vice's office. "You need to take a moment, and it'll be better to do it without people watching." He closed the door behind us. With his hands on my arms, he asked again, "Tell me you're okay."

My bottom lip wobbled. I'd never been good with people asking me if I was okay when I was highly strung. It made me worse, and tears filled my eyes.

Henley cursed. "Of course you're not. Stupid question. From what I gather, you were speaking to your ex?"

Nodding, I wiped at my face and cleared my throat. "Yeah. God, I shouldn't have taken his call at work. What will everyone think?"

"Who cares what they think? Besides, from the sound of it, he deserved everything you said."

"He did."

"See, so don't let what people think worry you." His hands rubbed up and down my arms.

Another tremble from my bottom lip. "Thanks for being so nice."

"Not a problem, darlin'." His hands moved up to my shoulders and dug his fingers into my tensed body. Closing my eyes, I dropped my head and moaned.

It just happened to be the time the door flew open. "What in the fuck is going on?" Vice demanded in a tone that could kill a person or petrify them at least, because it had me. I jumped quickly away from Henley.

"Vice. I mean, Mr. Salvatore, what are you doing back?" I stumbled over my words and realized it made me sound like I was guilty of something.

He stepped in glowering, and then another appeared behind him. Grayson also walked in, but he did it smiling. "Adalyn." He winked, closing the door behind him.

I watched the door shut and knew there went my chance to make a run for it. "Um, hi, Grayson."

"Someone had better fucking tell me what's going on, and goddamn now," Vice ordered, crossing his arms over his chest.

"Adalyn got a call from her ex, and things didn't go down well, so I brought her in here to calm down."

Vice's glare shifted from Henley to me and then back to Henley. "And you just happened to be the one to help her calm down by touching her?"

"Well, yes." He smiled.

"Shit," Grayson hissed from his spot leaning against the door.

"I could fire you."

"What in the hell for? Comforting a fellow colleague? That's messed up, Vice, and you know it."

"No, for touching a fellow colleague."

"It wasn't in an inappropriate way, so you can't fire me," Henley said smugly, crossing his arms over his chest.

"I can," Vice snarled.

"What for?"

Vice leaned in and clipped harshly, "For touching what's mine."

Puddle.

I'd melted into a puddle. His words caressed my skin and then tickled my nipples into standing to attention. I bit my bottom lip to refrain from grinning. Usually, I wasn't a woman who liked men staking their claim, but boy was I wrong about that, especially when it came from Vice Salvatore.

Henley jerked back. He swung his gaze from Vice to me, to Vice, and back to me. Then he grinned, and said to Vice, "I thought there was no fraternizing in the business?"

LILA ROSE

"In an hour or sooner, everyone will receive an e-mail from my legal team stating a change to the contract."

Henley's grin grew. "Really?"

"Yes. But what I said about Adalyn stays the same."

Henley chuckled. "Damn. All good, I get it, man." He looked at me and ran his eyes over my body. "Boy, do I get it." Then he clapped. "Right, better get back to work, and good luck to you both. Also for when the vultures come swirling for you both."

"W-what does that mean?" I asked, folding my arms over my stomach. What I needed was for the conversation to end so I could continue worrying about the words I'd had with John, and there I went asking a question.

Henley laughed. "Darlin'." He shook his head. "Is she for real?" he asked Vice, who sighed and nodded.

"Reminds me a lot of Kenzie," Grayson added.

The conversation was getting even weirder.

"I'll leave you to explain it,' Henley said, and then exited the room after Grayson moved out of the way.

"Are you okay?" Vice asked.

From confusion, I tilted my head to the side. "Henley didn't try anything."

He shook his head. "No. I meant whatever your ex said to you."

Straightening, I shrugged. "No... or I'm not sure. Honestly, I don't know what to think of it. Vice, I went off at John in front of everyone. I'm so sorry for—"

His hand came up before he stepped in front of me and curled me into his arms. "Don't apologize for it. I

couldn't give a shit how you acted in front of them, just as long as you're okay."

"Those type of words are panty-melting kind of stuff."

Vice chuckled. I stiffened when he said, "Good to know."

Grayson chimed in, "That's my cue to go."

Groaning, I thumped my head into Vice's chest, and asked, "Did I say that aloud?"

"You did," Vice said through his laughter.

"Adalyn, Vice, good to see you both. Vice mention to Adalyn what I said. Talk soon," Grayson said quickly, and then I heard the door open and close.

Sitting my chin on his chest, I met his gaze as he looked down and smiled.

"You changed the contracts so we could date?"

My belly was all warm and fuzzy, while my heart had other ideas and decided to do the mamba.

"Grayson pointed out how stupid I was for not doing it in the first place, so I did. But it also means… I don't want to sound conceited or anything, but some of the women around here may think I've done it for them."

"Alas, they will have to get clued up, fast. You did it for me, right?"

"No one else but you," he managed to get out before I attached my lips to his. It wasn't sweet and soft, but hard and hot. I couldn't get enough of tasting him.

Then there was a knock at the door.

"Ignore it," Vice mumbled against my lips.

LILA ROSE

"But—" All words left my mind when his hands gripped my bottom and pulled me forward so I could feel his hardness against my belly.

Ignoring was good.

Chapter TWENTY

ANOTHER KNOCK HAD Vice lifting his head and ordering darkly, "Go the hell away."

"Um, maybe you shouldn't have—" I didn't get to finish because his mouth claimed mine, and once again, I was lost in Vice.

Another knock, that one heavier. "Vice, sweetheart?"

We froze. With our mouths still glued together, we opened our eyes and stared at one another. Slowly, Vice pulled back, but not before laying a quick peck on my lips.

"Who's that?" I asked in a whisper.

"My mother."

"Yoo-hoo, Vice. We're coming in." It was a different voice.

"Who is that?" I hissed.

"My other mother, Molly's Mom."

With my hands still curled into his jacket, I pushed him back and straightened myself just as the door came open, and two women in their sixties stepped in.

Right then would have been a perfect moment to crawl under Vice's desk and hide. Both mothers looked from a scowling Vice to a nervous, smiling me, over and over a few times, as if they were at a tennis match. It was easy to tell them apart. Molly, like the woman on the right, was a little shorter. Both had light brown hair and matching eyes. Though Molly's mom's hair held some gray tinges. The other woman—gulp—Vice's Mom, was taller, and her coloring was so much like Vice's lovely tanned skin. Both women wore dark slacks with different color shirts.

Finally, they grinned at the same time and walked further in. "Vice sweetheart, aren't you going to introduce us?" Molly's mom asked.

Vice sighed, ran a hand through his hair, and gestured to Molly's mom, "Melanie, Molly's mom, and Grace, my mother, I'd like you to meet Adalyn Sage." He'd remembered to say my maiden name.

"Oh, gosh. You're Molly's friend. She's told us so much about you and Drew. But, what are you doing here?" Melanie asked.

"Um, I'm Mr. Salvatore's assistant."

"Your lips look well kissed, dear." Grace smiled.

My face went up in flames.

"Mom," Vice said in a tone of warning.

"Well, they are."

"Mom." Vice glared.

Fighting for something to say, I blurted, "I'm also his girlfriend." My eyes widened. I covered my mouth with my hand. I couldn't look at Vice. He'd said he wanted to see where it would go between us, but I'd just advanced us in seconds because I was scared they would think less of me.

"Adalyn." At least his tone was softer than he used on his mom.

But I was still in panic mode because a sudden thought popped into my head. I slid my hand to my neck, gripped, and rushed out, "I didn't pressure him into giving me this job. We hadn't been, um, seeing each other then. If anything, he peeved me off until, well, to be honest, he still sometimes does, but I don't mind so much anymore, and he's really great with Drew. Just last week we were at his house because he cooked us dinner—"

"Adalyn." I heard Vice laugh.

However, I powered through. "Which, by the way, I think is amazing, a man willing to cook, so thank you," I said to Grace. "And Vice played pool with Drew. He gave him one of his sweaters to wear outside. It was the sweetest moment I'd had in a long time. Drew just adores Vice, and I don't mean just because of his house either. I was sure Drew wanted—"

"Adalyn," Vice called louder.

Jolting, I whispered, "Yes?"

"Relax, baby." He smiled and tugged me to his side, where he placed his arm around my waist.

Flushing, I took a chance to look at both women. I was surprised to find they were smiling at us with tears shimmering in their eyes.

"Sorry," I mumbled, "I got a little flustered."

"It's fine, dear," Grace said. "We'd come to steal Vice away for lunch, but we'll let you get back to work." She winked, and I wanted to die since it seemed she thought I would go back to making out with her son.

"Adalyn," Melanie called. "Molly just rang before we came in. She mentioned something about a get-together for wedding talk."

"Okay." I nodded. "Thanks for letting me know."

"Fantastic. Kisses," she said with an air kiss and then walked out. Grace came up to her son, and he leaned in to kiss her cheek.

"We'll talk soon," she told him in a tone that brooked no argument.

"Yes, Mom."

"Adalyn, lovely to meet you."

"You also, Mrs. Salvatore."

"Grace, dear. Call me Grace from this day on."

I wasn't sure if I would ever see her again because I was terrified what Vice had to say about me telling his mom, *his mom*, I was his girlfriend. Still, I replied with, "Um, okay, thank you."

Then again, when he curled his arm around me, I took it as a good sign he hadn't minded.

I had to think positive.

He wanted me. I wanted him.

Stating I was his girlfriend to his mom wasn't too bad, right?

Once they left, closing the door behind them, I shifted away from Vice and faced him. "Can you please just kill me now?"

"Why?" He smirked.

"They knew we were kissing. Your moms knew. And then my mouth wouldn't listen to my brain when I told it to shut up, and I kept raving on about things they didn't need to know. I just made the biggest fool out of myself, and you ask why? And then I went...."

"What?"

"No, never mind. I really should get back to work. I've been in here way too long. People must be conjuring up stories about us."

"I don't care what they think. I want to know what you were going to say." He stepped closer, and I backed up, so he came forward again. When I was backed into a wall, he stood in front of me.

"And then you went...?" he asked again.

Expelling a heavy breath through my nose, I closed my eyes and muttered, "And then I went and told then I was... that I'm, um, your, you know."

"Girlfriend?"

"Yes," I cried, my eyes springing wide as I glanced up at him. "Girlfriend, Vice. And we hadn't even talked about anything. I'm not a clinger if you're worried about that."

"I'm not."

"And I don't want anything to do with your money."

"I know."

"I like your company, Vice. I like seeing you each day. I like talking to you, even when it's at times when we're going head to head about something stupid. I may have jumped us ahead, but I'd like to think you want the same thing here."

"I do."

My body deflated, relaxed. "Oh, well... good. So you're okay with me saying that G word in front of them?"

"More than okay," he growled low. Just before I got another taste of my boyfriend's—*cue giddy giggles, which makes me sound like a teen, so I mentally groan and think of Vice as my man without a giggle*—mouth, someone else knocked on the door.

"Fucking hell," Vice snarled and then moves off to open it while I once again straighten myself, and prayed I didn't have a guilty look on my face.

"Vice, I tried ringing your assistant's phone, but she's not even at her desk, and it's not her lunch break. I wanted to see if I could make a time for a meeting with you?" Kylie Whore-face asked from the doorway. Vice had hold of the door. She couldn't see me since I stood near the wall behind the door.

"Is this meeting about work, Kylie?"

She giggled, and I knew it had nothing to do with work, but the new policy on dating within the company. Kylie wanted to get her claws into Vice. My Vice.

"Of course it does," she replied, all sultry.

Stalking over to the door, I grip it and force it from Vice's hand to open it all the way. Kylie gasped, her hand fluttering over her heart. "Oh, you scared me." She laughed and glanced at Vice to see if he was watching, only he wasn't. His eyes were down on me with his perfect, twitching lips.

"Excuse me, Adalyn." Kylie sneered. I faced her again. "I tried calling your desk. It's not good to leave it unattended."

"Sorry, Kylie. I was busy. What can I do to help you?"

"I'd like to book in a meeting with Vice please."

"Oh, really? What time are you free, Vice?" I asked.

"I'm not sure—"

I interrupted him. "Never? Did you say never, because that's what I heard? Actually, Kylie, if you have any questions regarding anything, I'll be sure to help you out. If not, you can see Henley." Shifting to Vice, I grabbed the back of his neck, tugged him down and planted my lips against his quickly. "Now, honey. We'd better get back to work."

Oh, oh, oh... what did I just do? I overstepped, and it was the second time in a couple of minutes. Someone needed to lock me up and throw away the key or at least keep Vice away from me because it was his fault both times I overstepped.

Panic seized my heart to a point it hurt in my chest.

"Breathe, Adalyn," Vice's amused voice said in my ear. "As you can see, Kylie, Adalyn deals with all meetings. Also, if it has anything to do with the change in the contract, I don't want to hear about it." Once Kylie stormed off in a huff, Vice turned my still stiff form his way, using his hands on my hips. "Relax, woman."

Blinking, I asked, "How did you know I wasn't?"

"The freaked-out expression on your face. Don't second-guess your actions, baby. People now know, which means we can move things up...." *Move things up. Does he mean sex?* Vice chuckled and lowered his voice even more.

"I'm not talking about *that* just yet. Lunches are with me now. I get to walk you to your car, and when you arrive in the morning, I expect a greeting. We're still learning about each other. The other part will come. At least, I hope so." He winked, and I blushed.

Great, all I could think about was getting naked with Vice, and pondering it at work wasn't good.

Tapping his stomach, I said, "I'd better get back to work." And think about shaving my legs, underarms, and cleaning up down below.

"Where did your mind just go?"

"Hmm? Oh, nowhere." I grinned. "Don't you have a business or two to run?"

"I suppose I do." He gave me a quick peck and then went back into his office while I stepped out and walked to my desk. I didn't bother looking around. I knew I had eyes on me. They could stare all they wanted. I was more than happy, and no one was ruining it.

Then I remember my conversation with John, causing my stomach to sink. Even if I'd gone about it the wrong way, I was glad I'd mentioned me dating since I knew where Vice and I were finally at.

John would have to deal, and honestly, I didn't understand why he was so bent out of shape about me dating in the first place, not when he was the one who cheated and then left me for her.

Chapter
TWENTY-ONE

"DUE TO THE moms' visit and everything after, I forgot to ask what exactly happened with your ex?" Vice queried through the phone. I was sitting in the living room while Drew did his homework close by at the kitchen table.

"Ah, Drew is doing his homework right now."

"Shit, sorry. I didn't think."

"That's okay. I'll tell you about it tomorrow." I'd been surprised when Vice had called. Usually we stuck to texts, and then I'd see him at work. So when I saw his name flash up on the screen, my whole body quivered in excitement. He was moving up that step, straight into our relationship, right along with me, and knowing it made me dizzy with all the right feelings. "By the way, Molly rang me before and mentioned what her mom said about a get-together. I think we're looking at it for the following weekend."

"Sounds good. Just... don't listen to the moms too much. I know they'll say some embarrassing shit about me."

Laughing, I admitted, "I'm looking forward to hearing what they have to say."

"Damn," he muttered, amusement in his voice. "There was something else I forgot to mention. Grayson and Kenzie are coming over Saturday afternoon. I've invited Molly and Clint also. So I'd like you and Drew there as well. I know Drew has an early game that day... but that is if you can make it?"

"I'd like that. Can I bring Mom? Oh, maybe Kenzie can get Trent to come as well."

He groaned. "You and Kenzie are terrible, but I'll mention it to her."

"Actually, don't worry, I'll text her later. We have to talk about jewelry anyway."

"How is the business going?"

That right there, Vice calling my jewelry a business, and not a hobby, was something amazing. Just like the man himself.

"Good," I whispered, my voice shaking with emotion.

And he knew it. "And there's your sweet," Vice growled deeply into the phone. "You're voice does things to me, Addy."

My heart jumped in my chest. "Now isn't the time to be..." I lowered my voice and looked behind me to see Drew concentrating on his work, "hot, Vice Salvatore."

"So there will be a time for it? Say, when you're alone in bed?" he teased.

"Maybe." I grinned.

"Christ, woman, you surprise me all the time. What also surprised me was your reaction to the spanking DVD."

"You remember that?"

"Couldn't forget your cheeks heating or the sound of your voice when you cried spanking. It was like you were asking me to spank you."

"Um."

I did very much like a little rough in the bedroom. It was something John hated and would never do. But the way Vice was talking about it made it sound he wouldn't mind trying it out. Which of course thrilled me.

"Adalyn." His tone was rough. "Would you like that?"

"One day," I admitted quietly.

"Fuck. That pleases me greatly, baby."

"Vice," I whispered, getting hot all over.

"Mom," Drew called, as he came into the living room. "Is that Vice? Can I talk to him? He'll know how to help with this math problem."

Clearing my throat a few times, I said, "Ah, yes, it is, but I could probably help you." Drew just stared at me. "I could." Another stare and without blinking, which was kind of freaky.

"Vice—"

"Baby, any other time I would gladly help Drew out, but not while I have an erection."

"You do?"

He chuckled. "Yes, Addy. Tell him I'll call him in half an hour to help."

"You will?" I asked, surprised. It seemed Vice wasn't the only one getting surprised all the time.

"Baby, with you comes Drew. Half an hour," he said, and then ended the call.

Looking to Drew, I said, "He just has to do something, but he's going to call back in half an hour to help you."

Drew showered me with a bright smile before skipping back to the table.

Vice had turned my world upside down, and I wouldn't want it any other way. Heck, I still couldn't comprehend why he liked me, but I was going to go with it. Life was about chances, and Vice was a chance I was willing to take, even when it didn't make sense.

"Drew, do you need help with anything other than math?"

"No, I'm good, Mom."

"We'll read later. You wanted to start *Harry Potter and the Philosopher's Stone*, right?"

"Yes!"

"Great. I'm just going to call Molly from my room, and Nana should be home soon. She said she was going to bring takeout."

"Awesome. Will you bring your phone out when Vice calls?"

"Of course, honey."

"Thanks."

It was great to see Drew so taken with Vice, nearly as much as I was. In fact, it warmed me all over. I'd been scared to see how Drew would react when I finally introduced him to a man I liked. I was sure it had just been luck Drew liked Vice before I even admitted to myself I did too.

Closing my door behind me, I pressed Molly's name and placed my phone against my ear. I hadn't actually spoken to Molly about Vice and me. I felt it was time to do so. It had been on the tip of my tongue earlier when she'd called about a get-together, but I'd chickened out for some reason. Maybe fear she wouldn't like my dating her brother.

"What's up, buttercup?" she answered.

"Molly, there's something I need to talk to you about."

"Finally!" she cried.

"W-what do you mean?" My pulse quickened as I paced the room.

"You're calling me about Vice, right? My *brother* who you're *dating*..."

"How? When? Who?"

She giggled. "Vice called me a while ago and asked if I would be okay if he dated my best friend. I was down for it, but I knew things were new and fresh, so I let it go and waited for you to come to me. There's only one thing that sucks about this though."

Vice had asked Molly if he could date me.

Oh my God. Swoon and sigh happily.

"What?"

"I can't ask for any deets if he's good in the sack because that'd be just gross, him being my brother and all."

My whole body sagged in relief, right before I burst out laughing.

"This isn't a laughing matter, girlfriend. I need to know my friend is satisfied in every department, and every time I think I could ask you, I get hives."

"Stop. Please stop. You're killing me."

"I'm killing you?" she grumbled. "You're my friend. I'm supposed to live vicariously through you since I'll nearly be an old married couple."

"Babe, it's not like you ain't getting any," Clint shouted. "She may need to live through you because your brother's a dud in bed."

"Clint, shut the hell up. I do not want to think about my brother and a bed. That's so wrong," Molly screamed, while Clint laughed in the background.

"So you don't want to know anything?" I queried.

"Nope. Nothing, well except if he makes you happy."

"We haven't slept together yet, but—"

"I meant in a general happy sense, you bitch, not in bed happy."

I snorted. "Yes, Molly. He makes me happy, and even Drew thinks the world of him. Though, it is only new," I finished in a quieter tone.

"Don't go there, Addy. When it's the one, it'll be forever, and nothing nor no one will be able to come between the two of you. And, honey, my brother has never, and I seriously mean never, acted the way he does with you. He's smiling more, he texts me, calls me, *and* the moms. They see it as I do. He's taken with you in a big way."

My ears started to ring because my blood was coursing through my body in a rapid speed. I liked that a lot. No, more than liked, I loved hearing Molly say that because it made me feel special.

Vice made me feel special.

"Adalyn? Addy? Clint, I've lost her. Adalyn Sage, you talk to me right now."

"Here," I muttered.

"Honey, I see good, no… grand things for you and Vice. Take it, hold onto it, and make sure you enjoy it all. Even the bad time because let's face it, my brother can be a dick sometimes, but the good times will make up for it. Now, I'll see you this weekend. Can't wait to see you and Vice around each other. Even though I'll be barfing in my mouth the whole time."

"Love you, Molly."

"Love you, Addy."

Some days life could give you lemons when all you wanted was lemonade. It was what you did with those lemons, how you dealt with them that could make or break you. I wouldn't say I'd done well with those lemons, but I wasn't perfect, no one was. I let them beat me sometimes. But I also did the best I could and, if the lemons I had to deal with were what led me to my lemonade, I would do them all over again.

Great, now I want a lemon meringue pie with all the lemon thinking.

Seriously, why am I swapping lemons for life choices? What am I even talking about?

I even worried about myself some days.

My phone in my hand rang. I fumbled with it a few times, nearly dropping it, and then finally I managed to place it against my ear. "Hello?"

"Baby" was all Vice said, and I smiled like a fool.

"Hi," I whispered, and then I heard a herd of elephants running down the hall right before my bedroom door was thrown open.

"I was just coming to see if Vice rang when I heard it ring. Is it him? Is it? Can he help me now?" Drew puffed.

Vice chuckled in my ear. "I'll talk to you soon, Adalyn."

"You will." I grinned and then handed the phone out to Drew. He stepped forward quickly and snapped the phone out of my hand.

"Hey, Vice?" Pause. "Yes, I had a good day, but Mickey at school called me a douche. Do you know what that means?"

It was the first I'd heard of it, and I wondered why he hadn't shared it with me. Although, hearing him confide in Vice about it tickled me pink.

It was times like those I felt the need to break out into song.

As I hit the living room, the front door opened, and Mom stepped in. "I have food."

I placed a finger to my lips and scooted over to her. "Drew's on the phone to Vice. Since my son thinks I'm no good with math, he's asked for Vice's help."

"Oh my." Mom's eyes filled with tears. "And Vice was willing?"

Seeing the same emotions I felt mirrored in Mom's eyes, my bottom lip trembled. I nodded. "He said with me comes Drew. He wants us both."

Goose bumps spread all over my body at voicing what Vice had said. I honestly wasn't sure it had sunk in until then.

"That man." Mom wiped her eyes. "I knew he'd be the one."

"Well, I'm not sure—"

"Shut up. He is. Now, help me with these bags."

Smiling, I took some bags out of her hand. "By the way, all of us are going to Vice's on Saturday after basketball."

"Drew's told me so much about Vice's place, I look forward to seeing it."

"Good."

"Adalyn, what's that smile about?"

"What smile? I don't know what you're talking about."

"Adalyn Sage, you get back here and—"

"Shh, Drew's on the phone, and I have to get dinner on our plates."

"If you're up to something, I will kick your ass."

I only grinned back.

Chapter
TWENTY-TWO

ON THE WAY into the bathroom for a frantic shower, so we could make it to Drew's game on time, I hollered, "I can't believe you let me sleep in so late," down the hall to Mom.

"You needed it. You don't think I know how late you stay up working, but I do. A mother knows all."

"Hear that, Drew?" I asked with a yell.

"If a mother knows all, then how come you didn't know to set your alarm?"

That little monster. When I didn't reply, he knew he had me and started cackling.

Just before I closed the door, Mom called, "How about we meet you there? I know how long you take."

"No, I'll be quick."

"We're going. Bye," Mom shouted back.

"Mom!" I snapped.

"See you there, Mom," Drew yelled, and then I heard a door slam. Dang it. I wanted to take the one car since we were all going to Vice's after. I quickly got undressed and

started the shower. Vice was going to meet us at basketball, and I didn't want my mom and him alone for too long.
I didn't know what she'd tell him.

In record time I was done and drying myself. Since no
one was home, I walked from the bathroom to my room
naked, only that was when I heard a male voice speaking
low.

I froze.

Shit, was there a robber?

My mind panicked before my heart, but it soon joined
with a fast beat. Tiptoeing into my room, I grabbed the
baseball bat I kept for those types of occasions. Not that
we got robbed a lot. In fact, it was never, but I knew when
moving into Mom's, I would be the one who needed to do
all the protecting. Mom would probably offer a would-be
robber a cup of tea and a chat, while Drew asked them to
play a game.

So, with my heart in my throat, I snuck down the hall.
My ears pricked when I heard someone curse right before
something was knocked to the ground.

I jumped around the corner with a battle cry. "Get the
fuck out of my house."

Then I screamed myself.

That was before I tensed. My eyes popped open, and
I sucked in a breath only to stop breathing altogether.

Because Vice Salvatore was standing in the living
room.

Vice Salvatore was standing there as shocked as I was
with a phone to his ear.

"I have to go," he whispered. After he hung up, he slid it back into his pocket. His eyes roamed over my body and heated. "I didn't think we were at this stage yet, but I'm more than willing." He reached for his casual tee and pulled it up over his head.

"Oh, my," I mumbled, as my eyes scanned his body.

However, an issue soon registered in my head.

I was still holding the baseball bat up high.

And I was completely naked.

I let out a yelp, dropped the bat, and covered my breast with one arm, while the other went over my mound.

"OhmyGod, ohmyGod."

"So, we're not heading to the bedroom?" Vice asked. He sounded truly disappointed.

"No, yes, maybe. No, not yet. OhmyGod. I haven't shaved, trimmed, and plucked. Don't look at me. Are you hungry? Eat while I dress."

"I'm very hungry." His gaze again ogled my body.

"Um. I better dress, and you put your top on. You're very distracting." It would explain why I hadn't run from the room and instead stood there speaking to his abs.

He ignored me. "I knew you'd be perfect under your clothes."

Stunned. I was absolutely stunned by his words. However, my body wasn't. My nipples hardened, and my clit pulsed, while my core clenched, and I felt, *felt*, my hoo-ha dampen.

"So fucking perfect," he growled out and took the steps needed to stop in front of my dazed form. "Baby," he roughly clipped. His hands came to my waist and brought my body against his. My hands slammed into his chest, while I stared up at him.

My body hummed. I wanted the man in front of me. Oh, so very much.

"Vice," I whispered.

"Christ," he bit out, then lowered his mouth to touch mine, once, twice and then on the third, he slanted his mouth over mine and claimed it.

Wrapping my arms around his neck, he slid his around and cupped my butt. I moaned against him. Feeling his naked chest against mine was consuming. Having his hands on my bare ass was tantalizing.

Up on my tippy toes, I curled my arms tighter and rubbed myself against him. He groaned, pressing his hardness into me more.

He pulled back. "Shit," he puffed. "I didn't come here for this."

"I know." I nodded.

"You need to get dressed," he ordered.

"Do I?" I asked, because I wasn't sure I had to at that moment. I was enjoying the touch and feel of Vice.

"You must, or I'll have my mouth on your pussy next. Been dying for a taste, Adalyn."

My body shuddered. It wouldn't matter if I was a little late, would it?

"That, um, sounds okay."

His eyes widened, and with his strong arms, he gripped my ass again, only he lifted me at the same time.

With a huff of laughter, I wrapped my legs around his waist.

"Bedroom?"

"Second door down the hall on the right side."

His steps ate up the floor in his fast pace. We were in my room in seconds. Next, I was lying flat on the bed with Vice looming over me, his eyes roaming over my body.

"Honey, as much as I like you looking at me like that, we're going to have to hurry. Drew's game," I reminded him.

He nodded and nodded again. Then he kissed my neck, my shoulder, while I ran my hands over his amazingly wide back.

"Did you used to be a swimmer in school?" I asked, because his body was made to swim.

"Baby, now isn't the time for questions." He chuckled against my breast, only to then take my nipple in his mouth.

"Oh," I moaned. My back pressed against the mattress, and I slid my hands into his hair. So soft. "Do you use product in your hair?" I asked.

His lips left my breast. Dang it. He was laughing again. "I can see I'm going to have to distract you more to make you speechless. But don't hold back your moans or sounds of pleasure for me, Addy. I want to hear it all." He didn't see my nod since he started to kiss down my stomach and then the top of my mound.

"I didn't trim," I confessed on a yell.

He snorted. "Adalyn, baby, you think I care right now?"

214

"Um, no?"

"No. Now widen your legs more. I want to see your pussy before I devour it."

He slid to his stomach while I opened my legs, feeling suddenly shy and nervous. At his first touch against my center, my body jolted, and I glanced down to see his eyes were already looking up. "Goddamn perfect," he gruffly said and then leaned in, while still holding my stare, to kiss my clit.

My breathing was erratic as he swirled his tongue around my clit. I bit down on my bottom lip. He shook his head. "No, baby. Don't hold back," he ordered. I nodded, and when he flicked his tongue up and down, then over my clit again, I arched and moaned. If I could have Vice's head between my legs all day long, I would.

It was torture, but of the pleasurable kind.

He glided his hands under my ass and gripped before he tongued my center.

"Vice," I gasped, already close to climaxing. "Yes, please." Just when he inserted his fingers, and he paid special attention to my clit, I lost it, crying out as my walls convulsed and my body shook through my orgasm. He kissed back up my body, his smug grin coming into view.

"It's been a while, so don't think it was just you."

He winked. "It's all me."

Scoffing, I then smiled, running my hands up his strong arms. "True, it *is* just you. But now it's time for a nap."

He laughed. "No, we need to get going so you should dress."

Shifting one hand from his arm, I slid it between us and gripped his cock. He hissed. "I'd like to take care of this first."

His eyes closed. He cursed low and sat back on his knees. "Next time. This was all about you."

My head reared into the pillow. "Say what?"

He grinned, leaned down and kissed my lips quickly before climbing off the bed. "We have to get going, but I'll be sure to take you up on that offer real soon."

"But you're hard." I sat and grabbed the pillow to put in front of me.

"Very hard." He nodded.

"So I want to help you relieve that hardness."

Vice groaned and glanced back. "Soon, you will, but baby, we can't miss Drew's game entirely. I know once you start, I won't stop until I'm deep inside you while you scream my name as you come over my cock."

Oh, wow!

Vice's grin turned into a smirk. He knew my thoughts, how I wanted all that to happen and right then. "Soon." He walked to the door. "I'll wait for you in the living room."

"Hang on," I called, and grabbed the shirt I wore yesterday, slipping it over my head on my way to him. Placing my hands on his chest, I leaned in. "You're a good man, Vice Salvatore."

The corner of his lips tipped up in a wicked smile. His hands once again landed on my butt, where he applied pressure. I gasped. Then he said, "You wouldn't think so if you knew what I was thinking."

"Um...."

"Yeah." He grinned.

"You, ah, seem to like touching my bottom."

"Been staring at it a long time, baby. I totally love your ass. Now kiss me and get ready."

"Okay," I whispered.

It was after the steamy kiss, one I wanted a repeat of a million times over, when Vice asked, "How come you had a bat when you came down naked?"

"Mom and Drew left, and I'd just gotten out of the shower when I heard a voice in the house. I thought you were a robber."

His eyes shot wide. "And you were going for an attack while naked?"

Shrugging, I grabbed some panties out and nodded. "Sure."

He chuckled. "If it'd been a robber, you would have made him very happy. But, Adalyn, next time, you get dressed and hide, then call for help."

"Now there's an idea." I grinned, Vice frowned. He knew I wouldn't do any different next time. I was fiercely protective of Drew and Mom. Even though they hadn't been home, it was Mom's house I was keeping safe.

"Adalyn," he growled low.

A quick change of the subject was in order. "Hey, how *did* you get in?"

He sighed, shaking his head. "Was close by. Thought I'd call in to take you all to the game. Your mom let me in, saying you were running late and to wait for you while she took Drew on ahead."

LILA ROSE

I groaned. "She could have told me you were here be-fore she left."

Another wicked smile. "Then we wouldn't have had so much fun."

Chapter
TWENTY-THREE

DREW WAS ON cloud nine. His team won the game, so he was full of energy by the time we got to Vice's. Mom pulled up out front with us. I smiled when she got out with her mouth hanging open, staring at the home.

She glanced at me as I made my way over to her car. "This is where he lives?"

"Yes."

"Oh, my."

"I know."

"Nana, Nana." Drew cried, running over from Vice's car. "You have to see the game room, and the pool, oh, and the movie room. Vice's house is amazing. Come see." He took her hand and before she even had her car door closed, he dragged her off toward the house. Laughing, I closed the car door and made my own way up to the front where Vice was letting Drew and Mom in. Just as I went to pass him, with a warm grin, he grabbed my wrist.

"The entry code is 55478."

He was giving me the code to his house.

So I could enter whenever I happened to be over.

My heart swelled with the amount of emotions that bombarded me.

"Okay," I whispered.

"My sweet Addy is present."

"Yes." Going up to my toes, I pressed my lips to his. "I think my sweet side will stay for the rest of the day since you gave me an orgasm."

"Hmm, I'll have to remember that when fiery Adalyn is about."

Giggling, I leaned into him and kissed his neck. "Come on, we'd better save Mom from Drew." He started in the door with my hand in his, until I stopped. He faced me, and I admitted, "I know it's still new, but giving me your code means a lot, Vice."

"You mean a lot, Addy."

"Thank you."

His head jerked back. "What for?"

"For being you."

His lips twitched. "Okay?"

He didn't get it, and I knew he wouldn't. But I'd had to say it and I meant it. If Vice wasn't Vice, he wouldn't have annoyed me, charmed me, and consumed me in ways where I couldn't keep him out of my mind. If he'd been different, I wouldn't be standing in front of him with the feels I had for him.

Once again, I touched my lips to his.

Maybe Kenzie was right: people did eventually find their own happily ever after. And I had a feeling Vice was

mine. Not that I wasn't happy already; he just made life that much better.

Although, I could just be feeling extra happiness because I got a little somethin', somethin' that morning.

Heck, whatever it was, I was going to run with it.

"Come on, we'd better get lunch started before everyone arrives."

"Baby, it's a barbecue, not much to do."

My eyes widened. "Not much to do? Oh snap, the groceries are still in the car. Mom and I loaded them this morning. We've got all kinds of things for pasta salad, Waldorf salad, potato salad. Then there's dessert. We have—"

His hand covered my mouth. "Adalyn, all we need is meat and bread. We may be well off, but we're simple kind of people." He snorted. "By the way your eyes near came out of your head, I'm going to say how wrong I am right now. You're still going to make a shitload of salad no one will eat."

Glaring, I nodded, then grabbed his hand, removing it. "We'll see if no one will eat it, Vice Salvatore." Turning, I stomped back to Mom's car, grumbling about how we weren't in the prehistoric times any longer. I also heard his manly chuckle as he followed to help unload the car. At least he still had manners.

A FEW HOURS later, Molly and Clint were the first to arrive for the late lunch. I was in the kitchen finishing up the last salad and the dessert. The rest were all done in the fridge,

221

waiting. The whole time Vice had sat back looking amused and drank beer. Though to start with, he did ask if he could help, but I refused and told him I'd preferred having his company as I worked. Drew and Mom were in the pool mucking about. It was lucky Vice had messaged me the night before to remind us to bring our bathing suits. Though, I wasn't sure I would get in.

"What's cooking, good-looking?" Molly chimed in.

"I see you let yourself in," Vice deadpanned. "Remind me to revoke your access."

"Pfft, please. You adore me too much to do that."

"Hey, Addy, Vice, how you both doing?" Clint asked, walking around the bench to kiss my temple.

"I'm good, babe. How's work?"

Clint worked for the government. A couple of times he'd explained what exactly he did, but he went into too much boring detail, and I admittedly zoned out in the end.

"Same old. Vice, you want another?" Clint helped himself to the refrigerator for a cold beer. I was surprised Vice didn't say anything. Though since Clint had been around for longer than I had, he probably felt at home in any house of Molly's family.

"All good, thanks. Molly, please tell my woman we don't need salads and desserts for a barbecue."

His woman.... Swoon!

Molly scoffed. "Are you still trying to pull that crap? Mom and I kept trying to tell you barbecues aren't just about the meat, but did you listen? Nooo. However, you will now." She smirked. Molly knew the Sage family liked side plates to go with meat. I was a salad queen. I loved all types and as much as I enjoyed desserts.

Vice rolled his eyes and met my amused stare. "You know I'm only giving in because of you."

Grinning, I nodded. "I know, and I appreciate it."

He stood, leaning over the counter. "Kiss me before I go check Drew hasn't drowned Jenny."

"Good idea." I pressed my lips against Vice's. We pulled apart when we heard Molly cooing.

"I think I'll come with you, Vice, while these two women gossip," Clint said.

"No gossip here. Molly doesn't want to know anything about her brother and the way he uses his—"

"Shut it," Molly cried, hands over her ears. "La-la-la-la."

Clint brought her to his chest while laughing. Vice smiled, then winked at me while I giggled. Clint gave her a final kiss and left, following Vice out.

"You can't do that to me unless you want to pay for my therapy bills. And I'd go see the top doctor in the state."

"Promise, no more." I grinned. "Well, except this morning...."

She picked up a carrot and threw it at me. "You're evil."

"Why, thank you."

She came around the counter, grabbed a knife, and started cutting up the lettuce. Then she bumped my hip. "You do seem all gooey over him, and the same goes for him with you. It's good to see."

Smiling softly, I admitted, "It's good to feel."

"Did I tell you work has offered me a full-time position?" Molly, much to a lot of people's surprise, was a kindergarten teacher. Currently, she only worked as a substitute, and she'd been hanging out for a full-time position for a long time.

"That's fantastic."

"It is, but I'm not taking it."

Placing the knife to the counter, I turned to her. "What? Why?"

She kept cutting and shrugged. Then a smirk came over her. "At least not yet. Not until after the wedding, which Clint and I are moving up so we can have an amazing honeymoon. If I took the job right away, I wouldn't be able to take time off for any of it until I'd been there a full year. We don't want to wait to get married."

"That's a good idea. I still can't believe you two are getting married."

"I know. I thought he'd never ask. He seemed content with the situation we were already in. Anyway, I have a question for you."

"Hit me. Ow, I didn't actually mean hit me."

"That's for torturing me. Anyway, maid of honor… will you?"

I squished her side into mine as I hugged her tightly. "Of course."

"Thanks, babe. And now you've agreed, we really need to get things moving. We're thinking a November wedding."

"That's not far away."

"It's five months. Heaps of time."

"Oh, God, we need to go dress shopping and flowers and cakes. The venue, the—"

"Calm down. This is why I've enlisted the moms also. They're amazing at organizing functions. All you need to do is come dress shopping and work out my bachelorette night."

We looked at each other grinning. "Strippers," we cried together.

"No," Vice voiced grumpily as he stalked in. "Clint needs his clothes from the car."

"He's in already? And you have no say what goes on at my bachelorette night."

"Yes, Drew dared him to." We all laughed. "And I do when my woman will be there."

There went that word again. The term made me swoon so damn hard there was no way I could reprimand him for attempting to put a stop to strippers. "But no one could be as sexy as you anyway," I said. My attention was down on the cutting board, so when no one spoke, I looked up to see a smug grin on Vice's face and Molly sticking her finger in her mouth, pretending to gag.

"What?" I asked. "It's true. No comparison."

"Molly, you can do and have whoever you want at the bachelorette night."

Molly yipped with joy. "Well played, girlfriend. As if you'd have a say anyway, brother." Molly stuck out her tongue like a three-year-old.

Laughing, I shook my head. "Nothing played there. It's the truth."

"Yuck, there goes my stomach again. He ain't that good-looking."

"Oh, but he is." At first, my belly had been in knots with how Vice and I would be in front of company for the first time together, yet, since Molly and Clint arrived, I'd never known it would be so natural around them. We were just us, and it was amazing.

Molly gagged again. "Please, no more."

Vice came around the counter and took the knife from me to drop it down. He then spun me, so I was in his arms. His mouth came down on mine.

"Guys, seriously. I'll be sick." She groaned as if she were in pain. "Stop it!" she demanded, but it was only half-heartily.

The doorbell rang, and Vice pulled back. "That'll be the rest." He tweaked my nose and quickly left.

"Jesus. Do you go in a daze after every kiss?" Molly asked, clicking her fingers in front of my face.

Blinking, I giggled, then sighed. "Yeah."

"Dear God."

More than one set of footsteps approached. Vice, with Grayson beside him, walked in, and Grayson was a sight to behold since he was holding a baby girl who looked about one. She already had a head of wild black ringlets and was currently slapping her daddy's face.

"Ooh, come to Molly, cuteness." Molly dropped the knife and took off for the bundle of joy. Grayson laughed, and Vice rolled his eyes at his sister.

A boy about two ran in next. My eyes widened as he started stripping. Kenzie and Trent quickly followed behind him. "Noah, keep your clothes on."

"But swimmin', Mom. Swim."

"Buddy, Mom said after lunch you can go." Grayson knelt beside a muttering Noah and helped him get redressed.

Greetings were had, and when I saw Noah still pouting, I said, "Noah, maybe you can help Vice by telling the others in the pool it's time to hop out."

"'Kay." He nodded and since he was already standing by Vice, he reached up and took his hand. I had to thin my lips because seeing it was beautiful. I was already thirty-seven and had thought I didn't want any more children.

Until that moment.

Watching Vice smiling and talking about something with Noah, as Grayson followed, I knew if he wanted a child of his own, I would give him one.

Whoa! That thought was a bit advanced for our relationship. But now it was playing around in my mind, I couldn't stop thinking more about it. My belly swollen with Vice's baby, seeing Vice hold his own child for the first time, Vice and I being alongside each other through all the trials and tribulations of childhood, and lastly... Vice sitting down with Drew, reading, talking, and advising.

I wanted it all.

My hip was bumped. I glanced to find Molly watching me. She smiled. "He's always wanted children." She kissed Makala's cheek. "I can see you both with your own child to spoil right along with Drew, and right about now, I think that's on your mind also."

She knew me well. I smiled. "Maybe."

"She's totally thinking about his little swimmers and how many babies they can pop out," Trent boomed.

"Dad!" Kenzie snapped.

"What?" He grabbed a beer out of the fridge, shut the door, and opened his bottle, then took a long pull. When he rested his drink down on the counter, he looked at all of us still staring at him with shock.

"Jesus, I've stayed in the wrong room. Bloody women," he mumbled, then picked his beer up and quickly strode out of the kitchen.

"Sometimes I think super gluing his mouth closed would help." Kenzie sighed and took a seat opposite me on the bench. "Do you need a hand?"

"No, thanks." I smiled. "I'm almost done anyway. Tell me how you've been?"

"Good, great actually. I have something to show you." She grabbed out her phone and started flicking through things. Only before she got a chance to show me anything, Trent came barreling back into the kitchen.

"There's a woman in the swimming pool area." He glared at Kenzie.

"That'll be my mom, Jenny. Did you introduce yourself?" I asked, hiding my smile by biting my bottom lip.

Trent's narrowed gaze swung to me. "That's your mom?" He gulped.

"Dad, where's your beer?" Kenzie asked.

"Puddin', I think I left the iron on."

"You don't iron."

"We have to go."

"Trent, did you meet Jenny?" Molly asked.

A snort came from the doorway and then Grayson walked in. "He got in there, put his beer down, spo—"

"Son, if you say another word, I'll... shit, I don't know. Steal my grandkids."

Grayson's lips twitched. "As I was saying, he put his beer down, spotted Jenny, and made a run for it." Grayson chuckled. "Jenny wondered if you have irritable bowel syndrome to bolt from the room like that."

"I do not. Did you tell her I didn't?"

Grayson shrugged. "I wasn't sure, so I told her that."

Trent groaned. "Now she'll think I shit myself all the damn time. Great one, son. You're a pain in my ass too."

All three of us giggled while Grayson chuckled.

"It's not funny. I have to—" His eyes widened comically when he glanced to the doorway, and I knew why when Mom walked in.

She paused. "Sorry, did I interrupt something?"

"No!" Trent squeaked. Molly snorted loud. Trent cleared his throat. "Uh, no, you didn't. I just had to tell the ladies about, uh, something. That's why I rushed out. I'm Trent by the way."

Mom smiled. "Nice to meet you, Trent. I'm Jenny, Adalyn's Mom." She walked forward holding her hand out. Her smile faltered when Trent just stood there staring down at her hand. Like it was a tampon.

Then he boomed, "Right," and then laughed nervously. But instead of taking her hand, he patted her on the upper arm. Her whole body jolted. "Do you ever get the feeling you want to kill your kids?"

Mom glanced at me, then back to Trent. "Yes. Nearly all the time."

He laughed, then snorted, and lastly coughed. "Uh, good to know I'm not the only one." He turned back to the room and glowered at all of us. "Is dinner ready or what?"

Chapter
TWENTY-FOUR

VICE

ANOTHER LAUGHED FELL from my lips as Trent once again complained about how he'd acted like a fucking idiot. Not that he cared what Jenny thought, of course, nor was she his type, plus he was still in love with his deceased wife. Still, he wouldn't shut up about Jenny, which told me he was full of shit and wanted to get to know Jenny. Turning the steak, I glanced through the windows and saw Drew sitting at the table with Noah. Young Noah had taken a huge liking to Drew right away in the indoor swimming pool room; it was understandable since Drew was an amazing kid. Makala was sitting on the floor playing with toys and kitchen utensils that Adalyn had found for her.

"I think Molly's getting clucky," I told Clint.

Clint glanced in to see Molly sitting with Makala on the floor while Adalyn and Kenzie were in the kitchen getting the salads, no one would eat, out. "She has been for a while. So expect to be an uncle soon."

Trent scoffed. "The way Adalyn was eyeing you earlier with Noah, you'll have her knocked up just as fast."

I tensed. Adalyn wanted more children?

Trent barked out a laugh. "And the way you're smiling, you like the idea."

Grayson lifted his beer, his eyes meeting mine. The dick had been right all along. I'd found the one.

Shit, as sappy as that sounded, I was glad my one was Adalyn. Trent was right. Even though we'd be older parents, I still wanted my own child with the woman who was currently running from the kitchen outside.

"Careful, baby. It's been raining," I called and put the lid in the barbecue.

She didn't stop though. She came right for me, and it was lucky I had my feet planted firmly on the ground because she hit the front of me hard, grabbing my tee and shaking it.

"Did you see? Oh my God, Vice. I can't believe it. Mom left her phone in the car, and I left mine at home, so she's gone to get it to check my site, since she's in charge of all that, so I don't know if it's affected sales yet. But I can't believe she was wearing my work. Talking about my work online!" she cried.

"Baby." Taking her head in my hands, I ordered, "Calm down and—"

She spun out of my hold when her mom called, "Adalyn, Adalyn. Oh, dear it's, oh my, I can't believe...." Jenny came running out waving her phone around.

"Be careful, it's slippery," Trent called. We all looked at him, and he glanced back at us, then muttered, "Shit."

"Adalyn, look, come look. I don't know how you're going to make it all, but it's happening. It's finally happening for my baby girl."

Jenny thrust her phone at Adalyn. Once my woman had it, she looked at it for a moment before letting out an excited cry. Then her breathing changed. Her hand went over her heart, and her eyes widened with a shimmer of moisture.

"How am I going to do this? I can't... that's... I... never, how. Oh God." She groaned. "I'll be ruined before even starting." She spun back to me and asked, "How can I do this without failing?"

It struck me in the chest how she sought out my help right away, when whatever it was scared and yet thrilled her.

"Tell me what's going on, baby, and I'll help the best I can."

She nodded. Sucked in a breath and nodded again, more to herself. "Right, um, okay." While she worked out where to start, I glanced over her to see Molly, with Makala and Kenzie standing close.

Kenzie stepped up further when it seemed Adalyn was still struggling with what to say, or she was in shock about whatever it was. "I mentioned to Adalyn how Evelyn loved the site I showed her and brought some of Adalyn's work. She also wore it to an event, and when asked where she got it from, Evelyn mentioned Adalyn's site."

It happened. I hadn't actually asked Kenzie if she'd gone through with showing Evelyn, but she had. And Evelyn must have loved it enough to mention it to everyone.

"This is good, Adalyn. Many follow Evelyn and, once she shares online that she loves something, they'll want it too," Grayson said.

She nodded and then forced the phone in my face. I took it and… "Fucking hell."

"Yes," Adalyn whispered. Then she screamed, "Five thousand orders! How am I going to do it? I mean, I have some in stock already, but the rest I'll have to make." She threw her hands in the air and started pacing.

"I never thought something like this would happen when I mentioned to Kenzie to show Evelyn," I said, more to myself than anyone and certainly not to Adalyn, because she didn't know I was behind it… well, until then.

She turned, tangled, and would have hit the ground if it wasn't for Trent reaching out and straightening her up. He patted her back and ushered her toward me. "You?" she screeched. "You asked Kenzie to mention it to Evelyn?"

"Haven't we just been over that?" Clint asked. Adalyn and I sliced a glare to him. He zipped his lips with his fingers and took a step back.

"Adalyn," I started in a calming voice. "To start with, I only asked Kenzie because I had refused to change the contracts at work and I wanted you out of… fuck." I had really put my foot in my mouth.

"Idiot," Trent coughed into his hand.

"Keep going," Grayson urged.

"It's okay, Grayson. I don't think I need to hear any more. I can see it clearly now. Vice wanted my business to do well so I'd quit because he wanted to screw me. Simple." She went to walk away, but I grabbed her wrist.

"Adalyn, please it's not like that at all."

She snorted, shaking her head and frowned. "Mom, can you get Drew ready to leave—"

"No," she stated with a snap, causing Trent to laugh. "You'll stand there and listen to what he has to say. I will not let you walk off in a huff when I think he didn't mean to hurt you by asking Kenzie to help." She crossed her arms over her chest, and I wanted to pick her up and hug her tightly to me.

"Clint," Molly called. "Come inside and help with the kids."

"But I'm hungry," he whined. Grayson tagged the back of his neck and shoved him Molly's way.

When they left, Grayson picked up the tongs and opened the lid to the barbecue. "We'll take care of the meat." He gestured with his head to the end of the deck, where we'd be out of hearing distance.

Nodding my understanding, I pulled Adalyn along behind me and walked us to the end of the deck. I moved her around until she had her back to the house. Glancing back down, I saw Jenny eyeing us, while Trent stood quietly beside her. Grayson had Kenzie curled into his front while he flipped the meat over. It would probably be well done by the time we got to eat it, but I didn't care. I had to sort things out.

Looking down to Adalyn, who wouldn't raise her gaze to meet mine, I sighed and started anyway. "I hate you've taken what I asked Kenzie to do as a means to sleep with you. I didn't do it for that reason. I did it because I took a look at your site also and your work is amazing. It just wasn't getting noticed like it should have been. I wanted to help, that's all. I didn't want anything in return." I groaned in frustration when she glared up at me. "Okay, at first I asked because of the contract, but it was never with the intention of fucking you. I want more. I *want* there to be a relationship where it could lead to marriage and more between us. You mean so much to me, Adalyn." She bit her trembling bottom lip. "Do you trust me enough to believe my intentions were good?" Adalyn remained silent, her bottom lip disappearing completely beneath her top teeth. "I also asked Kenzie to show her *if* she thought she would like your work and to tell her not to buy it if she didn't absolutely love it."

When she continued to say nothing, and I still didn't have her eyes, I asked again, "Do you trust me?" Taking her chin between my fingers, I gently pulled her head up and saw tears welling in her eyes. My stomach churned, my heart ached. All in all, I was gutted from seeing the hurt on her face. "Baby, please. I don't want things to end when they've just started. We can be something wonderful, Adalyn. Do you still want that?"

"Y-yes."

My whole body relaxed. Christ, the thought of losing her cut me to the bone.

"I'm sorry for jumping to the wrong conclusion."

"Don't, baby. I get it."

"No, I should have trusted you right away, but I think things were overwhelming me, and I couldn't handle... I didn't want to think.... You mean a lot to me, Vice, and the thought that popped into my head, of you using me for one thing only, hurt. Still, I shouldn't have thought it in the first place."

"You're wrong. I went about things the wrong way. I should have come to you first and asked if it would be okay to have Kenzie share with her friends."

She smiled softly. "We're still learning about each other. Things will happen, but I'm glad I didn't walk out and instead listened to you."

"Listening is good." I smiled, until worry clutched my heart and I had to ask, "Are we okay?"

"Yes, of course. I may be stressed for a while though. I'll need to see if I can fulfill the orders before I, um, leave the job I have now. Vice, how will I do this?"

I let out a sigh of relief. I hadn't lost her. Happiness made my smile widen when she'd asked me for advice. "Hire some help."

Her eyes widened. "Can I do that?"

"Soon, yes, you should be able to, but for now you'll have to see what you have in stock, what you need to make, and figure out if you'll be able to make them by the set time. How much time do you give yourself?"

"I've stated on the site if it's not in stock, the turnaround time would be a month."

"Good. Until you have the answers, we'll figure the rest out after. But no matter what, you've got me, your mom, and I'm sure Molly, Clint, Grayson, and Kenzie will help you out. Although, not sure Grayson and I would be any good with delicate jewelry."

She wrapped her arms around my neck and brought me down to touch her lips to mine. Of course, every time I had a taste of Adalyn I wanted more, so I deepened the kiss, sliding my arms down to her ass and gripping.

"Hey, keep the PDA to a minimum," Trent bellowed, breaking us apart. Adalyn's cheeks heated, the way I liked to see them, especially if I was the one making them that way.

"We'll figure it all out," I said.

"Together."

"Yeah, baby. Together." Another peck and then, "Come on, I better rescue the barbecue from Grayson. He can't cook at all."

She gasped. Her hands landed on my chest, and she pushed. "Hurry then, we can't have our first dinner party ruined." Her eyes bugged out. "Have I already ruined it from having my little—"

"Hell no. This, the people here are family. They won't care about any of it." Taking her hand in mine, she nodded, and I led her back to the barbecue. I left her with her mom, who hugged her tightly and reassured her everything would work out, while I stole the tongs out of Grayson's hands.

"All good?" Grayson asked quietly after Kenzie went over to Adalyn.

"Yes, thank fuck."

My stupid move could have caused Adalyn to leave. If she had, I would have lost it... then soon after chased her to see reason and drag her back to my house where I'd lock her and Drew away forever.

Christ, that sounded crazed, but the thought of her walking away from me made me that way.

Chapter
TWENTY-FIVE

DREW TUGGED ON the sleeve of my sweater at the dinner table. He sat to my left and Vice was on my right at the head of the table. On the other side of Vice was Mom, then Trent, which I was pleasantly surprised to see was where he picked to sit. Next to Trent was Molly, who was still cooing over Makala in her high chair between her and Clint. On Drew's other side sat Noah and then Kenzie, with Grayson down the other end of the table. Thankfully, Vice had a huge dining table.

To start with, when Trent had sat down, he blurted loudly, "What's with the rabbit food?" Vice laughed straightaway, while I glared across at Trent, until he added, "Ah, it looks good?"

Drew tugged on my sleeve again, gaining my attention. "Mom."

Glancing down, I smiled. "Yes, honey?"

"Is Vice your boyfriend?"

The whole table silenced.

However, I couldn't look away from Drew. He was waiting for an answer as he stared back up at me. At that moment, I wasn't sure if telling the truth would be good or bad for Drew. Still, there was no way I would lie to him either.

"Yes, he is, honey."

"You okay with that, Drew?" Vice asked, his hand took hold on mine next to my plate.

Drew's eyes flicked down to our joined hands and then back up to Vice. "So does that mean you'll be around a lot more?"

"Yes, it does."

"Sweet." He grinned.

The others at the table laughed, but I met Vice's eyes and smiled warmly, blinking back the wetness in my eyes. Drew did in fact adored Vice. With my hand still in his, he turned them over and then pulled them to his mouth and kissed my wrist.

My emotions threatened to overwhelm me as I looked around the table and realized my family had grown. With my man, new friends, and my newly extended family, I was blessed.

"Hmm, salad's good," Trent mumbled around a mouthful. I glanced at him and smiled big before giggling.

Looking to Vice, I said, "See."

He snorted. "He's only stuffing it in to be polite." I moved my gaze to his plate and raised my brows at him. "And I'm only eating it because my woman made it."

Another hit to the heart.

LILA ROSE

If the man wasn't careful, I could easily fall in love with him. Though, I knew I was already over halfway there. Dang it, I was totally there, and it was a wonderful feeling. My hands shook in fear because what I already felt for Vice was new to me. John had never brought the heart-pumping, belly-fluttering, pulse-racing, and mind-whirling feelings from me the way Vice could with even a look, a smile, or a smirk.

I knew it was too soon to tell Vice, though. We all needed time to adjust, especially since Drew had only found out we were dating.

Dinner was amazing, and yes, all men ate a lot of the salad. I'd just gotten dessert out of the refrigerator when my phone rang from within my bag. I quickly grabbed it and my eyes widened. Glancing to Mom, to see she was already looking at me, I said, "It's Cammy." Mom gasped. "I'm sure everything's okay," I added. Grabbing Vice's eyes, I told him, "It's my sister, I'll just be a moment." He nodded. I made my way out of the room and pressed the answer button. "Cammy?"

"Hey, sis."

"H-hi. Are you okay?" I asked, unsure how the phone call was going to go. I rested my free hand on the back of the couch in the living room.

"Totes. Sorry been missing yours and Mom's calls. Been busy. I have a new job, and it's amazing. I'm really enjoying it, even if it's only a waitressing job."

"That's fantastic. I'm happy for you, Cammy. Where is this job?"

"Someplace exotic. But I just wanted to touch base and say I'd love to see you and Mom soon. I have some time off coming soon, was thinking of flying in."

My breath caught. "We would really love that. You just let us know when."

"Will do. How's my nephew?"

A normal conversation with my sister was new to me. Usually, she was snarky over everything I said or picking at me about my weight, my choices in life, and not once had she asked about Drew. Shock tangled with happiness ran through me.

"He's great, Cammy. Loves the new school, and he's playing basketball. Something he's wanted to do since he was six."

"That's great. How's the job at the sex shop going?"

My brows dipped. I hadn't thought she'd known about that job since we hadn't spoken since before I even started it. Even when, like she'd said, I'd tried to call her on occasion.

"I'm not working there any longer."

"Oh? How come, I thought you loved that job?"

"It was perfect for the hours and meeting people—"

She laughed. "Don't tell me you met men through there and dated them?"

"Ah, no." That was something I would never do. Well, until Vice came along. However, that was different. I hated him to start with.

"Oh, right. Anyway, I'd better go. It was great talking to you, Adds babe."

She'd never called me Adds babe. What was that about?

"Okay, um, we'll talk soon, yes? And Mom would love to hear from you."

"Yeah, yeah. I'll call her tomorrow. Later."

"Bye." I hit the End button, pulled the phone away, and then stared at it. That phone call was strange. It was as if someone had possessed my sister, only that someone was a nice person just calling to chat. She'd never done that.

"Adalyn?" Vice called. Turning, I saw him leaning against the wall near the closed door to the dining and kitchen. I wasn't sure how long he'd been standing there though; I hadn't heard him close the door on us. "I didn't understand your shock on getting a phone call from your sister. Wanted to be close if you needed me."

He wanted to be close if I needed him.

God, that man.

"I'm okay. I think."

He walked forward until one of his hands wrapped around the side of my neck and the other landed on my waist. "Talk to me, baby."

So I did. "My sister and I have always fought, even when we were young. I never understood why we did it. Maybe she hated how close Mom and I were, but she never wanted to help us in the kitchen or read with us or do anything we liked. My own sister confuses me, still, and I was sure she hated me, but that phone call..." I shrugged. "It was normal. Not one hateful word was thrown my way. I liked it, but it was weird too. Does that make sense?"

244

"Yeah, Addy. It does. What was she after?"

"Usually when she calls it's because she needs help from a situation, needs rescuing, but that time was to touch base, see how we all were. Maybe it's her new job? I don't know how or why the sudden change, but I like it. I think. She mentioned she'd like to see us when she gets time off."

"That good?" he asked, studying my face.

"I think so?" Another shrug. "I guess we'll see if this change of hers stays."

He nodded. "You know you can talk to me about anything."

I tilted my head to the side in confusion. "Yes?"

He smirked. "Baby, I didn't even know you had a sister."

"I don't talk about her much. She's been a troublemaker for so long I tend to not think about her too much. I wasn't keeping her from you. It's more like we're still learning about each other's lives."

Still learning, and yet, I'd still fallen for the man.

"This is true. Do you have any other siblings?"

"No." I smiled. "Do you?"

"No."

My eyes widened. There was something I didn't know yet, and I wasn't sure I wanted to know since Vice looked way younger than myself. Still, I blurted, "How old are you?"

"Old enough."

"Vice Salvatore... wait, do you have a middle name?"

"Nope. Do you?"

"Yes. Rogue."

His head jerked back while his eyes widened. "I'm sorry?"

Rolling my eyes, I said, "Mom's a huge *X-Men* fan, and Rogue was her favorite. She picked mine and Dad picked Camila's."

"What's hers?"

"Daphne, after his mother."

"Normal."

"Yes— Hang on, are you insinuating I'm not normal?" I asked, glaring and pushing at his chest to let me go. Only he wouldn't.

He chuckled. "Baby, you're far from normal, and I wouldn't want you any other way."

Groaning, I snapped, "How can you be sweet and annoying at the same time?"

"Talent."

I scoffed. "And don't think I've forgotten you haven't answered my questions. How old are you, Vice?"

"Forty-three, baby."

I gasped and slapped his waist. "You are not. Don't lie to me."

He threw his head back and laughed. When it dwindled, he pecked my lips with his. "Adalyn," he muttered, amused. "I'm forty-three."

Stepping back, I scolded, "Vice Salvatore, it is not nice to lie."

He threw his hands up in the air. "I'm not. I'm forty-three, Addy. Is that a problem for you?"

I blinked slowly, and then again. Next, I ran my eyes over his body. "You look thirty. How can that be possible? I worried I was a cradle snatcher."

He snorted. "No cradle snatching here, so you can stop worrying."

"Well... good." I smiled. "Forty-three, wow. You look amazing for your age."

He grinned and stepped up to me, claiming me back into his arms. "Glad you think so, baby."

Suddenly, the door to the dining room snapped open. Trent filled it. "Bloody amazing dessert, Adalyn."

My eyes dropped to his hand as he scooped a spoonful of apricot pie up from the baking dish and ate it. A gasp escaped me. I shifted from Vice to stand before Trent with my hands fisted down at my sides. Murdering was illegal, I reminded myself.

"I... you... why?" I cried, glowering at him. "Do you think, Trent, other people would like some?"

"Sweetheart, you made like a gazillion."

Stamping my foot, I yelled, "I didn't make a gazillion."

"Well, at least a pie per person. I picked mine." He grinned. "Any leftovers feel free to hand me the rest. Best pie out there."

At least he complimented my food.

Running a hand over my face, I took a deep breath. Before I could say any more, Trent moved, and Mom slipped into the room.

"Is she in trouble?" she asked, her hands fidgeting together in front of her.

"She's fine. It was strange how fine she was. Sorry, I should have come and told you right away."

She nodded, then smiled. "It's fine. If I had a man candy like Vice, I'd be also distracted."

Vice laughed. I shook my head, and Trent, oh wow, Trent glared at Vice. Then he clutched his pie to his chest, spun, and stormed back into the dining room.

With a smile, Mom winked at me and then followed Trent.

Vice's eyes met mine. He mock whispered, "I think I might have to keep one eye open while I sleep."

"I think it's great." I beamed.

"What, that I could possibly be killed?"

"Oh, no. Not that part." I patted his arm. "But how jealous Trent seemed."

Chapter
TWENTY-SIX

MOLLY OPENED HER door after she'd buzzed me up. The week had been frantic where I quit working for Vice and started full time on my own business. I still wasn't sure if I would get all my orders complete, but I was trying. So even though I should be working, I wasn't because I'd promised Molly I'd make it to her girls' weekend to drink and talk wedding stuff.

"Come in, come in. The moms are here already. So are Kenzie and Lori. We've just been waiting for you and Jenny."

Entering, I said over my shoulder, "Sorry to keep you waiting, and to add Mom can't make it. She's not feeling the best. She's home while Drew has a sleepover at Rick's." Which was how I met Rick's mom.

"Hope she's okay soon."

"She will be." I smiled. As I walked into the living room, everyone glanced my way. After a quick hello, I took my seat next to Kenzie on the couch. Lori was sitting on the floor with magazines spread out all around her, while the moms were opposite Kenzie and me on another couch.

Molly came from the kitchen holding two glasses of champagne. It was only *just* after lunch. If I started drinking so early, I didn't see good things for me. Still, I noticed everyone else had a glass already.

It was also Molly's girls' day, so I took the offered glass and had a small sip. "Okay, what's on the agenda?"

Everyone looked at me.

I flicked my gaze around the room. "What?" I asked.

"Grace and I would like to thank you for taking on our boy," Melanie stated.

Smiling warmly, I said, "I think it's my mom who needs to thank him for taking Drew and me on. I'm a lot to handle."

They all laughed.

"Do you plan to have children? How old are you?" Grace asked.

"Grace," Molly snapped.

"What?" she shrugged. "I need to know if I'm getting any grandchildren."

"You will, from me." Molly rolled her eyes.

Grace blew her a kiss. "I know, my dear. Still, I'd like to see Vice have one." She turned back to me. "So, how old are you?"

"Thirty-seven."

"Hmm. You'll both have to hurry if—"

"Grace," Melanie warned.

I cleared my throat. "Um, we're kind of just new. I'm hoping it will last, but no one ever knows what could happen."

"Pish posh, it will happen. You'll last the long run. I can see it already."

I loved she thought so, and that she seemed happy about it.

Still... insert freak-out mode because speaking about it with *his* mother made me feel I was overstepping once again. It was too soon.

"I like this dress," Lori called loudly.

We all faced her. She held up a page from a magazine with a dress that looked like something my mom would have worn back in the day.

"I'm not really sure it's something for me," Molly said.

"A little old, dear," Melanie added.

Then Melanie and Molly started talking about what type of dress Molly had always dreamed of. While they were and Grace's attention was elsewhere, I smiled softly to Lori. She'd saved my bacon from a grilling. Lori winked back and moved to a new magazine.

THREE HOURS LATER, we had a plan of attack. Though I wasn't sure attack was the right word for a wedding. Then again, I *was* sure, with the dress Molly found that Clint would be attacking her that night. Especially after she showed us the lingerie she would be buying. Heck, if I were a guy, I'd hump her leg from just seeing it.

"Another, Addy?" Grace asked.

251

My head was already a little fuzzy. "Please." I grinned. She smiled back. Even her cheeks were a little flushed; actually, all the women were a little pink. We were sitting around the dining table since we'd just consumed some dips, cheeses, and cookies.

"Molly, are you going to wear your hair up or down?" Lori asked.

"Hmm. Not sure. Kenz, how'd you wear yours?"

"Down." Her cheeks heated even more. "Grayson loves it down."

"Ooooh, look at that smile. I always thought Grayson a stunning young man," Melanie said.

"So did I," Grace agreed. "So glad he's finally settled down, and soon, my boy will be too." Grace's arm landed on my shoulders to hug me close. "I adore you, Addy. You're so sweet and the way you talk about my son, I can see you're totally taken by him. It's... well... I just can't put it into words how happy it makes me. In fact, I should call him and tell him." She grabbed for her phone off the table. Thankfully, Melanie was quicker and stole it.

"No calling Vice when drinking," Melanie stated.

"But—"

"No."

The kitchen door swung open and in strolled Clint, who paused with his hand on the door. It was funny how wide his eyes were. Mine grew too.

"Close the books, close the books!" I yelled, and all ladies went into panic mode while Clint stepped further in with a smirk on his face.

Lori practically lay over the table grabbing the magazines, while Grace was busy giggling. Kenzie knocked over her glass—thankfully it was empty—and Molly teetered on her chair since she liked to swing on the back legs all the time. Melanie grabbed her daughter's knee and pushed her chair back to all four legs.

"What are you doing here?" I accused.

Clint rolled his eyes. "I do live here."

"Yes, but this is ladies' day," Melanie said.

"He could make a cute lady." Grace smiled.

Everyone fell quiet as we looked at Clint. I wasn't sure what the others were thinking, but I found myself dressing Clint in a skirt to show off his nice calves, a tank to show off his arms, and some makeup. His hair was long enough I could probably get it up in a pigtail.

"Whatever it is you're all thinking, stop now." He glared. "I'll just grab a beer and head to our room."

Lori stayed on the table, and the magazines I had, I quickly placed under my butt as Clint made his way around the table to the fridge. He took a beer out, shut the door, and turned back to us smiling. He opened his beer, took a sip and then laughed. "Okay, I'll get out of here." He didn't leave right away though. He tugged Molly's head back by her hair and kissed her soundly.

Once he was out of the room, I sighed. "That kiss was smoking. Kind of makes me wish Vice was here."

All eyes came to me.

Grace giggled, so did Kenzie and then Lori as she moved off the table. Molly and Melanie only smiled.

"I said that aloud, didn't I?"

"I can call him," Grace offered.

"No!" I cried. The state I was in I'd probably jump him in front of everyone. I already couldn't keep him off my mind. Grabbing the magazines back out, I placed them on the table. "Right, we have the dress, the lingerie, the flowers, and the venue. Which by the way I think is a brilliant idea." I smiled to Grace; it'd been her idea. "Vice's backyard will be amazing. All we need now is to organize the bachelorette night."

Two glasses of champagne later, we had the night planned. I was in charge of the strippers and had already booked a function room for it. Only while I was on the phone a sudden urge to pee came over me, so once I hung up, I made a run for the bathroom.

Opening the door, I dashed in and slammed it closed.

"Hey."

My pulse kicked up as I spun around and found Clint in the bath... naked.

"Holy ship," I yelled. "You're naked."

"It happens when one takes a bath."

No wonder Molly was very happy with the man. He was nearly as big as Vice. I was happy for my friend.

"Addy?"

"Hmm?"

"Can you quit staring at me?"

There was a knock at the door.

"Hide it then. It's just hanging out floating for everyone to see."

The door opened and in the doorway stood a very pissed off Vice. He came in, covered my eyes and clipped, "What the fuck, Clinton?"

"She came in here while I was in the bath," Clint exclaimed.

"Cover your shit up." Vice snarled, and then I felt myself being dragged backward. I stumbled a few times, and if it wasn't for Vice's arm around my waist, I would have fallen to the floor.

"Vice, I have to pee," I admitted quietly.

"You'll not pee in front of him. You only ever do it in front of me," he ordered. Then he must have realized what he said when Clint burst out laughing. "Ah, not that... forget it," he barked.

A door slammed. Vice removed his hand, then took mine with it and led me down the hall to Molly's bedroom and into their en suite, which didn't hold a bath in.

"Pee," he demanded with a gentle shove to my back toward the toilet.

Glancing behind me, I asked, "Are you going to leave?"

"Right." He nodded, turned, and left the room, closing the door behind him.

Smiling, I did my business, washed my hands and dried them. I then stared at myself in the mirror. There was a glow to my cheeks, and a hint of red in my eyes; it all indicated I was indeed intoxicated. Then I remembered who was waiting for me outside the door, and a thrill ran through my body. Making my way out, I found Vice standing with his arms crossed, facing the door. He glowered down at me.

"I didn't know he was in there," I blurted.

He ran a hand over his face. "Didn't mean you should stay in there and eye his junk."

"I know. It's a habit of mine. I see men in bathrooms, and my evil eyes tend to look right there. I can't help myself."

"Stop being cute when I'm pissed."

"Why are you pissed?"

"My woman's seen another man's dick."

I shrugged. "And he's nowhere near as good as yours."

His lips twitched. "Really?"

"Yes." I nodded and made my way over to him, stopping to lay my hands on his chest. "In fact, there's only one penis I dream of."

He snorted. "Is that so?"

"Oh, yes."

"Fuck, Addy. How do you turn it around for me to want to fuck you instead of being annoyed?"

"I don't know, but I'm glad you do," I said against his lips. His hands came down on my butt, so he could tug me into him and slam his lips against mine. Breaking away, I asked, "Do you think it would be strange if we dry humped on Molly's bed?"

Chuckling, he nodded. "Yes, just a bit."

"Darn. What are you doing here anyway?"

"I've come to get Clinton. We're heading to the bar to meet Grayson and Dylan to watch the game and have a drink."

"Sounds like... a bore. Bedroom action would be better.... Um, fun?"

He grinned. "You do realize you said that aloud?" He kissed my nose. "I look forward to some bedroom action, just not in my sister's room."

"Never in your sister's room," Molly yelled from somewhere. "It's okay. She's making out with Vice in my bedroom, just better not be on my bed."

Groaning, I planted my forehead on his chest. When I lifted my gaze, my heart pounded. Vice was there, right in front of me. "Glad I got to see you today." Then again, if I had my way, I'd see him every day.

"So am I, baby."

Something thumped against the door. Then we heard "Are they making me a grandchild?" Grace's drunken whisper wasn't quiet.

"No, they're just talking," Molly replied.

"Oh, poop."

"We can hear you," Vice called.

There was another thump, then giggling.

"What's going on?" Melanie asked behind the closed door.

"They're talking," Grace answered on a sigh. It surprised me she actually thought we would be doing it in Molly's bedroom. Her disappointment was funny, yet disturbing at the same time.

"Maybe if you two left them alone, there would be some action happening," Melanie suggested.

Molly whined, "Not in my room."

Vice groaned, pressing his forehead against mine. Quietly, he said, "There's still time for you to run from a relationship. Those women are crazy."

I snorted. "You've met my mother."

He grinned. "This is true. Also, there isn't a chance I'd let you go."

My pulse raced as his words caressed my mind. He didn't know what they meant to me, and just as I was about to voice it, the door came open and three women stumbled in.

"Back away from my bed," Molly warned.

Vice turned, rolled his eyes at the women in his family and before he left, he leaned in to kiss me soundly, right in front of the three of them. Of course, I heard a content sigh from Melanie and Grace, while Molly gagged. He pulled back, wished me luck, and exited. I stood there staring after him and wished I had the time to tell him how his words made me feel. Then again, from the way things we're going, I knew we'd have a lot of time to share what I felt.

Chapter
TWENTY-SEVEN

TEARS WELLED IN my eyes as I waved once again to my son while Mom, with her hand in his, led him down the airbridge to the plane. Time seemed to have gotten away from me; it was already school holidays and Drew was leaving to go spend a week with John in Hawaii. I was going to miss him.

It was as if I'd blinked and the months had zoomed by. Although, I had been run off my feet with orders, and right up to the due date for deliveries to be sent out, I still hadn't been sure if I'd make it. If it hadn't been for Drew's understanding of how busy his mom was, or for my mom, who handed over her whole house for when my help arrived en masse, I would never have hit the deadline. Molly, Clint, Kenzie, Lori, and even Evelyn supported me, and as well as Kenzie friends from her work Dara, Angelia, Darby and Abby. Plus Vice, Grayson, Dylan, and Trent, of course, were willing workers. If it was not for all of them, I would have gone stir crazy, no doubt curling over in fear with the deadline looming.

My friends and family pulled through for me in big ways. After we'd organized a schedule for when they could help, we'd all put our heads down and bums up to make it work, and in the end, I got it all done. In fact, Darby, who was so very good using all the tools to make the delicate pieces, enjoyed it so much, I'd had no hesitation offering her a job just before everyone had left for the night.

Vice stumbled forward, Grayson coughed and then choked, and Kenzie cried, "Oh, yay. That would be so amazing. What do you think, Darby?"

"She already has a job," Grayson clipped.

I gulped and heard Vice chuckling. "Now she's not only my pain in the ass, but yours."

Rolling my eyes, I snapped, "I'm not a pain in your ass, Vice."

"Uh-huh," he murmured, wrapping his arm around my shoulders and kissing my temple. "Which is why you fight me at every turn."

"I don't fight you. I merely state my opinion, which you sometimes don't agree with."

"That's right, baby. And no matter how much cute you show me, I'll not allow you to buy me dinner when we go out ever. Or pay for the movie. Or the fucking carwash so we can—" My hand landed over his mouth.

"So you can what?" Drew asked. When no one said anything, Drew rolled his eyes and said to Grayson, "They do this all the time. Argue, and then BAM, next they're kissing.

I'm never getting a girlfriend. I think I'll have a headache all the time."

It was later that night, after Darby agreed to come work with me once her contract was up soon for Grayson, I asked Drew as I tucked him in, "Honey, is mine and Vice's arguing upsetting you in any way?"

"No, why?"

"I was just worried, is all."

"Mom, it's okay. I know it's different when you and Vice do it than when you and Dad used to do it. Vice gets this look on his face that tells me he likes arguing with you and then when you're kissing, that tells me you aren't too much annoyed with him for it."

Smiling, I nodded. My boy was so dang smart. "That's right. It's more playful when Vice and I bicker."

"I know. He's cool for you, Mom."

"Thank you, honey. However, no matter what, I need you to know if anything bothers you, you can come to me and tell me. Anything at all. We're a team."

He holds out his fist, and I bump it with my own. "Our team is awesome. We have a big one now."

"How?"

"Well, it's not just me, you, Nana, Molly, and Clint anymore. We have Noah, I suppose Makala too, but she dribbles a lot. And Mr. Grayson, Ms. Kenzie, and all their family." He searched my face. "Why are you crying, Mom?"

I laughed. "Because I'm happy you're happy."

"'Kay. Can Vice come in and read with me again tonight?"

"I'm sure he'd love to." With a kiss, I walked out, taking the darn cat with me again, and went to find my man. He saw me enter the living room and was standing in seconds.

"Reading?"

"Yeah." I sighed contently. *"He wants you to do it again."* His own soft smile could melt hearts and make women swoon. As he walked past me, I got a quick lip touch, and once he was gone, I turned to Mom.

"You won the lottery in that one," she said.

"I honestly did."

Vice's days, as always, were busy, but his evenings and nights had become mine and Drew's. Even if he was tired, he'd come to Mom's to either help me or spend time with Drew. Actually, Drew and Vice always seemed to be hanging out with each other while I was neck deep in bling. It was beautiful to witness the two guys in my life sharing their time and watching them care and love for one another grow. They shared words, looks, and even hugs. If Vice wasn't helping Drew with homework, he was taking him to the skatepark to teach him to scoot.

Vice Salvatore was something special.

"Baby," he whispered into my temple before kissing me there. "He'll be back in a week." Vice stood next to me, his arm tightly around my shoulders, while I cried over my boy leaving.

"I know." I sniffed. "I-it's just hard to see. I've never been apart from him. Oh, God. How am I going to handle his first school camp?" Turning into him, once Drew and Mom were out of sight, I gripped his tee and rambled,

"Maybe I could go with him or at least follow and book into the same place they'll be staying."

"Adalyn, he'll be fine."

"But the teachers might not know what to do," I whispered, my tone frantic.

He tried to keep his smirk at bay, but he failed, and I glared up at him. As I was ready to bite his head off, he leaned down and touched his mouth to mine. What started out as a touch of lips, soon changed when I slid my arms around his waist and held on tight. Vice took the kiss to the next level, and when I had Vice's mouth on mine, everything else around me and in my mind disappeared. It was just Vice and me.

So when we broke apart to gain oxygen, I realized we were still standing in the airport kissing like we were teens.

Vice chuckled, ran the backs of his fingers over my cheek. "There it is." I knew what he was talking about, my blush. "Want to know one good thing about Drew going and having you caught up with your orders, for now?"

He was right, the orders were constant, but I'd caught up with most of them. "What?"

"Means you're staying at my place, and fucking finally, I'll get the chance to be inside you."

My clit spasmed along with my walls. Due to everything going on, Vice and I hadn't really had a private moment... until then.

Biting my bottom lip, Vice smirked, and I asked, "Can we go back to your place now?"

His eyes darkened. "Yeah, baby."

THE DRIVE GAVE my nerves time to appear. The walk up to Vice's front door gave me time to second guess my skills in the bedroom, and the front door being pushed wide from Vice gave me time to ask myself if it would look bad if I made a run for it. What happened if I couldn't please Vice in some way? Heck, I hated the smell of semen, and I hadn't even told the man of my dreams yet.

Once I stepped in, I faced Vice. He came in studying me and shut the door behind himself with a flick of his wrist, not even looking at it. "You okay?" he asked.

"I hate semen."

His approach stopped, his body locked, and he muttered, "Sorry?"

Throwing up my arms, I paced in front of him and admitted, "Ever since I was young, well not too young, but when I became sexually active, I discovered the smell and taste of semen makes me gag and feel nauseous." Sighing, I ran my fingers through my hair and added, "I'm sorry, I should have told you right from the start. Then again, no man would want to hear his partner could vomit from his scent or taste. God, I've led you on, and now we're finally at this stage, I wanted things to be perfect because you're perfect, and I was really looking forward to getting horizontal with you in so many ways. I swear just the sight of your naked body I could climax over it, but now I've ruined it. I should go."

I started to walk around him when my waist was seized in a strong grip.

With his front pressed against my back, his mouth touched my ear. "Been waiting a bloody long time to have you in my house alone. You're not leaving, baby. You're scared. I get it. Don't care about your dislikes, Adalyn. Well, I do, but we'll do it in a way you'll never have to care about it."

"O-okay."

"Good," he clipped roughly and then sucked my lobe into his mouth. I gasped and shifted my head to the side, while he licked and sucked on the outer shell of my ear.

Never thought I would be an ear woman, yet there I was getting drenched from it.

Vice took one hand from my waist and slid it around to my breast. He gripped. My head fell back and hit his shoulder.

"Want me to stop now?"

"Don't you dare."

He chuckled. "I want you on my bed, baby. Been picturing it for a long time."

"Yeah?" I breathed.

"Oh, yeah."

"D-do you touch yourself while thinking it?"

He pinched my nipple, and my legs shook. Dipping in, he bit my neck and then glided his tongue up to my ear again. "All the damn time." He sucked in my lobe, and I quivered. "Jesus, I bet you're wet already."

"Are you hard?" I asked, then gasped when he thrust his cock into my lower back.

"That answer your question?" He massaged my other breast.

"Vice?"

"Right here, baby."

"Please."

"What do you need?"

"Take me to your room."

"Gladly."

I let out a squeal when he swooped me up bridal style and stalked toward the hall.

"I'm too heavy. Put me down."

"Shut it."

"Vice," I snapped. "Do not tell me to shut it."

"I will when you talk silly about yourself."

I wasn't sure if he realized my heart just contracted hard, but it did, which was why I exclaimed, "God, I love you."

His steps faltered for a second. He glanced down at me, and I had never seen his eyes so soft or warm. "What did you say?" In his room, he let go of my legs. They dropped to the floor, and before I could step away, he swung my front into his. "What. Did. You. Say, Adalyn?"

"Um... I love dew? It's lovely to see in the mornings."

"Baby, say it again."

"I love dew?"

"No. What you really said."

Sighing, I glanced to the left, the right, and then up at the man who held my soul. "I love you. It just popped out. I'm so—"

His hand covered my mouth. "Don't. Don't take that away from me by apologizing."

When he slid his hand from my mouth, and both palms cupped my cheeks, I took it as a chance to start talking. "But—"

"No," he clipped, interrupting me. I glared, and he replied with a smirk. Leaning in, he touched his mouth to mine, once, twice. "I was enchanted by you from the first sight, I was falling when you pissed in front of me,"—I groaned—"and I fell in love with you when you searched my pants for stains."

Blushing at the memory of eyeing his crotch, I licked my dry lips. His hands went to my waist and mine to his chest. "You love me?"

"Yes."

"Are you sure?"

He grinned. "Yes, baby."

Nodding, I shifted my gaze to his neck and nodded again. Okay, Vice loved me… *holy shit.*

"Adalyn, are you going to stay shocked for a while or can we move things forward?" Vice asked, humor lightening his voice.

Clearing my throat, I met his gaze. "Moving forward sounds good to me."

Chapter
TWENTY-EIGHT

REACHING UP, I kissed him with everything I had while I fumbled with pulling his tee from his jeans and sliding it all the way up. We broke apart enough to discard his tee to the floor and the same with mine, which he'd tugged from my body roughly. Our mouths slanted together again. His hands went around my back to unhook my bra before he dragged it between us. The whole time I was busy fondling his hot-as-sin butt.

Vice glided his mouth from mine to my cheek, and then ear where he bit down. My body quivered, and I moaned, my breath coming in and out rapidly.

"Christ, are your ears your magic button to lose control?"

"M-must be."

He licked, sucked, and then another bite. My fingers dug into his butt harder, and I yanked him closer to me.

"Oh, yeah. They're your magic button." A hand of his slid down from my waist to my hip and then over my belly to sink into my jeans and panties. My head dropped back, my mouth opened, and I closed my eyes as he skimmed his fingers over the outside of my lower lips. "Fuck, already soaked. Looking forward to being inside here, Addy," he said gruffly and pushed his fingers inside of me.

"Please," I begged. God, I'd never begged before, but the man in front of me... I needed more than I needed to breathe.

Mind jumbled, desire took over. I wasn't sure if I was fully with it when Vice leaned in and took my nipple into his mouth and sucked hard, while his fingers pumped in and out of me fast. All I could do was feel and let my mind go blank.

"V-Vice," I stuttered, moving my mouth to his shoulder where it was my turn to bite something of his. He cursed but didn't let up the glorious torture. Instead, he moved his mouth to my other breast. "Vice... need you."

Lifting his head, his smoldering eyes bore into mine. He touched his mouth to mine and ordered, "Take your pants off."

If it meant action with the hottest man ever, I didn't care he was ordering me around. Heck, he could do it all he wanted in the bedroom if in the end it would bring me a climax. Well, I hoped.

Moving quickly, I undid my jeans and with a hop, skip, and a jump, I had them and my panties off. Glancing at Vice, I saw he was smiling sexily at me with amusement shining in his eyes. His fingers were still frozen on his top button while he watched me.

"Bend over the bed, Addy. I've wanted to do something to you since I met you in the adult store." Only, I was too busy gazing at Vice while he finished undoing his button and slowly slid down his zipper. My eyes hooded when he reached into his jeans and gripped himself. A hiss escaped his lips. "Baby, I love you looking at me, but I need you to bend over the bed."

"Bed. Right." I nodded and dragged my eyes away from Vice. Once at the bed, I placed my hands on the edge and stuck my bottom out. Glancing over my shoulder, I wanted to take a photo at what I saw: Vice eyeing me like I was a treat as he ran his hand, still in his jeans, up and down his length.

"Vice," I whispered, my voice low from the desire running through me.

"Shit. Fucking gorgeous, Addy. Gorgeous," he said gruffly. Vice stalked his way over to me. My body shivered, and I gasped when his hands flattened on each butt cheek and then ran down to the backs of my thighs, only to run up again and glide a couple of fingers over the lips of my vagina. "Hmm, so goddamn wet for me."

"It was the ear action," I blurted, then blushed and cringed when he chuckled. *It's not time to make funnies, Adalyn. It's naughty seductress time.*

As if he read my mind, he ran his hands up and down my back, rubbing his erection into me, when he said, "Don't hold anything back from me, Addy. With me and anywhere we are, be yourself. Let whatever you want to say or do happen." He took hold of my shoulders and tugged me back so I stood, and he wrapped his arms around me, kissing my neck. "I'll love you no matter."

No words came to mind because I was feeling too much.

"You good?" he asked.

"V-very much so." I nodded. "Vice...?"

"Yes, baby?"

Reaching up, I held onto his arms, which wrapped around my shoulders and chest. "I'm not good with words, but I love you, like a lot."

He chuckled. "That's all I need, and having my dick inside you every chance I can."

Giggling, I said, "Then let's make that happen." One arm moved from my chest, and next, I cried out when it landed on the side of my ass in a fast-action strike. My legs wobbled, my breasts swelled, and my core became saturated. "More," I breathed.

"Fuck yes." Both hands landed on my shoulders, and as I bent over the bed again, rubbing my thighs together because I felt so needy, Vice glided his hands down my back to my butt where he palmed each cheek. "Love my mark on you. Want to make more marks and not only by my hand, Addy."

"Yes."

"Perfect," he clipped, right before I lost one hand but gained it back by him slapping down on my skin. I screamed his name, and my body jolted forward, but I loved it all the same. Vice circled his hand to lessen the sting. "Again?"

"Please."

"Christ, made for me." His hand came down in a loud crack in the silent room, except for our heavy breaths. My pussy clenched, and when Vice dipped his finger into me, he found out how wet I was. "Drenched. Spread your legs, baby." I did as asked, unable to speak, just feel. Vice got to his knees behind me, spread my lower lips apart and lapped up my juices. "Jesus, delicious." He groaned.

"Oh, God. Vice...!" I cried out as he again inserted two fingers inside of me and his tongue slid lower to play with my clit. I slowly rolled my hips up and down, lost in the best sensation I'd ever felt.

Noise from the back of my throat erupted when I lost Vice's mouth, but then I hissed his name when his hand once again slapped down on my ass.

"Vice," I moaned after.

"What do you need, Addy?"

"You."

He leaned over me and licked my earlobe before taking it into his mouth and sucking on it hard. My legs nearly gave out on me. If it wasn't for his arm snaking around my waist to hold me up, I'd be a puddle of lust on the floor.

"Say please, Adalyn."

"Vice," I warned.

He thrust his hardness against my butt. "Say please, Addy."

"No," I teased; he wanted it as much as I did.

"Addy," he bit out. "Say please."

His hand dropped from my waist to cup my mound, and then one finger glided up and down over my clit. "Addy?"

"P-please."

"Good, girl." I would have told him to shove his good girl, but I felt his other hand come between us and I heard his jeans hit the floor right before he rubbed his cock up and down my opening. "Condom?"

"On pill."

"I'm clean."

"Me too, and if you don't… oh, God," I yelled when he thrust all of his length deep inside of me. I gulped in air and let it out slowly. I'd forgotten how big Vice was. He took my breath away, but filled me nicely.

"Baby?"

"More, please."

He gently pulled out to the tip and slid back in slowly. "Fuck, you feel so good, Addy."

"S-so do you," I panted. He pulled out again, nearly all the way. I wasn't one for slow, gentle movements, at least not right then. So I pushed myself down on his cock, causing us both to cry out. "Faster."

"Christ," he grunted. I lost him. I turned my head to look at him, ready to complain, but he slapped my ass and then climbed on the bed, sitting back against the headboard. "Ride me, Addy. Take control. Fuck me how you want it."

"You don't want to go fast?"

He smiled. "I want it fast, slow, hard, and hot. I want it all, but I also want to have your eyes and mouth close, so I can kiss you and then watch you come undone while riding my cock."

Well, okay, then I was down with that plan.

Climbing onto the bed, kneeling beside his hip, I hooked one leg over his waist and then leaned up to grip him between my legs and guide him to my entrance.

"This what you want?" I asked.

"Yes," he growled, his hands running up and down my waist.

Smirking, I teased the tip of his amazing cock at my entrance, and then said, "Say please."

His brows shot up. A chuckle left him before he pulled my mouth down onto his and kissed me, hard. I moaned into his mouth. His tongue slid against my own for a moment, then lips touched, and he mumbled, "Please."

Grinning, but only for a second because he gripped my hair tightly and slanted our mouths together again in a passion-filled kiss. Lost once more, I pushed my ass down, his cock filling my pussy. I planted my hands on his shoulders and broke our kiss to gaze into his heated eyes while I lifted and then sank down on top of him. His jaw clenched, his nostrils flaring as I did it over and over. I started out slow, but when his hands slapped down to each cheek of my butt, my pace increased.

Closing my eyes, I arched my neck and just *felt*. The way Vice's hands ran over my skin, from my ass to my waist and up to cup my breast.

"Vice," I whispered. Opening my eyes, I watched him suck a nipple into his warm mouth and swirl his tongue around it. "Yes. I-I'm close," I warned, riding him faster than before. My fingers dug into his shoulders, my legs tightening at his sides. His hand cupped the back of my neck, and he lifted his mouth from my nipple to pull me close and claimed my lips with his. Only, when his mouth trailed to my cheek, to my neck and up to my ear... I lost it all completely.

"Vice," I cried, as my walls contracted around his cock. "Oh shit, yes!" I yelled as I kept coming and Vice kept sucking.

He splayed his hands at my waist and kissed his way back up to my mouth. "Fuck, Addy," he growled against my lips. "Christ. I'm...." He wrapped me up tight, kissed me hard, and his cock swelled. Then he grunted into my mouth through his own release.

Breathing heavily, he rested his forehead against mine. "Meant to be mine."

Smiling, I said, "Or you were meant to be mine."

Vice chuckled and then kissed me on the nose. "Either way, we're good for each other."

"Yes, honey, we are."

"Slip off, baby, I'll get a cloth."

Holding my breath, I got to my knees, and Vice pulled out. I was about to reach for the tissues I'd spotted on the side table so I could make a run for the bathroom to get clean because I could feel myself leaking when Vice picked that moment to bite down on my earlobe. My body shuddered, my hands landing on Vice's shoulders to hold on.

"Fuck, do I love your ears." Vice chuckled.

Breathing deeply when he did it again, I realized an important thing.

"Wait," I said suddenly and pushed against his chest.

He shifted back and looked at me. "What's wrong?"

Smiling brightly, I told him, "You don't stink."

His head jerked back. "Huh?"

"Your cum, it doesn't stink." Ignoring his laughter, I climbed off him and got close to his cock, taking in a breath. I didn't gag, *thankfully*. Vice's scent was so different to any other I'd smelt. "Holy ship, Vice. You were made for me. Do you know what this means?"

Grinning, he asked, "What?"

"A shower while I give you a blow job." I clapped, and jumped off the bed. "This'll be so much fun. Come on," I waved back to his stunned form still sitting on the bed. "Come on, I want to suck you off."

It only took a second. He blinked and was off the bed running for me. I let out a squeal when he caught me and picked me up, heading for the shower.

He placed me back down, got the water running and curled me unto his chest. "You know you're crazy, right?"

"Yes." I nodded.

"Love you the way you are, Adalyn."

Swoon!

Chapter
TWENTY-NINE

IT WAS NEARLY the end of the week, and I was excited to be seeing Drew come the weekend. Vice and I were lounging on the couch at his house; it was after I'd been back to Mom's to feed and check on Puss-it. I'd decided to have another night off from making jewelry. Vice was a bad influence; then again, I was happy to spend some one-on-one time with him because it usually led to naked, orgasmic time with him.

After a sip of my wine, I curled back into Vice, and asked, "Do you like it?" We were watching *Kingsman,* one of my favorite movies.

"I have you pressed up against me, and it's an action movie. What's not to like?"

I smiled, looping my arm around his waist and felt him press his lips against my temple. We went on our first official date the other night where Vice took me to a restaurant. It had been amazing, especially after we tried out his Jacuzzi in his bathroom. I wanted to spend every moment I could with the man beside me. I wasn't sure I'd ever find my happy ever after, but I did. Kenzie had been right.

His hand on my hips tightened. "Addy?"

"Yes, honey?"

"Love that."

"What?" I asked, shifting my head back on his chest to meet his gaze.

"You calling me honey. You use if for those you really care about." He shrugged. "Love that I'm one of them."

"Me too."

"That wasn't what I was going to say though."

"No?"

He shook his head, leaned in, and touched his lips to mine. "You still looking for a place to live?"

Thinning my lips, I nodded. "Have you found one?"

"Yes."

Grinning, I said, "Great. Is it on the net? Can you show me it?"

"You're in it now."

My brows dipped, even when my stomach woke with butterflies. "Sorry?" I breathed.

"Would you and Drew think of moving in here?" He watched my face, but I wasn't sure I had an expression on there because I was frozen.

"A-are you asking us to move in with you?"

He winked. "Yes."

"Move in with you?"

He chuckled. "Yes, baby."

"Are you sure?"

"Been waiting for the right one. Never thought she'd come along until I found you. We're not young, Addy. I don't want to waste time with you living somewhere else when I have the room here, and I'm not up for only seeing you every second night or something. The thought of having you and Drew living here is the right one. Where I want us to go, means we have a future. It's about moving forward together to make sure that future is the best one we can have."

Sitting, I straddled his waist and threw my arms around his neck. A sob took hold. I buried my head into his shoulder as he wound his arms around me.

"Is that a yes?"

"Yes," I mumbled, then sniffed. "I want a future with you too."

He kissed my neck. "You've made me happy, Adalyn."

Pulling back, I wiped under my eyes. "I've always been a happy person, content in life, but you've made my dream come true. I never thought fairy tales were real until my annoying, but charming prince came into my life."

His grin was big. "Love you, baby."

My eyes widened. "Are you sure it's not too soon? How do you think Drew is going to take it? I mean, I know he loves you and your house, but it's a big step."

He tucked my hair behind my ear and then played with my earlobe. I closed my eyes and just about purred. Of course, he laughed. "I think Drew will be fine as long as you are."

"I know I will be."

"Then everything will be good. We'll talk to him before it happens. Even though everything in me wants you to move in right now, we'll wait for Drew to come home. And if he doesn't go for the idea, we'll wait."

"You would?"

"Of course. But if he's okay with it, are you happy to run your business from here instead of at your mom's?"

"Heck yes."

"Good, there's also something I have to tell you—"

My phone chose that moment to ring. "Hold that thought. I have to check it." Twisting around, I grabbed my phone off the coffee table. "It's mom."

"Grab it." Vice nodded.

Hitting Accept, I placed it against my ear. "Hi, Mom. Not long until you're both back." I smiled at Vice.

"Adalyn, sweetheart, we have a problem."

"What?" I breathed like I was just punched in the stomach.

"Addy?" Vice called.

Looking up from his chest, I asked Mom, "Is Drew all right?"

"Yes, but there's something else."

Moving off Vice's lap, I gripped the top of my hair and snapped, "Mom, talk to me."

She sighed deeply. "The week has been great. John's been fantastic with Drew, spending all his time with him."

"I don't care about that, Mom. Tell me what's happened that has you worried."

"Sweetheart. Is Vice with you?"

Glancing at him, I said, "Yes, he's here."

"Good. Because what I have to tell you, you'll need him."

"Shit, Mom, you're scaring me."

Vice's arm came around my shoulders. I felt like shoving him off and pacing, but I knew from the way his jaw ticked, he was just as worried as I was, and he was seeking the comfort I needed also.

"Your sister is here."

"What?" I screeched. "Hang on, what's my sister being there got to do with anything?" I hadn't heard from Cammy since the last time she called. She never rang Mom the next day, and when we tried again, she didn't answer.

"Okay, all right. Apparently, she works at the resort. I didn't know this until she and John came to my room while Drew was sleeping. To say I was shocked to see her was an understatement. Adalyn, they're threatening to keep Drew here with them."

My body solidified.

"They think they have a case against you for being unfit to look after Drew. It's all bullshit of course, but they told me they'll be in contact with you soon about it. However, they would have known I'd call you. Sweetheart, Cammy is with John. As in they're getting married soon, and they think Drew is going to love the idea of living with them here."

"Addy? Baby?" Vice called. But I wasn't there. I was in my mind ripping John and Cammy apart. My sister, my own flesh and blood was going to fight me for my son.

VICE

FUCKING HELL, FEAR burned in me from Adalyn's frantic voice and solid body. I could hear her mom calling for her through the phone, but my woman's mind was elsewhere. I took the phone from Addy's hand and watched her arm drop. Then she sat there glaring out into space.

"Jenny? Vice here. What in the fuck is going on?"

"Vice, thank God you're there. I knew she wouldn't take it well."

"Take what well, Jenny? Tell me so I can help her."

"Right. Long story short. Cammy, whom I'm unsure if I can love after this, and that says something about a mother losing love for her own daughter—"

"Jenny," I clipped.

"Okay. Sorry. Cammy's here, and she's gotten in John's ear. They're going to try for full custody over Drew."

I sucked in a sharp breath and moved my gaze to my woman. No wonder she was lost. Drew was her world. If she lost him, she'd lose a part of herself.

I wouldn't let that happen.

"We'll be there shortly."

"What?" Jenny asked, shock evident in her tone.

"I'll get Addy packed and on a plane. We'll let you know when we land."

"Okay. God, thank you, Vice."

"Keep watchful and talk soon."

"Yes, right. I'm on it."

As soon as she was off the phone, I placed it back down on the coffee table. Picking Addy up in my arms, I put her ass to my lap and turned her head so I had her eyes. They were dark. She was probably murdering her ex and sister in her mind. I'd let her have her time to process. I had to get us moving though.

"Right, Addy. We're going there. They aren't fucking keeping Drew." After I got nod from her, I helped her up and into my room. Her overnight bag was already packed so I threw some of my shit in there and ordered Addy to get some bathroom items. Robotically she did. When she was out of the room, I took my phone out and hit Grayson's number.

"Vice, how's things?"

"Not good."

"Talk to me."

Cursing every second word, I finally told Grayson what the deal was, and his reply was "I'll make sure the plane is fueled and ready for you both. Do you need me to come?"

"Thanks, Gray. But I've got it."

"Call me if you don't or if I need to bail you out."

Snorting, I said, "I will."

"Is Addy okay?"

"Shit, I'm not sure. She hasn't said a word."

"It's a lot to take in, especially with her sister involved."

"I know. I'll get her through this somehow. No one will take Drew from her."

"Good luck."

"Thanks. Talk soon."

LILA ROSE

Adalyn walked back into the room. Her fists were clenched around a moisturizer bottle and a bottle of pain meds, from when I injured my back a while ago. I wasn't sure if she was going to massage them into backing off or just poison them. I knew I'd prefer the second option.

"Addy, come here." Once she was close, I wrapped my arms around her. "We'll get there, baby, and sort it all out. One way or another, we won't be leaving without Drew."

She nodded and then I heard a sniffle before her body stiffened. She wanted to stay strong. I understood that. So I took her hand in mine, grabbed the bags, and we made our way out of the house. Fuck the toiletries. It was time to fight for Drew.

Chapter THIRTY

BY THE TIME Vice and I stalked into the Hawaii resort, I was frantic to see my son and find out what in the hell John and Cammy were playing at. What Mom said couldn't be real. John handed over his rights to me for Drew. All he wanted was every second weekend, and that was until he'd up and moved away. He wouldn't fight me for Drew. *Not now.* Rationally, I knew he didn't have a chance in hell at succeeding in a custody battle, but that didn't make my fury or anxiety lessen.

God, I wanted to throw up my stomach was in so many knots of worry.

Vice steered me toward the front counter, while he organized a room. I turned and looked around. Having a chartered flight by private plane organized by Grayson had made everything so much easier. I had no idea how I'd ever repay him, or Vice for arranging everything. It also meant nobody knew we'd arrived.

LILA ROSE

It was nearing dinnertime, so the foyer wasn't too busy. There were only a few people milling around.

"Adalyn," Vice started and placed his hand on my lower back. We headed away from the reception desk. "They're taking the bags to our room. Text your Mom and find out where they are. It's time to deal with this bullshit." He rubbed his hand up and down my back. Nodding, I grabbed my phone out and shot a text off and then leaned into Vice while we waited for a reply. Thank God, I'd been around Vice when Mom called. If it weren't for him, I wouldn't have moved from my shocked state to make it to Hawaii in the first place. He helped me pack, rang Grayson for his private plane, got us to the airport, and on the plane, all while I screamed, ranted, and silently maimed in my mind.

I wasn't even sure I'd spoken to Vice after he hung up from Mom. Although, I did remember his first words after the call. "Right, Addy. We're going there. They aren't fucking keeping Drew." Then it was full of frantic movements to get us both here while I silently freaked the hell out.

My phone vibrated. I jumped, and Vice's arm around my shoulders curled me in tighter again him. "Calm, baby. We're not leaving without Drew. Do you hear me? No matter what, Drew will be with us."

"Okay, honey," I whispered, and opened the text. I believed him. He was Vice Salvatore, after all, and I was sure he'd move heaven and hell to make sure Drew was with us.

Mom: In the hotel's restaurant.

Me: Coming.

Taking a deep breath, I shook out my arms and came back to myself, then admitted, "I'm not sure…. Vice, I might lose my control in there. If I look like I'm going to hit someone, hold me back because it could cause more trouble."

He smiled, probably glad I wasn't a zombie any longer. He kissed my temple and then shifted to take my hand. "You'll be fine."

I wasn't so certain about that.

We made our way toward the restaurant, and each step I took, I kept reminding myself I couldn't go in there kick John and Cammy's ass, take my child back, and run from the room. Even when it sounded like a grand idea. If it hadn't been for Vice's thumb making lazy circles on the top of my hand, I would have stormed in there like a mad woman. Maybe even grunted and yelled like cave women used to do.

Believe. I just had to believe things would be okay. We'd work everything out calmly, and no one would get hurt in the process. Especially Drew. I wasn't sure what he knew, or even if John had told him anything or even asked Drew if he wanted to live in Hawaii with him permanently.

Holy shit. What happened if Drew did know everything and wanted to stay?

I wasn't sure if I could cope with losing my son and only seeing him holidays. I'd have to move to Hawaii myself, but then I'd lose Vice because he had businesses to run.

I clutched my chest. I wasn't getting in enough air.

"Addy, baby, please, calm down." Vice brought me around to face him. His hands landed on my shoulders, and then he ran them up and down my arms. "Slow your breathing, sweetheart."

Nodding, I took a deep breath in and then slowly exhaled. Rubbing at my chest with my knuckles, I face planted into Vice's chest. I couldn't lose either one of them.

"Everything will be fine, Adalyn. Promise." We stayed that way for a while longer, until I was calm enough to function, and then Vice kissed my temple, took my hand, and led me the rest of the way in.

Thankfully the restaurant wasn't busy, which was how we spotted them quickly. John was talking to Drew about something, Cammy was glaring at Mom for some reason, and Mom was wiping her eye with her middle finger toward her other daughter. That actually brought a smile to my face.

"Ready?" Vice asked as we made our way through the tables.

"No, but yes." I squeezed his hand, and he returned the gesture. We'd nearly made it to their table without being noticed, until Cammy looked over her shoulder for some reason, and the evil smile that graced her face I wanted to knock right off.

"Oh, look. Adds is here."

"Mommy! Vice!" Drew cried, his beaming face misted my eyes and wobbled my bottom lip. Yes, I would do anything to make sure my boy was still with me. He was out of his seat in seconds and ran the few steps to land in my arms first. After he got a forehead layered in kisses from me, he moved into Vice's arms for a big, tight hug. With his arm still around Vice's waist, he planted his chin in Vice's stomach and looked up at him. "What are you both doing here? This is so awesome. I can show you the beach."

Vice smiled down at Drew. "Looking forward to it. We thought we'd fly in to surprise you before you come home." Drew missed the evil eye Vice sent John because Drew was telling his nana how cool he thought it was we were there.

Cammy scoffed, rolled her eyes and muttered, "We'll see about that."

"Mom," I called. "Great to see you. Drew my boy, can you take Nana to the ice cream shop I saw on the way in. I just want to talk to your dad for a bit."

He sat on Mom's knee and eyed me, then Vice, then John. He didn't bother with Cammy; it showed me he wasn't a fan of hers.

"Why?" he asked.

"Just adult talk, kiddo." Vice winked. "We won't be long."

Cammy snorted. Drew swung his gaze to her and lowered his eyes into a glare.

"Okay, Mom." He stood and gave us another hug before taking Mom's hand. On her way past me, she took my arm and gave me a reassuring squeeze.

Cammy got up and moved to Mom's seat and then took John's hand on the table. Vice moved forward, took her seat and Drew's, shifted them close to one another, and then he waited for me to sit before he did.

289

Cammy sneered at me. "You going to introduce us, Adds?"

"Vice, Cammy and John."

Vice nodded to them both but said nothing. I glanced out the corner of my eyes to see he had a death stare going on with my ex.

"John," I started. He looked at me. "Why are you doing this?"

Cammy rolled her eyes, leaned forward and said, "John was telling me how you worked in a sex shop, Adds. That wasn't a suitable place to be in when you have Drew living with you."

"I don't work there anymore, you know this," I pointed out.

"So, that doesn't matter. You chose to work there in the first place."

"Maybe you should stay out of mine and John's business over Drew." I glanced to John. "You know it was the only job I could find at the time."

John opened his mouth to reply but Cammy butted back in. "You should have waited for another. John left you with money to get you by."

"I'm leaving it for Drew's college fund." Every word out of her mouth was pissing me off more and more.

"Do you have anything to say?" Vice asked. I saw he was watching John.

John smiled, and it wasn't a pleasant one. "Actually, I do." Cammy smugly sat back in her chair and wrapped her arm around John's. My ex finally looked at me. "I don't like the company you keep, Adalyn."

My head jerked back. "What do you mean, who?"

"The man next to you."

Vice snorted, relaxed back into the seat, and placed his arm around the back of my chair. "I had a feeling it would be this type of play."

"What type of play?" I asked.

"Please, continue," Vice gestured to John. Then he leaned in and kissed my temple. If I hadn't been looking Cammy's way, I would have missed her deepening glare. "It'll be fine," Vice whispered into my ear.

"Adalyn, I'm filling for full custody for Drew to come live here with Cammy and myself. He'll be safer here."

Shaking my head, I asked, "Safer from what?" I pointed to Cammy. "And you hate kids. You've always told me this."

"I've changed. People can change."

Shaking my hands in front of me, I said, "Wait, how and when did this happen? I thought you were with Daphne."

"Cammy and I got to know one another again, and I realized I've always had a thing for her. We're in love."

I snorted, then laughed and laughed some more. I laughed so hard my eyes were watering, and I had to hold my stomach it ached so much.

"Adalyn," John snapped.

"Oh, God. Really? In love? Wow, congrats and happy Tonka, wait." I turned to Vice, "That's a toy car isn't it."

He smirked. "It is."

"Well then, happy whatever it is. I wish you all the happiness you both can carry." Vice chuckled. "One thing though, Drew is not staying here with two people who are mean, hurtful, and fucked up in general."

"How dare you," Cammy cried.

"He *will* be staying here, and he'll never want to be around you again because of the man beside you."

"Vice is safer and more normal than you'll ever be," I bit back to John.

Cammy's smile grew vindictive just before John's hand slammed down on the table. "He owns sex shops and porn studios, Adalyn, and you have my son around that man."

My eyes widened. Cammy looked like the cat that got the cream. Still I asked John, "How did you know?"

"Cammy found out his name from Drew and re-searched him. Are you seriously with a man who films porn for a living? What would Drew's school think? Or the parents of his friends? Did you think about Drew at all?"

"That's rich coming from a man who cheats on women," Vice snarled.

"I don't even want to speak to you or hear anything come from your mouth."

I wanted to slap John in the face. He had no right to speak to Vice like that. Heck, if Vice wanted to own strip clubs, I wouldn't care because he was an amazing man. He was caring, sweet, smart, the perfect man my son could look up to. He was driven, courageous, and looked around ready to blow his top. Maybe it wasn't me who would have to be held back, but Vice.

"You think this shit will keep me from her?" Vice asked deeply. "You think you can keep Drew away from us? Think again." Vice stood, held his hand out to me. I took it and straightened beside him.

John jumped up, so did Cammy. "My son will never be in your presence again."

"Yeah? Why? Because of the businesses I run? Tell us the real reason you want to drag this crap up? Is it maybe because you don't want Addy to move on? You discard her and expect her to listen or do everything you want or say. Tell me, how long have you and Camila been together? Camila's been in your ear for a fucking long time, and because she has some serious issues against her sister, she's making you do things you're not really thinking about, but instead jumping into because that trash there tells you to. How do you think Drew will feel without his mom? Has Camila proved herself to be a good role model like his mom already is? Addy works her ass off to make sure Drew and even her mother has everything they desire."

My hand went to Vice's chest. It was bouncing up and down from his rapid breathing. But what he'd said made a lot of sense.

"Tell me it isn't true, John. Was Daphne even here, even the girlfriend you left me for?"

"I'm sorry, but yes, it's true. Cammy and I hooked up for a few nights a long time ago. And Daphne was real, until I rekindled things with Cammy while staying here."

"So, you and my sister… years ago started something while we were married?"

He actually looked remorseful.

"John, you don't have to say anything," Cammy said.

Turning my gaze to Cammy, I asked, "You slept with my husband before we'd even divorced? What did I ever do to you?" My eyes welled. Vice's arm wrapped around my shoulders. "Why do you hate me so much?"

Sick, I felt so sick in the stomach from the thought of my sister betraying me so long ago along with my ex. It wasn't that I lost John out of it all, but Drew lost his father. All because of her and the way John couldn't keep it in his pants.

Cammy's hands fisted. She then placed them flat on the table. "You always got everything. I got nothing."

"Jesus, Cammy," John sighed. He shook his head. Maybe he was finally realizing her play had nothing to do with Drew's safety, but to hurt me some more.

"How can you say that? Mom and Dad always tried to bend over backward to make you happy. I didn't get to do dance or tennis or anything else you tried."

"You said no to be the good, perfect little girl, so they felt they had to spend the money on me. They hated me, loved you."

Throwing my hands up in the air, I groaned and then wiped my face. I would not cry over her any longer. "You can think what you want. I really don't care anymore, Cammy. Do you hear me? I don't care about you because I no longer have a sister."

Her eyes widened for a fraction before slanting into a scowl. "Whatever. At least Little Miss Perfect can't have everything. Drew will be staying here with us or else your man there will be paying big bucks to shut us up about his

life and what trouble it could cause for Drew now at school and when he's older."

"Drew won't be staying with you," Vice growled.

"You can't—" Cammy started.

"Cammy," John warned, his eyes searching Cammy for something before they flashed with disappointment. "This has nothing to do with what Addy has or hasn't got, and it certainly hasn't got a goddamn thing to do with money. We're doing this for *Drew's* sake." Cammy reached over and patted John's leg.

"Of course." She nodded.

"Are you seriously going to stand there and listen to your woman's words? She hates her sister to a point she'll use anyone to bring Addy down. I know I won't let it happen ever again. You need to think of your son, not the woman who's leading you around by your dick."

"I am thinking of my son. I won't let Drew be around a person like you if it could cause problems for him in any way. Kids can be cruel."

Vice smiled. "Then it's a good thing two weeks ago I sold those businesses."

"You what?" I gasped.

"Yeah, baby. I sold them because I knew having you and Drew in my life were more important than those businesses. You think I want Drew to come home one day asking if I make porn? I don't, so I made sure that won't happen."

"But, but...," Cammy began.

"No one knows. It isn't public. The change is happening though, and everything about my name associated

295

with porn and adult stores will be gone from any search engine on the net. The films I've already produced will have a cover change with the new owner's name on there." He turned back to look at John, with his lip raised in disgust. "Adalyn and Drew are my world. I'd do anything for them. It's something you should have done because, man, they make my world shine bright. They would have yours if you hadn't fucked them over. Your loss, my gain, and I'm gaining big."

"This... you... fuck." John turned to Cammy. "You egged me on and all for what? To mess with Adds more and because you saw dollar signs." He shook his head and glanced back to John. "I don't—"

Vice's hand came up. "I don't want to hear anything you have to say right now. Take the trash at your side and go. We'll be leaving tomorrow *with* Drew. If you want to see Drew the next school holidays, organize it, but you'll fly to see him in our town and without her. If you think you can play more games with us, think again. I have the means to tear your lives apart even before it went to court."

Holy shit.

Vice was so getting lucky.

I was giddily ecstatic with how my man handled the situation.

"Adds, I'm sorry, I—"

"Don't you apologize to her," Cammy screeched, stamping her foot.

"Shut up, Cammy," John barked in her face.

Running my hand up from Vice's belly to his chest, I caught his eyes when he looked down. "Can we get out of here? Drew wants to show us the beach."

"Sounds good to me." He smiled, touched his mouth to mine, and we walked away.

Getting closer to the doorway, I said, "You know I wouldn't have cared if you kept the business?"

"I know. But I wanted to. I'll have people living with me soon. I didn't want to be run down with work. Besides, I'll have to keep up my energy for all the sex we'll have to make more babies."

I stopped. "You want to have children with me?"

"Fuck yes," he whispered against my lips and then ran his tongue around to my ear. My legs quivered along with my clit when he bit down before adding, "Speaking of which, I'm not getting any younger, we should start tonight."

Pulling back, to see if he was serious and he definitely seemed it, my heart jerked inside my chest and then galloped along in excitement. Even my belly was tumbling in joy at the thought of having Vice's child. Still, no matter how big I was smiling, I had to ask, "Can we wait at least until Drew and I have moved in?"

"We're moving in with Vice? Wicked!" Drew yelled.

Epilogue

THE BED DIPPED, and I blinked through the haze of sleepiness when Vice wrapped me up in his arms. Rolling, I cuddled in close and kissed his chest. It was mornings like this I loved. Actually, I loved every moment with Vice.

"Is Drew awake?" I asked. I knew it wouldn't be long. He was a very early morning riser, especially when it came to days he was excited about. Like Christmas. We'd been living with Vice for six months, and it was our first Christmas together, I think I was as excited as Drew.

"Not yet, but he'll be awake soon."

Pulling back, Vice dipped his head so our eyes could meet. His eyes held a glint to them, meaning he'd done something.

"What did you do?"

"Baby, get your pj's on."

"Vice, what did you do?"

He smirked, leaned in and kissed me. Once his tongue touched mine, I was on my back with him hovering over me. Only when things had heated, his lips trailing down my neck, that he shifted back and got out of bed.

"Hey," I called, annoyed.

He chuckled, and while putting on warm clothes, he said, "It seems my girlfriend can't get enough of me." He faced me, smiling. "I had you last night, twice, baby. Thought it would get you through the day. I see it won't, but baby, you're going to have to wait. I promise I'll make it up to you tonight. Quick, Addy, get dressed."

My brows dipped, but I slipped out of bed and pulled on my pj's Vice had taken off the previous night. "I don't understand why it's so urgent when Drew isn't even—"

"Mom!" Drew yelled, his voice full of awe and elation.

Vice winked. "Come on, baby. Santa's been." Vice took my hand and tugged me out of our room, down the hall to enter Drew's room. I'd thought Drew would already be in the living room where the Christmas tree was with all the presents under it. A Christmas tree we all went shopping for and one we'd all decorated. It had been another perfect night, one of many nights, days, and mornings we shared. Of course, everything couldn't be all roses. We had our days where we went head-to-head against each other, but even on those days I loved him.

Because the making up part I looked forward to something fierce.

Vice stepped away from the doorway, and my mouth dropped open. Drew, still in his bed, held a blond Labrador puppy, who he was cuddling tight.

"Look what Santa brought me." Drew beamed up at us. His eyes held wetness. He'd been asking for a dog since he could talk. When Puss-it had rocked up at Mom's place, his need for an animal settled a little. It wasn't until after we'd moved, and Drew wanted Puss-it to stay with his nana in case she got lonely without them there, did he start hinting at a dog again.

As Drew shoved his face into the dog's neck, I turned to Vice and whispered, "You got him a puppy?" That must have been why he kept going into the garage the night before; he said he was doing some work on the car. Of course he knew I'd tune that out, not wanting to investigate when it had something to do with a car. He was a smart cookie.

"He's wanted one for a long time, baby. Couldn't not get our boy his first puppy."

Our boy.

I loved hearing Vice call Drew *our* boy.

He'd been wonderful with every aspect of altering his life with ours. Once we moved in, he made sure he was home to each dinner with us. He came to all the basketball games, helped Drew with homework, and loved reading with him. After we'd got back from Hawaii, John called, and when I refused to answer, Vice had.

"No, you've got Vice," he answered. "Not sure she's ready to talk to you." He frowned, listening. "Right. You know where I want it to lead with Addy and Drew, so you have to understand I'll be in their lives from now on." He paused. "Good to hear. You're still his dad. I'd never stand in your way, but if you fuck with either of them again, I will come down on you like a ton of bricks." My va jay jay danced at his words. "Okay, I'll let her know, and come back to you once we've talked. Later."

As soon as he hung up, he pulled me onto his lap on the couch and told me, "He didn't like I answered, but he knows

I'm a part of your world now. He wanted to apologize. Said he's kicked Cammy to the curb and wanted it clear he was still Drew's dad. He's moving back, baby. Wants more time with his son."

"Vice...."

He tucked my hair behind my ear. "He's getting his thumb out of his ass for Drew. It's a good thing. Wish my dad would have thought of his kids instead of his dick. But we'll sort it so you and Drew are comfortable with whatever you want to give him."

"Before everything, John was a good dad. Turned out, he just wasn't great at being my husband. I'll never forgive him and my sister for what they did. I have a lot of hate inside of me for them lying to me for so long. However, I couldn't have Drew miss out on time with his father since John and I did do one right thing together. Bringing Drew into the world. Doesn't mean I'll ever be happy to be around John. You may have to deal with him."

"I can do that. Anything for you and Drew. Anyway, it won't be for a while until he moves back, so we have time to organize the times he has Drew."

"Okay, honey."

"You good?"

"Yes." I smiled.

That was no lie, I was good because I had Vice at my side.

John moved back two months later, and he now had Drew every second weekend. Both son and father looked forward to those times, and maybe, eventually, we'd come to some type of agreement where John could share the special events with us. Though, it wouldn't be just yet. We were still working on a congruous relationship between us.

Watching Drew lavish the puppy with attention, my eyes misted. Stepping close to Vice, I wrapped my arms around his waist. "Love you, Vice Salvatore."

"Love you, Addy. Always."

"Can I name him? Can I?" Drew climbed out of his bed with the dog in his arms.

"Careful," I said.

"I know, Mom," Drew replied, then looked at Vice and rolled his eyes.

Snorting as Drew got close, I tugged him into both Vice and me. "Kiss and hug first. Then you can think of names while you take him out the back for a bathroom break."

Drew sighed and puckered his lips up to me. I leaned in for a quick kiss and then wrapped him close to Vice and me. Vice placed his arms around the both of us.

"You happy, kiddo?" Vice asked, gazing down at Drew.

"Totally."

"Good." He ruffled Drew's hair and then added, "Now go do what your mom said, and no peeking at the other presents."

"That's like when Mom asked us not to touch the cake she made yesterday, but... nothing." His eyes flicked to me quickly and then away. He wiggled his way out and started for the door.

"Drew, did you have some of that cake?"

"Um. Sorry, gotta take Optimus Prime out. Ask Vice."

Turning my glare to the man at my side, I placed my hands on my hips. "Vice Salvatore. Tell me you didn't let Drew touch that cake."

His lips twitched. "God, you're cute when riled."

"Vice?"

The doorbell rang. Vice smirked. "Saved by the bell." He dipped in for a quick touch of my lips and dodged my fist. He chuckled as he made his way out of Drew's room.

It was just lucky my guys were cute, and I'd made a second cake hidden at the back of the refrigerator because I'd known, once I saw them eyeing it, they wouldn't be able to resist.

"Merry Christmas!" was shouted from the front door. Mom had arrived.

"Jesus, woman. Warn before you do that" was boomed just after by Trent.

Grinning, I made my way out of Drew's room and down the hall. Since the barbecues, Mom and Trent were getting to know one another. Well, that was what they both told Kenzie, Lori, and me, but we were sure it was more since they spent a lot of time together. Of course, we teased them about it all the time. That was until Mom sat me down and said if I didn't act my age soon, she would go into great detail about her time between the sheets with Trent. Then she'd added not that she had as yet. Since I never wanted to hear it, I cut my teasing back to the bare minimum and mainly focused on Trent because when he blushed, he went bright red, and then he'd start stuttering or calling us every name under the sun.

LILA ROSE

"Merry Christmas!" I called, walking into the living room to find them already sitting on the lounge, waiting for Drew to come back in.

"Merry Christmas, sweetheart." Mom smiled.

"Merry Christmas, shithead," Trent grumbled.

"Hey, I haven't even started." He rose a brow. "However, I have a question." He sighed, Vice chuckled, and Mom glared. Still, I went on. I just couldn't resist. "Since being here so early, did you and Mom have a sleepover, Trent? Do I call you my stepfather now?"

He coughed, glared, pointed his finger at me while opening and closing his mouth.

Drew came running in. "Nana, Pop. See what I got? His name is Optimus Prime, but Prime for short."

One day when we were at Mom's, and Trent was there, as he usually was, we were all sitting down to a meal when Drew turned to Trent and asked, "You're always with Nana so can I call you Pop?" It was another time Trent blushed, coughed, choked, and spluttered words without a real answer. So Mom came to his rescue, placed her hand on Trent's thigh and said, "Drew, my boy, that would be fine, and it's really sweet of you."

"Yeah!" Trent yelled. "What she said."

Vice came up behind me and circled his arms around my waist as we watched Drew fly at Mom and Trent, then drop his wiggly, bouncy puppy onto their laps.

"Oh, wow, a puppy," Mom cooed.

"You must have been a very good boy to get a puppy, Drew-Boo," Trent said, ruffling his hair before pulling him onto his lap.

"I was. I ate all my vegetables, even though I hate them."

"Say what? All of those pesky vegetables?" asked Trent with mock horror.

"Yep."

"Good job, boy."

Drew looked up. "Can we do presents now? Can we?"

"How about we get Prime into his playpen, so he won't eat all the wrapping paper first," Vice suggested.

"Good idea." Drew nodded, scooping up his puppy and walking to the pen Vice must have set up in the night, before he placed him in. Warmth flooded me when I saw Drew kiss Prime's head. "Presents?"

"Yes," I cried, clapping. Then I ran over to the tree and picked up a bracelet-sized box. I couldn't wait any longer to give Vice his present. "Drew, can you give this to Vice?"

"Sure can." He skipped over, just as thrilled as I was over the gift since I'd told him about it the night before. Anything earlier and he would have spilled the beans about it. Drew was terrible at keeping a secret.

Drew made it to Vice with the gift and when Vice took it, he met my gaze and said, "I thought we were doing ours after Drew's done his."

"Just open, open, open," Drew told him.

Vice chuckled. "Okay, kiddo."

Wrapping my arms around my middle, I rocked back and forth on my feet while my nerves bombarded me. If he didn't like it, I was screwed. He had to like it. No, he would like it. He would.

Biting my bottom lip, I watched as he finally got the paper off and then lifted the lid of the bracelet box.

His eyes widened, his mouth dropped, and slowly he lifted his head to look at me. "Really?"

Once more, tears filled my eyes, and I nodded.

"What?" Mom asked.

"We're having a baby!" Drew shouted. He spun around and did a jig, while Mom screamed then burst into tears. Trent, with his own eyes filling, pulled Mom into him.

"Addy?" Looking up, I found Vice right in front of me. "How far are you?"

My bottom lip wobbled. "Three months. I didn't know for two, being so busy and you know how I suck at keeping track of my period. Then I wanted to make sure everything was perfect for us, and it was so close to Christmas, I thought I'd wait." Second-guessing my choice, I asked, "I hope that was okay?"

"Fuck," Vice clipped. "I don't care when or how long you've known. You've made me so goddamn happy, baby." He ran his fingers through my hair and dragged my body against his while his mouth came down on mine.

"Yuck!" Drew yelled.

One of Vice's hands slid from my hair down over my shoulder to land flattened against my belly. He broke the kiss and looked down. "A baby," he sounded in awe.

"Yes, honey."

"Mom, can you make sure it's a boy? I want a brother," Drew stated, which made everyone laugh. "What?" Drew asked. "I do."

"Sweetheart," Vice whispered. I raised my gaze to his from my son. "Your present outweighs mine. Still, I'm going to give it to you." He smiled softly. Then... my heart twirled in my chest because Vice got down to one knee. When I sniffed hard, he chuckled. "Never thought I would find my happy ever after, but I have with you and Drew. I made sure Drew was cool with this, and he was. Adalyn Rogue Sage, will you do me the honor of becoming my wife?"

"Yes!" Mom cried.

"Darlin', I think he was asking your girl, not you," Trent said.

Vice Salvatore asked me to marry him.

Vice Salvatore, the man with my dream penis, asked me to marry him.

Marry him.

Out loud and in front of people.

Wiping the back of my hand across my tear-streaked face, I nodded.

"I need to hear it, baby."

"Yes, you crazy, bossy man."

He slid the ring, a stunning diamond, onto my finger, stood, and picked me up in his arms. Before his mouth claimed mine, he said, "Best Christmas ever."

It was the best Christmas ever.

That was until the next year, when I surprised him with his second child, a daughter, and sister for Drew and Toby, who Drew helped name.

Actually, every year onwards was a best because I had my family, friends, new and old. I had my booming business, which I'd expanded and hired more staff, and most of all, I had Vice Salvatore.

Finally, my life was making sense.

Acknowledgements

Becky, Donna, Randi, MariaLisa, and Rachel, thank you for working on Making Sense with me. The help you all gave was very appreciated.

Wander Aguiar, you've done a marvelous job on the cover photo. I love working with you!

Nazarea at InkSlinger, thank you for all your help on the release launch.

Neringa, you rock woman!

To the readers, I hope you enjoy Vice's happy ever after as much as I did writing it. Thank you for your continued support

ALSO BY LILA ROSE

Hawks MC: Ballarat Charter
Holding Out (FREE) Zara and Talon
Climbing Out: Griz and Deanna
Finding Out (novella) Killer and Ivy
Black Out: Blue and Clarinda
No Way Out: Stoke and Malinda
Coming Out (novella) Mattie and Julia

Hawks MC: Caroline Springs Charter
The Secret's Out: Pick, Billy and Josie
Hiding Out: Dodge and Willow
Down and Out: Dive and Mena
Living Without: Vicious and Nary
Walkout (novella) Dallas and Melissa
Hear Me Out: Beast and Knife
Breakout (novella) Handle and Della
Fallout: Fang and Poppy

Standalones related to the Hawks MC
Out of the Blue (Lan, Easton, and Parker's story)

Romantic comedies
Making Changes
Making Sense

Fumbled Love

Trinity Love Series

Left to Chance

Love of Liberty (novella)

Paranormal

Death (with Justine Littleton)

In The Dark

CONNECT WITH LILA ROSE

Webpage: www.lilarosebooks.com

Facebook: http://bit.ly/2du0taO

Instagram: www.instagram.com/lilarose78/

Goodreads:

www.goodreads.com/author/show/7236200.Lila_Rose

www.ingramcontent.com/pod-product-compliance
Lightning Source LLC
Chambersburg PA
CBHW071534110726
47908CB00007B/1876